SOUL KEEPER

*Book One
of
The Dark Portal Mysteries*

Alice Keynes

Copyright © 2020 Alice Keynes

All rights reserved

Cover Images © 2020 Genevieve Lovelock

Website: genevievelovelock.com

The characters, names, locales and events portrayed in this book are fictitious and a product of the author's imagination. Any resemblance to real persons, living or dead, or actual locales or events is entirely coincidental and not intended by the author.

No part of this book may be reproduced, or stored in a retrieval system, or transmitted in any form or by any means, electronic, mechanical, photocopying, recording or otherwise, without express written permission of the publisher.

Alice Keynes was born in a rambling house in the countryside of Hertfordshire, England, with a love of the paranormal in her blood. She devotes her time to writing, psychic development and travelling; always looking for mysteries and inspiration for her stories.

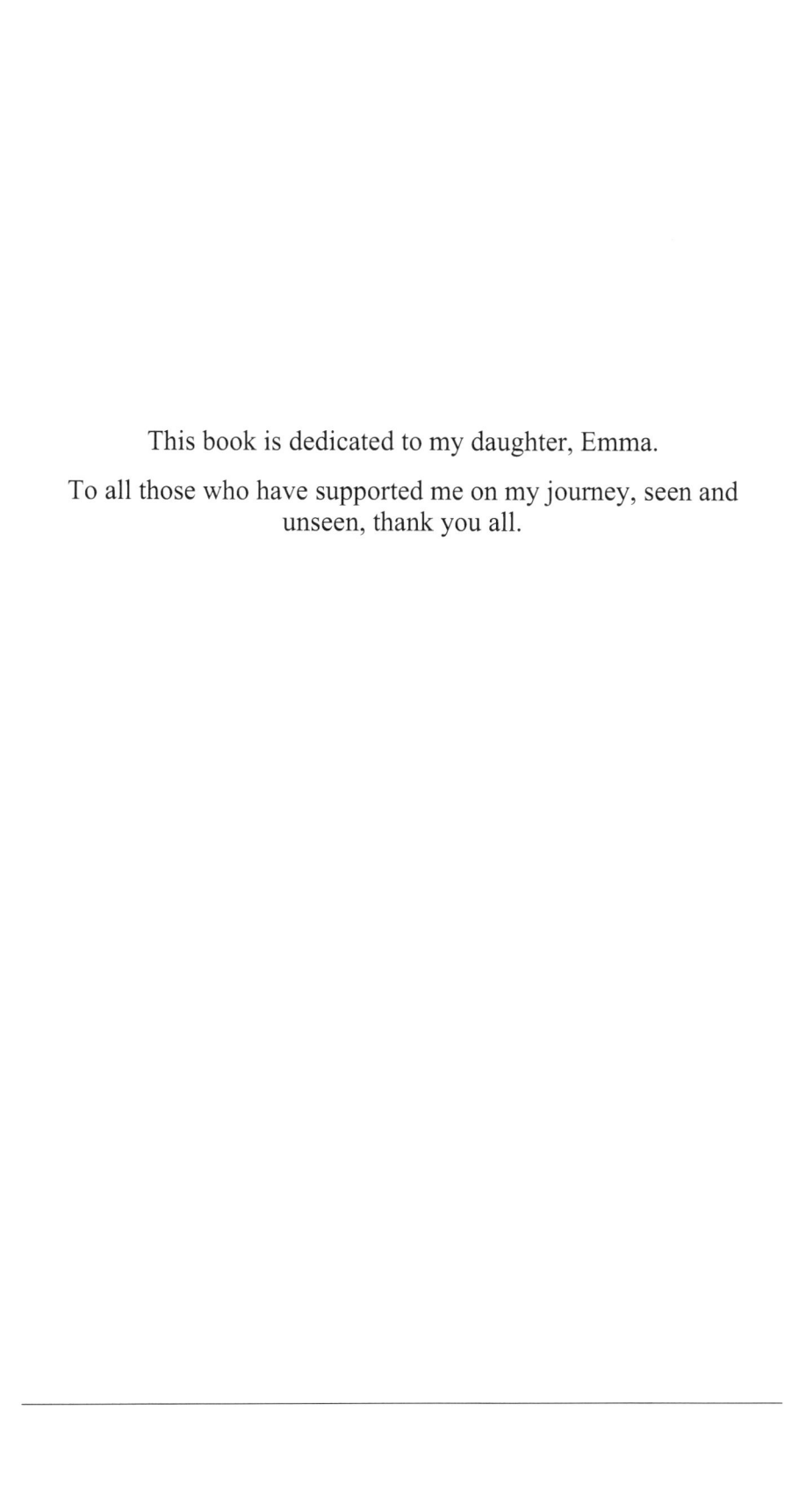

This book is dedicated to my daughter, Emma.

To all those who have supported me on my journey, seen and unseen, thank you all.

Foreword

To all those readers who love nothing better than to curl up in a cosy armchair on a dark and stormy night; this book is especially for you.

Chapter 1

Edinburgh, Scotland, Present Day

Her murder had been easy. Quick and unnoticed by anyone. The girl's face, smudged with heavy black kohl and red lipstick, was now lifeless, staring glassy-eyed into the void. Her body lay crumpled and motionless; her white naked shoulders tinged purple with the tattoo of a butterfly now spattered with the misty rain of a cold, autumn night. In the alleyway of industrial buildings, locked gates and high wire fences, she was like the masticated remains of a spider's prey, splayed over a web of metal railings and plastic rubbish bins. No-one, not even the lone security guard, knew that she was there.

Painter looked down at her body and laughed to himself. She was what humans called a Goth. What a ridiculous term! And the butterfly was supposed to represent a new beginning. Transformation of some kind, giving her earthly life some hope for the future, a new regeneration. Painter's lips drew back in a sneer. What did humans know about regeneration? Their paltry lives were always a mess of chaos, lived as a string of misery-laden experiences that could never by anything other than dull. They grabbed hold of a glimmering light bulb of hope at the start of their birth, only for it to be snuffed out at death in a frail ping.

Ping. Painter liked that word. The more thoughts he devoured from humans, as their souls slithered into him at the point of death, the more he liked to toss random words and language around in his mind. Some didn't make sense, just as humans were too diverse to contain in one broad sweep of culture or belief system, and that made Painter's task easier. Humans could barely even communicate with each other, let alone care about one another. And who would miss the unemployed, single teenager who had run away from her abusive father and fallen into a crack den of vice, only to be spat out in a discarded heap of human wretchedness?

Painter looked down at her corpse and sighed. The heavy kohl was now a black trail, a jagged mess of makeup which made it look as if she were crying. She had been so trusting. There had been little challenge in taking the life essence of a girl who would have killed herself eventually anyway. And that was Painter's problem. He was becoming bored with the tediousness of wrecking lives. He craved more excitement, a new challenge and he yearned to savour the soul of a true opponent; someone who would put up a desperate fight for their existence and not make it so damn easy for him.

And to make him fully immortal, that special soul needed to be truly gifted. To be able to transcend both worlds. Painter knew such individuals existed on the earth plane but they were proving hard to find. He yearned for the essence of a true psychic. Perhaps, he sniffed, holding back a laugh, a human who was now termed as a *Lightworker*. Either way, whatever the label, the sudden and immediate pull to consume such a life force flooded afresh around his body and he groaned. It was becoming harder and harder to ignore.

It was strange, he thought, as she lay there lifeless, just how little resistance she had actually put up in the last few moments of her life. She had possessed very little physical strength, but, surely, she could have questioned him; wondered at his motives? No, she had not. She had offered herself to him on a plate, like most of them did, and her life force, her spiritual essence, had just willingly given itself up to him. The deliciousness of her last moments of agony still resonated within Painter's blood. Her final gasp as he had sucked in her soul had given him such immense pleasure that he could barely contain his instinctive urge to immediately harvest more. But he couldn't. The time wasn't right and his voracious urge to feast would have to wait.

A sudden sweep of yellow from a car headlight beam lit up the wall behind him and Painter cowered down, covering the girl's body with his long black coat. He wondered for a moment if he had been seen, but he was safely blocked on all three sides by warehouse buildings and an ugly metal brace of a fire exit bolted up one wall. She would soon be buried in the skip behind him, lost amongst a ton of industrial waste. Just an empty shell of a human being, as disposable as shredded paper and crushed metal cans.

He stayed low, crouched in the shadows, until the vehicle had swung around and disappeared from view. Then Painter hauled the girl up over his shoulder; her arms flailing down his back like a limp ragdoll and he paused to balance her weight. Though she was petite and weighed less than a normal sized teenager, he was still in the initial throes of acquiring a new life force and it always took several moments to assimilate into his system. Her essence had been lighter and purer than he expected. It was like trying to synchronise water and oil, proving painful as he staggered over to the far wall. There was just one final thing he needed to do; a last flourish of finesse that he had dreamt up after observing the delicious and barbaric tortures which humans inflicted upon one another.

Pushing his hand deep within his black coat, Painter withdrew a green glass phial of inky black liquid. He had found the potion in a backstreet Apothecary's shop in the rundown hovels of Whitechapel over a century before and experimented on victims until it was just to his liking. And so he might have stayed longer in that abysmal place, had not some other fiend found occasion to satisfy his murderous whims on the poor, unfortunate women of the East End of London. It had suited Painter to flee into the night and move on, leaving another, more infamous than he, to carry on his own barbarous mission to inflict pain and suffering. It had covered Painter's tracks perfectly.

Painter grinned, running his fingers over the glass, enjoying its touch as if re-acquainting himself with an old friend. The dark green bottle was deeply grooved, as was the nature of old Victorian bottles containing poison and could have passed for any corrosive cocktail of substances posing as a remedy for disease, but this was special. This liquid had a quality that both excited his desire to wreak havoc on his victims and also assisted his haste in disposing of their identity. A drop of his own blood, mixed in with the lethal concoction, had proved to be the perfect way of erasing human tissue and eating away layers of skin. But not too much; delicately, with a little dash of piquant humour. After all, he wanted to retain a little something of what they had been. To remember their features for long enough to transfer them in paint onto his beloved wall, where they would remain for all time, staring out helplessly at him.

That's why he called himself Painter. A demonic Da Vinci of genius with a twist; one who could replicate their stupid, trusting faces with coloured swirls of oil paint and the surprising delicacy of his brushwork. It was an art form that he had liked since he had consumed the soul of his first artist, a young and opium-addicted Victorian painter who would have been feted and famous in Society, had he lived long enough.

Propping the young woman's lifeless body up against the metal railing, Painter hooked her by the neck of her leather jacket over one of the steel prongs and smoothed back her hair from her face. How young, innocent and tortured she looked. A sort of cracked Madonna who had seen a vision of her very own Hell. Painter traced her features with his gloved finger and felt a quiver of ecstasy as he remembered sucking in her soul. It made him want to burst out in pleasure all over again. But there was nothing left of her now worth keeping and she had served her purpose.

Painter felt no pity as he withdrew the pipette from the bottle and let the corrosive liquid drip carefully over her features. Each drop hit her skin with deadly accuracy, burning instantly through the layers of skin and dissolving tissue. He watched, awed for a moment, breathing in the delicious aroma of the deadly poison and then lifted her up and flung her, head first, into the skip, to be immediately buried amongst the mass of black rubbish bags and cardboard boxes.

By the time anyone found her, Painter knew he would be long gone.

He smiled to himself as he edged back along the streets, unmolested and unchallenged. The Dark Ones would be pleased with him. As a Youngblood, he needed to prove his worth. He knew that they were expecting powerful things of him but as yet, until that chain of trust had been fully forged and he had earnt his place among them, he had not been allowed to see them in their true form. They were ancient; created before the fabric of time and constantly tracking the human realms from their dimension of darkness. Painter understood that the Dark World was not made of blackness as humans understood blackness to be. It had its own light, of demonic making, having consumed the life essence of countless stars and species. The light burnt orange, glowing for all time over the Dark Realm and needing more and more star matter and living organisms to sustain it. Human beings were especially prized for their inner light and ability to transcend spiritually to a place of peace and purity. Painter knew that the purer the soul of the prey species, the more powerful the demon would become. The demons of the Dark World could take on the appearance of any species in any solar system and dimension that they wished, but the result would always be a counterfeit copy; a clone devoid of any feeling, empathy, compassion or the ability to feel love. A being completely black inside and intent only on destroying all it came into contact with.

Painter flashed his teeth and grinned. One thing he had learned about humans was that they liked to put labels on people. He was therefore, in their words, a killer; a psychopath perhaps? It amused him to toy over the various meanings and descriptions that could be applied to him.

Carefully making his way across the old City, avoiding any traffic and open spaces, Painter eventually crossed the street and crawled over the iron gates that led up to the stark black skyline of Greyfriars Kirk, slinking into the macabre sprawl of eroding tombs and edging along their cold stone with his hands. Of all the areas in Edinburgh that he come to know, this was his favourite place. It was the nearest he could find that reminded him of his true home and for a moment he felt a pang of longing for the Dark World. Whilst he liked the graveyard and its smattering of grey and black memorials and weathered gargoyles, he utterly detested the church and all it stood for. The pretence that man had any sort of salvation was laughable.

The Dark World existed between the physical, earthly state and the highest realm of The Source and its angelic beings. The dimension of the kingdom that humans termed the land of God was an age-old realm of light that his own kind detested more than any other spiritual world. It was a place that disgusted and repelled him with every ounce of his being. The Dark Ones wanted dominion over that realm, The Source, and all human beings who were stupid enough to believe that they could be saved from demons who had been raging this battle of souls for eternity.

But the Dark Ones had evolved a way to unlock the gates of Purgatory, to invent themselves as demonic Gatekeepers. They could take the life essence of their prey and lock up their souls in the forlorn and forgotten realms of Purgatory forever, never to escape again. Not even the hand of their so-called God could probably reach down that far and extricate them.

Therefore, thought Painter with a surge of contempt, the Kirk of Greyfriars was frankly pathetic and as useless as a paper bag in a storm. He was a fledgling Gatekeeper, earning his right to sit amongst the Dark Ones until such time as the earth and all its miserable inhabitants would be merely consumed into the orange Hell of the Dark World. Not so much consumed, Painter rebuked himself sternly, but annihilated.

Bending his tall body over, almost double, Painter scraped aside the gravestone marker of the mausoleum that he had habitually used for many a night, before he had been able to recreate his current human identity well enough to blend into the populace of the Scottish capital. He looked at the dismembered, rotten corpse and shroud which had once covered a stalwart member of the City and kicked it over into the corner in distaste. After the graveyard bodies had long since decayed, fought over by rats and having dissolved into a mass of maggots and foul stinking mush, the bones were nothing more than arthritic bits of pathetic brushwood, which Painter had used as torches rag-rolled until they burnt with flame and lit his way through the underground tunnels of Old Edinburgh. It suited him now, in his new venture as the owner of a nightclub situated within a street connected to the tunnels and vaults, to know every inch and corner of the passageways and caverns that had once housed the social deprivation and criminality of the City.

He climbed down further into the dark, dank recess, beneath the iron grille in the floor, aware that time was now against him, and entered the tunnel that led to his lair; The Nightshade Club. Making his way along the damp and cold passageway, Painter finally entered the vaulted nightclub through his secret door, unseen and with ease.

The Nightshade Club, his human residence, was popular with the alternative scene and he did not look out of place in it. The Club could have been a theatrical stage, with its low-level ceilings and wooden bars crisscrossing the venue, studded with a mixture of candlelight and red and green neon that gave the cavern intimacy and privacy.

Each area around the central flagstone dancefloor was divided into wooden cubicles, individually named after notorious Scottish characters. There was the Jekyll and Hyde, draped in red velvet and lined with crimson and red cushions, the MacKellar, resplendent in deep blue and black brocade, with its hanging black wrought iron pendant chandelier, and the tartan Brodie, where most of Painter's staff seemed to prefer to hang out after the end of their shifts. No-one entered the Moriarty Suite at the far end of the Club. This was reserved for Painter's use only and was always locked.

Taking the key from the inside pocket of his caped overcoat, Painter slid it quietly into the skull-shaped lock and realised that his hands were shaking. It was now almost six o'clock in the morning and he needed to sleep, to conserve his energy. The night had been productive and had yielded him some sustenance, but it wasn't enough.

Painter closed the door behind him and pulled the mortice bolt across. He went over to the large mirror and stared at his reflection. His aquiline, lean face was as white as the candles which surrounded the mirror. His shrine. They covered every spare inch of the table below, constantly flickering in the darkness. Painter would never allow them to go out. He liked the fact that they were easier on his constantly sore eyes. Beneath the ice blue contact lenses, his eyes were the darkest black, the colour of his true self, but no-one had ever seen his real state and lived to retell the fact.

He sighed with exhaustion and ran a trembling hand through his white blond hairpiece. It was slicked back from his forehead and tied in a velvet band at the nape of his neck. It made a striking contrast to the black clothes he always wore and he edged back his lips in a smile. Some customers of the Nightshade whispered that he was probably a real-life vampire, and they loved it.

Taking up the goblet of wine, Painter drank deeply, watching in fascination as the rivulets caught on the corners of his mouth and trickled down his chin. He wiped away the liquid fastidiously with his beautifully embroidered black handkerchief. No, vampires did not exist. They never had. They were just old folklore and media creations, dreamt up to terrify and entertain the masses. They weren't real. But demons were real and did exist. He knew, because he was one of them. He had existed for over a century in human terms and being classed as a Youngblood rankled him. He had amassed enough kills to progress and devoured more souls than other demons of his age and yet the Ancient Ones still demanded more from him. Painter knew it; *felt* it, in every moment of his existence.

For a moment, he despised his fate. He was just one of many other demons. One come to the abysmal junkyard of a planet called Earth, to fulfil the Dark Quota; a list of living human souls, now drained of their life essence and trapped forever in the darkness, having fed those others like him who despised everything that the miserable human race stood for.

Painter moved slowly over to the chaise longue and laid down, resting his weary head on the plump, velvet black cushion. He always knew when it was turning into daylight outside, even in the colder months. It came with a crushing urge to rest, to sleep and offer his mind to the dark recesses of delicious dreams, which people on the earth-plane habitually called nightmares. Painter felt his eyelids closing. The dreamscape, the astral world, was very different for humans. They wandered around aimlessly, picking up random, useless spiritual snippets of experience which they thought denoted the meaning of life. Painter thought it hilarious. What did any of them know about the true meaning of life? All of them had been force-fed garbage like that since the day they had first begun to carve animal pictures on cave walls. He was far greater than that, and far more powerful than they would ever be.

As Painter sank into the blackness of his mind and opened himself up to his true existence, he sensed the incoming rush of evil and shuddered in submissive ecstasy. Tomorrow, he would add the girl's image to the wall of his office; hidden beneath a deep crimson velvet curtain. He enjoyed painting their features onto the cold cavern stone, seeing their contorted faces stare back at him, contorted in agony and begging him for pity, and each one now sucked dry of their soul and life essence, consigned to the void, *Purgatory*, or whatever the stupid human race wanted to call it. Painter smiled hideously as he thought of his secret Sistine Chapel of disembodied faces, their features twisted in pain and terror. Yes. He would rename his masterpiece of blood-etched diabolism *The Wall of Purgatory*. It summed up their miserable, wretched existence, perfectly.

Chapter 2

He was a drifter with no name. No-one knew anything about him; where he lived; if he had any family. There were no clues on his body and no distinguishing marks on his weathered, rough skin. In a society full of self-absorbed and disinterested people, the only reaction the man's death elicited was a passerby's attempt to take a photo of himself with the corpse, before being sent off by the police with a robust indication of where he could safely store his mobile phone.

The policeman in question had seen such sorry endings to an unknown victim's life many times before and yet he was still unhardened to the sadness it always evoked in him. It was the same deep void of loneliness which resonated with him on a soul level and somehow, Detective Inspector Chris West had never managed to completely resign himself to it. As he crouched down, all six feet two inches of him, next to the crumpled, disheveled body of the vagrant, Chris let out a deep sigh of frustration. It would be another case of trawling through Edinburgh's missing persons' data, trying to put a name to a face.

Except that the man had no face. His features had been burnt off with some sort of acid, but carefully. As carefully as if someone had poured icing on the top of a cake and taken care not to let any drip down over the edges. The man's neck, covered in patchy red-brown stubble, a few days' growth, was barely marked at all. And that made it seem worse, for the man had obviously attempted, at some point, somewhere, to try and take care of himself by shaving and even washing. For despite the man's shabby army store khaki shirt and grubby jeans, the remainder of the man's skin was clean and his fingernails were short and scrubbed. Chris felt a surge of pity. Why had he ended up on the streets? What was his story?

Chris sniffed the air, wrinkling his nose at the reek of acid. It had penetrated down into several layers of the man's skin and melted his eyeballs. There was nothing left in the socket recesses except a mess of solidified jelly and blood vessels. The man's nose had ceased to protrude out from his face, instead collapsing into the centre in a sickening yellow spread of puss-filled gunge. The post-mortem results would come but Chris estimated the man's age to be close to his own, around forty-five years. The flecks of grey in the man's stubble and at the temples reinforced the fact that he was nearer to middle age than anything else. There were no documents in any of his pockets, and Chris didn't expect to find any. When people wanted to disappear from life, they usually did a good and thorough job. But some aspects of him didn't add up. Chris just had an inkling that here was a guy who had attempted to stay trendy at some point, judging by his half decent trainers, and who had then given up and dropped out of the whole rat race. Bloody knackered and out of ideas. No direction, no hope and no-one to pick up the pieces of his sad waste of a life.

"Hey, don't look so fed up. We're still on tonight, remember?"

The sudden onslaught of the man's voice pulled Chris out of

his thoughts and he looked up, shielding his eyes from the vivid burst of late, watery autumn sunlight. "Oh yeah, I'd forgotten about that. Where are we going, again?"

Sergeant Ben Miles rolled his eyes and shook his head in exasperation. "Out on the razz. It'll be a laugh." He held out his hands in an effort to prompt Chris' memory but when that didn't work, he gave up. Crouching down next to Chris, he let out a low expletive. At thirty-one years old, he hadn't yet seen as many corpses as his boss. "Poor sod. What happened? Looks like someone didn't want his own mother to recognise him. Foul. Actually disgusting." He paled for a moment and had to wipe his mouth with the back of his hand.

"Yep, it's grim." Chris nodded in agreement. "Acid. Not a bucket load, but drip fed. Probably with a pipette. Precise and careful. The murderer paid a lot of attention to detail. Forensics are on their way but I want you to go back to Base and see who's been reported missing."

"Fine, but don't forget about picking me up tonight."

"*Okay.*" Chris sucked in a deep intake of breath in irritation. He wasn't in the mood for any stag do, a strip club, or anything else Ben had arranged for their soon-to-be-married colleague. All he wanted was to go home to his apartment on the edge of Leith, shower, get in a Chinese takeaway and watch the endless grey sea. He was tired and de-motivated and nothing seemed fun right now.

Ever since Kirsty had left him, there seemed little remaining in his life to fill Chris with any inspiration. Maybe he had just spent too many years on the job, seeing the worst side of humanity and no longer able to muster up any enthusiasm for something as superficial as a night out on the town with a group of other coppers, mostly younger than him, who were only interested in pulling some skirt and seeing who could drink the most shots.

Chris pulled himself up to his full height and ran a hand through his hair. It had once been blond. Now it was more silver than blond, but he guessed there must be something still vaguely attractive about his appearance, judging by the admiring looks he still got from women, although none of them were Kirsty. Her leaving him had made him feel like shit. She said he was boring. That they didn't go out and never did anything interesting. And worst of all, that he was unambitious and didn't mix with the right people to better their lifestyle. Perhaps she was right but he didn't, and never had, given a crap about mixing with the right people.

Chris stared down at the body and felt a rush of bile in his throat. It was putrid, all of it, and Kirsty had never understood that, after a day dealing with murderers, rapists, pedophiles and drug-dealers, the last thing he wanted to do, was go and sit at a dinner party with her and smile like everything was great in his world.

"Anything else, Guv?"

"Sorry?" Chris turned around to look at Ben.

"Do you want me to do anything els...."

"No." Chris moved his hand abruptly with a sigh. "You're fine. And stop calling me Guv. This isn't the bloody Sweeney."

Ben gave a smirk and headed over to the patrol car. He had nabbed a lift back to Murray Road Station with the uniforms and left Chris to finish up and sort forensics out.

This suited Chris perfectly. Time alone gave him the opportunity to think, to start mentally building up a profile of the man's killer. The woodland clearing where the man's body had been discovered was a notorious haunt for local kids. There were signs of various makeshift dens around the edge; stamped out fires and empty lager cans littered around what was effectively one large campsite. It probably stood to reason that someone would die there someday, but at least it hadn't been a little kid.

Chris was glad about that. The worst thing in the world was telling a parent that their child had been killed. Chris had no real notion of what that must feel like, having never had any kids, but he could tell, during his time rising through the ranks, that something in them had died too. He felt true empathy with the family liaison officers, the bereavement counsellors. They had the job from hell as nothing, and no-one, could ever truly heal those parents or bring their kid back.

The trouble was, the more he came across the dark side, the underbelly of human civilisation, to try and make the world a better place, the more the slimy bastards who killed, raped and abused just kept coming out of the woodwork.

Chris gave a short smile to the man who lifted up the cordon of yellow police tape to join him. "God, Eric, any more curries and you'll go up like a balloon."

The man in the pale blue overalls gave him a sarcastic grin in reply. "Shut up, West. Women love my physique. Even more so when I'm wearing my finest."

Chris chuckled as the zip on his colleague's stomach was

clearly strained to bursting point. "No accounting for taste. Anyway, if you want any background on the poor guy, there isn't any. Homeless, from the looks of it. Discovered this afternoon by an elderly dog-walker who is now in hospital with shock and a little shit with an iPhone." Chris held up the offending mobile phone, glinting in the sunlight. "One less piece of crap on YouTube now, thanks to me. You'd think I'd made his world fall in, the fuss he made over losing his phone. He cared more about taking a selfie with the victim than anything else."

"Better let me get on with it, then. Leave it to the experts. We *always* get better results than you lot."

Chris shrugged his shoulders in nonchalance, but in reality, he was pleased to have Eric on his side. He was one of the best forensics in the business and nothing, not even the tiniest detail, ever escaped his eye.

As he made his way back to his car, Chris paused for a moment and looked around him. It should have been a fun place for kids to hang out with their mates, away from the dark, looming tenements of old town Edinburgh, but like everything else he had seen in his life, it was now tainted and spoiled. What sort of perverse killer used acid to destroy his victim? Chris could only hope that the poor guy had been dead first but, knowing the sort of evil bastards that roamed the streets, somehow, he doubted it.

Chris started up the engine and drove the car purposefully down the hill towards Murray Road Station. He flicked on *Dark Side of the Moon* by Pink Floyd, humming tunelessly as he sat back in the driver's seat and wondered again why the hell he had agreed to out that night.

Chapter 3

Tia Olsen picked up the auction house particulars and looked again at the photographs of Redfield Grange. It was like some Victorian Gothic monstrosity, rising up from the countryside surrounding Edinburgh in dark grey stone, a morbid mausoleum to a long-forgotten member of the elite had who wanted to be remembered for posterity through his architecture.

Something niggled at Tia, poking at her memory with insistent fingers, but there was only the same vaguely familiar sensation that she had seen Redfield Grange somewhere before. Tia frowned at the flamboyant descriptions and artfully shot angles of the house's shabby, faded rooms and wondered why it made her feel uneasy. It should have been perfect but somehow it was odd. It was as past its sell-by date as an old Hollywood actress who liked to pretend she was still beautiful. Just as the cracked façade of heavy face powder and garish slash of over-ripe lipstick looked too sad to be credible, Redfield Grange, too, looked worn out, isolated and strange.

As Lars Olsen drove the Audi carefully away from the main road and into the narrow driveway that led up to the house, he sighed in heightened anticipation of what they were going to find. "Well, this is as far as the sat-nav takes us. We're on our own now," he said, turning to smile at his wife. "Better get unlocked and ready for the removal men. They can't be far behind us."

Tia shivered and looked up at the passing trees. It was growing dark already, with the autumn sky turning yellow and purple above them, but the atmosphere had changed. It was as if they had left the busy, modern world and entered some long-forgotten reality where time now stood still.

"Are you okay, babe?" You don't seem very happy." Lars took hold of Tia's hand and gave it a reassuring squeeze. "Are you regretting it already?"

Tia shook her head and gave him a glimmer of a smile. It was pointless lying to Lars when he could read her like a book. "I'm just…a bit overwhelmed, I think. We've spent all our savings on this house. Suppose we have made a really big mistake?"

Lars grimaced as the car lurched over an unseen pot-hole. "It'll be fine. We've seen the auction particulars. I've made enquiries and there are no major structural problems. What's the point of marrying a solicitor if you can't get *some* use out of me?" he finished, suggestively.

Tia managed a laugh, despite her growing sense of foreboding. It wasn't that she didn't trust Lars' judgement, or even that they had to make it work or they would be homeless and penniless. No, it was something else, like a feeling of impending doom, but as Tia sought a sideways glance at his excited expression, she shoved down her inhibitions and made an effort to go with the flow of the whole adventure. It was supposed to be a good thing. A brand-new beginning for both of them.

When Lars finally drove between the open gates and switched off the engine on the gravel drive, they both looked at each other in silence. The purr of the well- maintained Audi stopping stark dead in the countryside made them even more aware of how isolated they were.

Nothing moved. No birds in the trees, no breeze lifting the crispy, fallen leaves, nothing.

"It's like some sort of Hammer Horror house, isn't it?" mused Lars, lifting off his driving glasses and leaning back into his seat with a sigh. "Kind of peculiar. As though the architect couldn't decide quite what style to use. Have to admit, though, it's a lot more substantial than it looks in the photos. I hope it's not going to take too much more than a lick of paint and a tidy up."

Tia bit the inside of her lip. The place already gave her the creeps. "One man's fixer-upper is another man's fast track to ruin. I hope this doesn't ruin us."

"Oh Tia, for God's sake, lighten up, eh? You've been miserable even since we sold the flat. London isn't our home anymore. This is. You made the choice with me, remember?"

Tia's green eyes filled with unshed tears. "Stop having a go at me. I just need time to get used to this. Everything's happened so quickly."

"You're too sensitive. Where's your spirit of adventure? You used to have one. Anyway, I thought it would be a good idea after …" Lars stopped abruptly. "Let's stop this. It isn't getting us anywhere. How can we have a fresh start when we keep arguing?"

Tia sighed. He always stopped short of mentioning The Affair. The one he had had with his PA. The one which had very nearly broken them up and wrecked their lives. She sought another glance at him. His handsome profile used to make her go weak at the knees with love and desire. Now it only made her feel anxious all the time. How many other women thought he was gorgeous? And would he betray her again? He just didn't seem to understand that she was risking everything on a dream that would either work or it wouldn't. And right now, Redfield Grange loomed over her like some kind of mad old Aunt, grinning a maniacal smile of welcome in the fading daylight.

It made her feel even more lonely at that moment.

Lars released his seatbelt and got out of the car first. He was like a puppy with a new toy between his teeth, any sense of negativity drowned out by his excitement and determination to turn Redfield Grange into something amazing. He was already at the front door when Tia joined him on the porch, desperate to get inside and look around. "I can imagine a butler opening the door and offering us a glass of brandy, can't you?" he joked, fumbling with the set of keys. "At least it would save me trying to find the stupid key. There must be at least twenty of the damn things on this keyring." Lars was irritated for a moment. He always got irritated quickly and it was a trait that Tia was used to.

Tia swallowed and glanced around her, feeling suddenly exposed and vulnerable. "Well, it's got potential…" she said, arranging an expression of positivity on her face, but the task of taking on such a huge house seemed so overwhelming. "I'm sure it's nothing we can't manage…"

Lars frowned. "You don't like it, then."

Tia made herself laugh. "I didn't say that. It's just…different, that's all. Entirely different to what I expected. I didn't realise quite how…isolated it is." She pushed the unsettling sensation of unease to the back of her mind and tried to lighten up. It was a good idea, of course it was. People bought renovation projects all the time. It was just sudden fear that so much was now invested in Redfield Grange. And it wasn't just the money. This really was make or break for both of them, for their marriage and any real hope for the future.

Lars softened and drew her close, caressing her hair with tenderness as Tia nestled her head into his shoulder. "I know it looks a bit of a mess but I think we can fix it up in no time. It'll be perfect for having the family to stay, don't you think?"

"Sure." Tia imagined his mother moaning about the lack of central heating, overgrown gardens and the fact it was miles from Marks & Spencer and all her expensive London friends. "As long as no-one expects it to be perfect. It'll be fun."

"That's the spirit". Lars kissed the top of Tia's head and then continued to push the appropriate key into the front door. As he walked inside, his smile of triumph glimmered and then fizzled out like a used firework. The smell was the worst thing. It was the acrid odour of decay and neglect, of old musty wood and damp, mouldy curtains and carpets. Lars wrinkled up his nose in distaste but doggedly persisted in pursuing his dream. "Better get a skip in then, I suppose."

They both stood, dejected, in the hallway, Tia's nose muffled in the sleeve of her padded jacket. It looked even more horrendous than it smelt and she found herself beginning to giggle. "Well," she managed to say into a mouthful of material, "it's nothing a lick of paint can't fix".

Lars caught the twinkle in her eyes and his mouth twitched in response. "Oh God, it's crap, isn't it?" he rued, his handsome face turning pink with a mixture of embarrassment and sheer laughter that they had just spent their savings on the House from Hell. "I guess I just got carried away with the whole romance thing. You, me, real log fires and four poster beds…"

Tia looked up into his blue eyes and felt a long-lost twinge of desire coming back to her, but it was tainted with distrust and as much as she wanted to believe him, she still couldn't. He had told her similar things so many times before, even when he was having an affair. That was the worst part. Knowing that he was sleeping with his PA when he was also sleeping with her, his wife. Such dark thoughts, never far from her mind, continued to torture Tia by making her stomach churn over with anxiety. The damage had been done, no matter how hard Lars was trying to make them forget it. All smiles dissolved, Tia found herself keeping her emotional distance and changing the subject.

"Look at this place. It looks really baronial. There's a horrible, moth-eaten stag's head on the wall. I think that should be the first thing to throw in the skip." Tia walked over to the window and smudged the dirty stained glass with her sleeve. "It has some sort of description on it. 1875… I think. I'll Google it. See if I can find out who originally built the place." She turned to look at Lars but he had already gone over to the staircase.

Thankfully, the light switch worked and the electricity buzzed into life when Lars flicked it on. "Once we have the place brought into the twenty first century, the heating bills shouldn't be too bad," he mused, staring up at the galleried landing above. "Apparently the old girl who last owned the place used a hell of a lot of wood. The parkland around here used to be a wild hunting forest, back in the day. Probably a haunt for witches and vampires,"

Tia shuddered, knowing that she would be on her own in the house during the day, when Lars went back to work in his law firm's Edinburgh office. She peered through the glass and could see the dense shadow of the trees in the distance. She didn't want to think about horrible things living in the woods. Her imagination was vivid at the best of times and it certainly didn't need any colourful local folklore to help it along. The silence of the house was strangely loud as Tia looked around her, tentatively. In old houses, one normally could imagine the clunk of an out of time Grandfather clock, the creak of a worn floorboard. Perhaps even rats in the attic. But there was nothing to break the sound of her breath. It was eerily quiet. As if the house was watching, studying them, waiting for them to make the first move.

Tia shivered and folded her arms around herself, protectively. She didn't know why she felt so overly-sensitive, but she seriously needed to get a grip.

"The removal lorry should be here in a minute. Let's get the tea and coffee unpacked. I'll get the stuff from the boot, if you want to find your way to the kitchen." Lars turned and went back outside, leaving Tia standing in the entrance hall.

"Wait, I'll help…" Tia responded, suddenly not wanting to be left alone, but it was too late. Lars had already gone outside and

Tia felt goosebumps rise on her skin. Looking up at the galleried balcony, she could easily envisage the shade of a grey lady or a disgruntled spirit groaning down the staircase at her. Tia closed her eyes and willed herself to stop being so pathetic. "Get real, girl," she muttered to herself, "or you're not going to last five minutes here." But she knew it was useless trying to tell Lars about her feelings. He wasn't the slightest bit sensitive to atmospheres, or old buildings, or psychic abilities, or anything of that nature. He was strong, capable, bossy and practical and never gave any of her thoughts or experiences any sort of credence whatsoever. And so she had learned to shut down most of the time and become, in his words, 'normal'. Sometimes though, like now, it ripped through the veil and got her attention, whether she liked it or not.

Making her way over to the passageway that led off from the entrance hall, Tia finally found the dilapidated kitchen and switched on the light. It flickered on and she could see an old pine plate rack, suspended over an original butler's sink, a large bar of old carbolic soap left on the draining board, and a mouldy tea towel hanging from a hook on the wall. Tia pulled aside the flowery curtain beneath the sink and shuddered, half expecting to see a large rat feasting on a lump of green cheese or something just as hideous, but apart from a box of cook's matches and a rusty old tin of brass polish, the shelves were thankfully bare.

"Well, what do you think?" smiled Lars, as he brought in the cardboard box full of mugs, coffee, biscuits and the fresh pint of milk they had picked up, en-route at a petrol station. "Look at the old Aga. That will look amazing when it's cleaned up. Another job for you, Tia. You can't say you will be bored."

"No, but I'd rather have my old job back."

"It's not my fault the firm restructured, is it? They didn't need so many paralegals, you know that. They had to get rid of the deadwood."

"I didn't call myself deadwood, thanks. I was doing really well. Or so I thought. You're a partner in the firm. You could have warned me."

Lars slammed the coffee jar down on the work surface, aggressively, "For crying out loud, Tia. How many times have we got to go through this same old shit? I'm not responsible for running the whole bloody firm! You weren't the only casualty. There were at least five other paralegals, plus admin staff."

"Plus Sophie." Tia moved away from him and went over to the grimy kitchen window. "You forgot to say that she was a casualty. Oh wait, no, that's because she *wasn't*."

Lars sighed and ran a hand through his light brown hair in frustration. "She put in for a transfer to another office. You know that."

"Do you miss her?"

"What?"

"Do you miss her? It's a simple question." Tia was on the verge of angry tears but continued to probe him. It was almost compulsive, despite it causing her deep pain. She needed to have an answer. She felt so raw, so exposed in that moment and there was no familiarity to help her stay grounded and strong. She didn't feel rational or in control of her emotions at all.

"Do you know what? Right now, it might be better if I don't answer that question."

"Don't worry, Lars. You already have."

"Oh, for Christ's sake…" Lars turned away from her abruptly and went to the doorway of the kitchen. "Make your own bloody coffee. I'm going to wait for the removal men. At least then I can talk to somebody bloody sane."

"Fine. You do that," she whispered, picking up the kitchen and going to the tap as calmly as she could. "Walk away. *You always do…*"

As Tia turned on the stiff tap to fill the kettle, she flinched in shock. The water was red, like blood. After running it for a few moments, the colour began to disappear and become normal, but Tia was shaken. If houses could bleed, perhaps this is what it looked like, and it mirrored her own feelings. Sometimes she felt as if she had lost the stomach for a fight and resolved to make the best of the situation, but today she felt like she had been pulled into an arena against an opponent intent on knocking her out. A heaviness, an invisible threat, a feeling of doom. The whole business of moving into Redfield Grange just compounded her sense of loneliness and Tia tried not to break down and cry. Lars was trying hard to make a go of it and all she kept doing was ripping off the sticking plaster and exposing the same old wound, time after time. Tia brushed away the trickle of tears from her eyes. Selling up and moving had been a mistake. It was the last thing they should have done.

Unable to stand being alone with her feelings any further, Tia swallowed the beginnings of a sob and went out of the kitchen towards the front door. She would apologise to Lars again, like always, and smooth things over between them. She would try to push the horrible feelings away into some void that she could put a mental lid on so that they couldn't do any further harm. Sometimes it was just too hard to be anything else but meek and compliant, even though her heart raged and her blood still boiled at the thought of Lars' betrayal.

Chapter 4

Painter was hungry. He sat back in his leather office chair and watched the customers start to gather at the entrance of The Nightshade Club outside, He could see them but they couldn't see him, thanks to the one-way glass and blacked out exterior. He liked to study them in some depth, to admire them or sneer at them as he thought fit, constantly turning over in his mind who he could choose as his next victim. He fancied another female this time as they were usually more compliant and easier to flatter. But she had to be willing. A snack was better than nothing, despite his craving for a real feast.

    Painter clutched hold of the arms on his chair, feeling the familiar rise of frustration threatening to burst out of him. It was so predictable. He would smile and caress her, seduce her with wit and flattery, and when she could stand it no more, he would move in for the kill. It was so, so easy and human women were virtually begging to be taken over by someone like him. He made them feel wanted, desired, protected. Whatever they wanted to feel, he could provide it, and that was part of the delicious game. But he always pulled back before they got too intimate. The thought of their clumsy hands and slobbering, usually drunken kisses repulsed him. Humans were like animals; only good for prey and stooping that low made him want to vomit in disgust. He would never even sully himself with the thought of having sex with them, let alone leave any physical evidence on his victims.

Leaning forward in his chair, gripping the leather with his white hands, Painter spotted a pretty girl in the queue outside dressed in a long black skirt and heavy biker jacket. She looked like easy prey until he scanned her mind and realised that she was sleeping with her own mother's boyfriend. Painter chuckled in appreciation. Whilst he enjoyed psychically finding out about his customers without their knowledge, their duplicity always made him laugh. They really thought that no-one suspected them of anything and it made him almost empathise with them. Perhaps empathy was too strong a word but he certainly found them entertaining. Humans could sink to almost subterranean levels of degeneracy in terms of morals and debauchery, but that was why he had to select his victims very carefully. They needed to be pure, morally innocent, kind, even gentle. And what he desired most, the most powerful soul of all, was that of a gifted psychic, A human whose feet stood in both worlds. They possessed a talent, an ability that made him crave them. He could almost go out of his mind with the taste of their souls. It was beyond satisfaction of hunger, it was the most intense pleasure he had ever experienced, and Painter wanted to taste it again. But he didn't need a charlatan, or a fraud, he needed a genuine soul who would fight him to their death, thus in return granting his own soul immortality for all time.

Painter looked at his pocket watch. It was midnight and the Club was filling up nicely. It was time for him to mingle and be seen. The customers liked him and wanted to be singled out by him, with a word or a favour. Men and women both enjoyed his touch and Painter took little sips of their energy as he talked to them, leaving them totally unaware that he was draining them. It passed the time and gave him interest, but nothing was as good as satiating his hunger. Painter wanted to feed again. He needed to feel another soul slide into him.

"Hey, Mr P, can we please bring some more kegs in? There's 'ardly enough in the bar…"

There was a thump on the door and Painter felt himself stiffen. He knew it was the annoying bar worker, Kevin Stone, an idiot with shit for brains. Painter had only taken him on because he needed someone of basic enough intelligence to do all of the menial tasks and not get in his way.

Arranging a smile on his face, Painter opened the door and looked down at the young lad. "Just get whatever you need. And why are you asking me? Where is Paul?"

"Paul's an arsehole. He didn't turn up last night 'an 'e never turned up tonight, He's a joke. I can't work with a joke."

Neither can I, thought Painter, surveying Kevin, sarcastically, but nevertheless continued to perfect his plastic smile. "Very well, Kevin, I will deal with Paul. You deal with bringing in the kegs. Agreed?"

"Yeah, alright!" Kevin grinned all over his face and turned back down the corridor looking pleased with himself. "Cheers, Mr P."

Painter stood on the threshold and sighed. They really were all morons. Paul was a bar manager who couldn't be bothered to get out of bed and Kevin Stone was a lackey totally devoid of any intelligence whatsoever. Painter needed someone he could ensure would run things smoothly. Someone he could rely on whilst he went out hunting, Some-one who wouldn't ask any questions.

In the cellar vault which was buzzing with life and pumping with music, Painter let himself be fawned over by his fans; young people who couldn't get enough of his presence and personality and, for a while, Painter basked in the vain glory. It allowed him to get a feel for who was in the Club and any potential victims. He went from table to table, smiling and elegantly taking the hand of everyone, ordering free drinks on the house for anyone who was celebrating a special occasion, or who just took his fancy. It was expensive, but it kept the clubbers coming back for more, which was exactly what Painter intended.

His attention was caught by a table full of men who were clearly on a mission to get completely inebriated by alcohol. Their inane and childish laughter reverberated around the Club, even causing some of the quieter groups to glare over at them. He sighed inwardly and arranged his famous, all-inclusive smile. Wafting over in his black cloak, he ignored an attempt by one of the men to pull on his cloak and try to look underneath it. He could have killed the man in an instant if he wanted to, but he could not bring any suspicion as to his true motives and instead brushed away the immature attempt deftly, with a well-rehearsed laugh.

"Well, gentlemen, I would hazard a guess that you are enjoying yourselves? A stag night, I presume? Let me extend my compliments by giving you all a drink on the house to mark this momentous occasion."

The man who had tried to pull at Painter's cloak fell about laughing. "Seriously, are you for real? No-one talks like that. Mind you, I *am* getting married, so you're right about that. Don't think I'd call it momentous, though. She's up the duff, so I'm doing the *honourable* thing, mate."

"So, why are you called Painter, then?" Sergeant Ben Miles, already pretty drunk from their previous pub visit, slid across the table, folded arms on elbows, and looked up at him with as much focus as he could manage. "Is it a nickname?"

"No, it is my real name."

"Did your parents like art or something?" Ben laughed at his own level of wit, which was entirely lost on Painter, and even more on Chris West.

Chris gave Painter an apologetic expression. "Sorry about him. He's had enough to drink already, as you can tell. Thanks for the free drink."

"Think nothing of it. I'm used to being asked about my name. My name *is* Painter. It is as real as I am." Painter stifled a sneer with his handkerchief, pretending to clear his throat politely. Of course it wasn't his real name. He didn't even have a name. Names were for pathetic little humans who needed such stupid terms to tell each other apart. "And you are…?"

Ben sniffed and looked forlornly at his empty glass. "I'm what's known as a co…" He stopped short and looked at Chris. "I'm sort of… under cover. I can't say because if I did, I would have to kill you."

Chris sighed and pushed back his chair. "Come on, Ben," he said, picking up Ben by his arm. "I think you've had enough now. I should get you home. Sandra will be wondering what's happened to you."

"Oh yeah, I forgot about her. She couldn't care less. She fancies you, anyway. She told me."

"Somehow I doubt that. Come on. I've had enough of you. Let's go." Chris smiled awkwardly at Painter and took out his wallet. "How much do we owe you?"

"It's on the house, as I said." Painter waved his hand in an elaborate gesture. "I hope you will come and visit The Nightshade again?"

"Of course," Chris lied, giving Painter the best smile his frayed nerves could manage. Why did all his nights out with Ben always end up with him acting like Ben's dad, taking him home and plonking him on his poor wife's doorstep like a belligerent, drunken teenager. God only knew what that poor woman had to put up with. Not so much abuse as trying to put to bed a grown man who was too drunk to stand and couldn't even string a couple of words together. If it wasn't for the fact that Ben was bloody good at his job, Chris would have given up on babysitting him a long time ago.

"Thank you." Chris nodded to Painter in appreciation and mouthed over to the rest of his colleagues on the dancefloor that he was taking Ben home. None of them paid him any attention so he knew he wouldn't be missed. It was 1.00am and he had had enough. Stringing Ben's arm over his shoulder, Chris bypassed an amused Painter awkwardly and made his way out of the nightclub.

The cold night air took his breath away as Chris eventually managed to get Ben into the passenger seat of his car and start the engine. The soft rhythm of the engine was a kind of comfort as the interior dashboard lights sprang into life and the radio started playing. Ben lolled against the window glass, his eyes closed and moaning as Chris glanced at him in distaste. What was it with younger guys who always wanted to get wasted all the time?

"God, Ben, you're a disgrace. Why can't you get your shit together and start acting your age?"

"We're not all Saint bloody Christopher," Ben slurred, putting a hand to his head. "I'm gonna be sick..."

"Not in my car, you're not. Just sit back and enjoy the ride. I'll make sure I put my foot down."

"Bastard."

"Whatever."

Chris plunged the car into gear and pressed on down the road until they reached a set of traffic lights. As the lights turned red and Chris slammed the car in irritation to a stop, Ben suddenly opened the door and vomited heavily onto the side of the road. As he moaned and clutched his stomach, Chris felt his own stomach turn over. "Nice one, Ben. Leave a little present for the poor sods crossing the road tomorrow."

"Better out than in. I can't help it..."

Chris sighed as Ben closed the car door again and fell back into the seat. Even Chris had to admit that Ben looked like death warmed up; a peculiar mixture of green and grey. Flecks of vomit were already beginning to crust around his lips, which drooled and quivered as he was clearly struggling not to throw up again.

"What the hell were you drinking, Ben? "

"God knows. I lost count. Something called The Vampires Revenge, I think."

"Well, he bloody did get his revenge. Just don't bother coming in tomorrow. Sleep it off and make sure you come in sober."

"Yes, Guv..."

Chris swallowed a further retort and concentrated on the road. He didn't have the energy to respond and wanted to get some decent sleep before he started on the acid murder victim. It was a bizarre crime that just didn't fit the usual pattern. No drugs had been found on him and no obvious injuries, apart from the deliberate acid attack. Eric had confirmed that it had happened after death. Worst still, Eric had not yet been able to pinpoint what the cause of death had actually been. It was as intriguing as it was bizarre.

Listening to Ben groaning on about how hard his life was, just made Chris want to dump him out of the car and leave him to sober up in the cold night air.

"Ben, for God's sake, give it a rest, will you? You're always so miserable when you're pissed up. Your life is as hard as you make it. You've got a good job, a nice wife who puts up with a lot of crap, a decent place to live. It's a damn sight more than the poor bloke who hasn't even got his face left."

"You still going on about that? That's why you're on your own, mate. You live and breathe work all the time. You don't have a life."

"Right," Chris murmured, "that's it. I'm dropping you off

here..." It wasn't too far from Ben's house, and Chris had had enough of his comments. "Give my best regards to Sandra, won't you."

Ben mouthed an expletive in reply and got himself out of the car, before heading up the path towards his house. Thankfully, Chris could see that Sandra had left a light on outside, otherwise the stupid idiot would probably half kill himself stumbling through the gates and up the garden path. "Good riddance, Ben," he sighed and swung the car around in the opposite direction.

Heading back towards his apartment, Chris felt a sudden and inexplicable pang of loneliness. Ben was probably right but Chris would never give him the satisfaction of knowing it. There was only work to concentrate on now but at least he was trying to do something positive with his time. What else was there, except wallow in his own self-pity and he wasn't going to start doing that. It was a road that only led to despair and he had seen enough people do that over the years. It never ended well. He wondered, just for a moment, what Kirsty might be doing now. Despite what had happened, he still sometimes missed the warmth of her body next to him in bed; the cosy feeling of comfort when he opened the front door after a long shift knowing that there was someone waiting for him.

The small group of teenagers hanging around the base of his apartment block soon dispersed when Chris pulled up outside. They knew who he was and there was always a silent understanding between them that they wouldn't cause him any trouble. Chris got out and clicked the alarm on his car. They were just kids playing at being hard. They were nothing like the real thing, at least not so far, anyway. He hadn't yet had to go and tell their parents that their son or daughter was dead, killed by a drug overdose or suicide.

Chris climbed the short flight to his apartment and eventually unlocked the front door. The passageway inside was dark and quiet, just as he had left it earlier that morning. Nothing and no-one was there to meet him and ask him how his day had been, and, just for a moment, he felt so alone that he almost went straight back out again to the Station, where at least he could get on and do something useful in the remaining hours until dawn.

Chapter 5

Up at Redfield Grange, the house was bathed in silence, surrounded by nothing but mist floating down from the great glens of the north and chilling the dark passageways and rooms as it crept beneath the nooks and crevices. The curtains were still open, and the full moon lit up the night sky beyond the window, encasing the fields and woodland in a caste of silver. Frost was already glinting on the windowpanes outside; the branches of the trees and the sheep were but distant dots of white, cloudy with wool and the curling of their own breath. The house slept, resting in stillness, but all was not well.

From the master bedroom came the sound of whimpering and moaning. Tia tossed and turned beneath the blankets, murmuring in discomfort. The nightmare had come back.

It was growing stronger and more vivid in its intensity; entangling Tia is its terrifying, lucid clarity and each time, Tia awoke from its grasp sweating, upset and feeling horribly vulnerable. She sat up in bed and pushed a damp strand of auburn hair out of her face, straining all her senses, willing them to come back to reality. Trying to regulate her breathing, Tia was acutely aware of the silence for a moment, broken only by the dull clunk of the mantel clock, its antiquated mechanics echoing the thud of her own heart.

Tia looked again through the half-darkness towards the

further recesses of the bedroom and tried to hold back her tears. It had been the same scenario, night after night, for nearly a month now. She had been running, fleeing for her life down the dimly lit corridor of a house. The house felt familiar, as if she knew her way even in the sheer panic and terror that almost blinded her. He was coming to get her. The man in black. Although she never saw his face, she knew that he was evil and would stop at nothing to kill her.

Swallowing a gasp of frustration, Tia buried her face in her hands. As much as she tried to scan every recess of her memory for any further indication of what the nightmare meant, it always evaded her. It was as if she wasn't supposed to know; that it couldn't be revealed to her yet.

Lars turned over in his sleep and threw out a hand which landed on Tia's empty pillow. As his fingers spread over the damp cotton, his eyelids fluttered and half-opened, blurry with sleep. "Tia, honey, what is it?"

His muscular body, dressed only in pyjama bottoms, reached out for her but this time, she evaded his arms. He was just another thing that wanted to constrain her when she felt compelled to jump from the bed and run away. But from what? The feeling refused to leave her tired body and suddenly she could have wept with a sadness that made her soul ache.

"I'm alright," she whispered, levelling her voice as steady as she could. "Go back to sleep. I'm just a bit thirsty. I need a drink of water."

Lars turned over and feel half on his face back into the pillows. "Well, don't be too long or I'll have to come and drag you back to bed." He smiled in an effort to look enticing but within a moment, he had fallen back to sleep.

Carefully and quietly, Tia eased herself out of bed and pulled on an oversized warm cardigan over her pyjamas. It was cold in the bedroom and she felt washed out and exhausted. Taking a spare blanket, she went out into the corridor and made her way downstairs to the library. It was the one room that was the most welcoming and not too cold, with the remnants of the day's fire still smouldering in the hearth. Lined with faded red flock wallpaper and old bookcases, it still retained the atmosphere of a genteel Victorian study and Tia had already put throws over the sofa and large armchair, giving the room a relaxed and more contemporary atmosphere.

As she eased open the library door, Tia smelt the sudden scent of beeswax polish and cinnamon spice room spray, which she had used lovingly that morning to clean and freshen up the room. It was a pleasing scent and somewhat comforting. Tia wiped away a sudden tear of emotion, surprised at how something so insignificant and small as a homely scent had unlocked another small part of her heart which had become embattled and defensive following Lars' betrayal of her feelings and their marriage. What she had thought had been solid and life-long, was now just a sore, wrenching sensation that made her feel devastated and sad. She felt a gut-churning sense of failure for not having kept him interested enough and now not even having a job that could help alleviate the loneliness which had followed the law firm's clinical decision to cut her out. Rejection on both fronts had been very hard to assimilate into her normal ability to stay calm and grounded.

Tia switched on the table lamp and settled herself on the sofa, covering up her body with the blanket and wrapping it around and under her neck like a soft cocoon. She felt tired and drained but more at ease away from Lars and his demands. It wasn't that she didn't find him attractive anymore; it was the way he acted like nothing had ever happened. Each time any kind of desire built between them, it was always ruined by the thoughts of Sophie doing the same thing with Lars, and how he had obviously found Sophie sexy and gorgeous. Surely Lars had compared her to Sophie in bed and found something in Sophie that he preferred. Even now, Tia was unconvinced that Sophie would give up on Lars. Worse still, that Lars would probably encourage it.

Feeling her eyelids trying to close, Tia struggled to stay awake, dreading the images that always came with sleep. Scenes of unknown people and places she could deal with; premonitions were also something she had become used to over the years. But why hadn't she seen Lars' betrayal coming? Every time she had tried to read the Tarot cards, nothing, not even an image, had come to her inner vision. Nothing had been revealed. It was easy enough to read for friends but for some unknown reason she was not allowed to see her own destiny.

With a sudden determination to stay awake, Tia withdrew her copy of the Psychic Times, which she had kept hidden beneath the sofa away from Lars. As she scoured the pages in an effort to keep her eyes open, it was almost 5.00am before she could hold out no longer and finally succumbed to a dreamless sleep.

"Hey, sleepyhead, aren't you getting up today? And why are

you down here, anyway?"

Tia felt a hand brush over her shoulder and shake her. She sighed and tried to snuggle further into the blanket but Lars was insistent.

"It's half past seven. I'm going to take a shower and get in early. I've got a departmental meeting and as it's my first one in the new office, I'd better show willing."

"Do you really have to go in today? We've only just got here and there's so much to do." Tia peeked out from the blanket. "I wish you could stay at home."

Lars stretched out his arms and sighed, looking at her intensely. "I don't have the luxury of staying home, Tia."

"Being made redundant isn't a luxury, Lars. Anyway, I couldn't sleep."

Lars picked up the magazine from Tia's lap and scanned the page. He read aloud a random paragraph with an amused expression on his face. "*Nothing sends a shiver down the spine like a good ghost story. A tale of the supernatural, told on a dark and stormy night, has the power to invoke ancient fears and fill the imagination with all things macabre...* Seriously," he laughed, "no wonder you can't sleep, reading crap like this."

Tia sighed and held out her hand. She felt cold and nervous, despite the warmth of the blanket. "Give it back, Lars. It's not crap."

"What is it, then? Entertainment? You're so weird." Lars shook his head and dropped it nonchalantly on the sofa. He walked over to the door. "Do you want a coffee?"

"It's okay. I'll do it. You get a shower." Tia pulled back the blanket and eased her legs onto the carpet. Despite her woolly fisherman's socks, she shivered. "I'll get the fire going again this morning. It's going to need more wood already."

Lars ran a hand through his sticking up hair and laughed. "We do have some central heating, Tia. But if you want more wood, I think there's a store of it in one of the out-buildings. And a wheelbarrow."

"Great."

"Fine. I'll be upstairs."

"*Fine*."

When Lars eventually came back into the library, fully dressed and munching on a slice of toast, Tia was ready for him. Leaning forward with her hands clasped around a large mug of comforting and fortifying coffee, she kept her voice deliberately calm and steady.

"I'm going to apply for another job. I'll make a start today trawling through the local vacancies online."

His eyebrows raised in response and for a moment, Lars looked as though he was about to laugh. "Okay," he sighed, lifting up his hand to deflect any confrontation. "Whatever makes you happy. There are plenty of other law firms in Edinburgh."

"I'm not going for another legal job. I want a complete change. New house, new job, new me."

"Tia…" Lars leant forward and suddenly tried to take her hand in his own. His fingers still had toast crumbs on them. "What is the point of getting a law degree if you aren't going to use it? What do you want to do, then? Work in the local corner shop?"

Tia took back ownership of her hand and her determination. "I don't see what's wrong with that, particularly. No, actually, I thought I might try for a managerial role somewhere. I'd like to have a go at something new."

Lars stood up and sighed, straightening up his clothes. "You haven't got managerial experience. You were only a paralegal, for goodness sake, not a bloody partner. Why can't you stay at home like we agreed and get the house straight first? At least one of us would then be able to focus on their career. And it is my salary that makes a difference, Tia."

Putting the now lukewarm coffee onto the side table, Tia fought back tears. "I'm doing it, Lars, whether you like it or not. I need an income, too. I'm not some loser with no talents who has given up on life."

"Oh yeah, sure. I don't call this," Lars lifted his hands around, "giving up on life. We've got a fabulous home, Tia, think yourself bloody lucky."

"I do...I am," Tia struggled to hold back the tears, which threatened to come thick and fast again. Lately they constantly been under the surface, ready to flood her cheeks in a torrent of pain and hurt. "but I need to get out, to have something of my own. I thought you would understand, Lars."

"I do. Or at least I try to. But you are such a bloody enigma, Tia. I think I know you but I don't. And you're not," Lars paused, searching for the right words, "...you're not even stable at the moment."

"Stable? What's *that* supposed to mean?"

Lars looked down at his feet and sighed. "Just forget it. Forget I said anything. Get a job if it makes you happy, Tia. Anything for a bloody quiet life. Just don't come moaning to me when it all ends in tears because you've cocked up."

"Thanks for the vote of confidence, Lars. And stop swearing at me all the time. I'm not your PA, you know."

Lars gave a half smile, shaking his head as he left the room, leaving Tia trembling with anger.

Fighting back an almost overwhelming sensation of despair and frustration, Tia picked up her laptop from the side table and flipped it open with renewed determination. As she punched the ON button and it whirred into life, Tia bit her tongue in defiance and threw herself into the task of finding new employment, not even caring to answer when Lars hurled a goodbye from the passageway a few moments later and slammed the front door after him.

Chapter 6

"There's been another one." Ben looked up from his computer when Chris walked in. He had the grace to appear sheepish and Chris knew that neither of them would mention Ben's drunken episode again.

"Give me what you've got." Chris sat down at the desk opposite and switched on his computer. As the mountain of paperwork stared back at him from the collection of stuffed wire trays, Chris felt his stomach sink. He already knew what was coming. "Our friend, the acid freak, again?"

"Yep. But we do have a name for the victim this time. Katie McGlynn. A security guard was on a cigarette break when he saw something in the skip, just as the bin men were about to take it away. Lucky for us, not so lucky for him. He's a jibbering wreck. We could barely get a word of sense out of him. He did find her bag, though, thrown into the bushes. It had a prescription for birth control pills in it."

"Well, that's a start." Chris steeled himself for the next step, which would be looking at her body, or what remained of it, in the laboratory. As much as Eric, their Forensic Pathologist, liked his job, Chris had to psyche himself up at the prospect. "Poor kid. Did she have anything else on her?"

Ben shook his head and took the pen from behind his ear,

pointing at the screen. "About five quid in change. And she was wearing this on her toe." He stabbed at the picture on the computer. It was an enlarged photograph of a toe ring, silver and in the shape of a pentagram.

"So, she wasn't robbed, possibly into Wicca or some sort of Pagan thing. Was she raped?" Chris looked hard at the picture of the ring. Her naked toe still had the remains of chipped, red nail polish on it. His stomach turned over.

Ben chewed on his pen and then threw the wet, squashed pen lid into the waste bin beside them. "Not that Eric thinks so, no. But there were signs of consensual sexual activity. She'd definitely had it off with someone within the last few hours of her life."

Chris looked at Ben in distaste. "Let's give the lass some dignity, shall we?"

"What did I say, now?"

"Just forget it." Chris picked up his jacket and phone from his desk. "I'm going to see Eric. Can you do some digging on her background? If she was still living at that registered address when she died, any relatives, God forbid, even a parent?"

"Sure." Ben nodded and then sat forward in his chair. "Something else the security guard said. Apparently, the CCTV camera was acting weird. Our guys are looking at it, now."

"Get any footage up for me to look at as soon as you can. And question him again. I want to be sure it's not an inside job."

"Sure. Okay." Ben didn't say Guv this time. He knew better. "Where are you going?"

"Hell."

"Okay. Give Eric my regards."

A short drive away later, Eric was already gowned up in his laboratory and casually probing through the intestines of the male acid victim when Chris entered the room. The room was tiled from ceiling to floor with pale green tiles, scrubbed clinically clean, and two large basins were located at one end. In the centre were three long tables, upon which lay the bodies of a middle- aged man and a young teenage woman. Both were easily identified to Chris as the acid victims by their lack of any facial features. Even from a distance, the scene was like something out of a Gothic Victorian horror story. He didn't want to look but felt compelled to. Besides, it was his job.

Chris cleared his throat, having mentally prepared himself by staring through the square of glass in the door for a full five minutes. No matter how often he went into the room, he always dreaded it. He hated the gore, he hated the sound of the various electrical tools and, worst of all, he hated seeing the victims stripped of all their humanity and dignity. Naked bodies were one thing, but lifeless bodies robbed of any hope and chance of reprieve were beyond sad. Someone's son, daughter, spouse even, lay on those tables and it would fall to him, yet again, to hunt down the bastard who had committed their murders.

"Alright, Chris? How's the world treating you, then? I hear you've been out on the lash."

"Don't. Keeping my sidekick from being sent to juvenile detention camp, more like. I see news travels fast."

"Nothing's a secret from us, mate, you know that. Anyway,

have you come to see our new beauty?"

"Yeah." Chris put one steady foot in front of the other and tried not to look at the suspicious, bloody contents in the sink. "Jesus, Eric, you really enjoy your job, don't you?"

"Someone's gotta do the crap or we'd never catch the villains. Present company excepted, of course."

"Of course. So this is Katie McGlynn. She's so...fragile. How the hell could somebody do this to a young woman. She looks so...defenceless...", he muttered, already annoyed for her sake.

"Yeah, but that's the strange bit. No sign of struggle, no skin under her fingernails. Nothing to say how she died. One thing is for sure, though, both of our victims died before the acid was applied."

"How do you know that? Tell me, Sherlock."

"Sarcasm will get you nowhere. Look for yourself."

"Where?" Chris looked down at the young woman's slender, naked body and was none the wiser. She looked perfect, apart from her lack of facial features. No bruising, no scratches. "Where am I supposed to be looking?"

"Basically, in layman's terms, it comes down to timing. After primary flaccidity at the time of death and then the stiffening of rigor mortis, both of our victims are doing what nature intended, varying of course in slightly different degrees allowing for build, muscular structure, that sort of thing. Going into corpse-mode, if you like. But the acid is still congealing in the tissues. In other words, it's still working. I've got the lab to run a few tests on it. I have no firm conclusion on what the composition of it is yet."

Chris frowned. At least they had been spared being burned

through the eyes and face whilst still alive. "So, it was just an attempt to remove their identity. All rather old-school, don't you think, what with fingerprints, dental records, DNA..."

Eric lifted his shoulders in response as he wiped down the surface of the table. "That depends on how rational and clued-up your average psychopath is, I suppose. Ain't no rhyme or reason why the nutters in this world act the way they do. That's what my old dad used to say and he was right."

"Great source of wisdom, yep..." Chris responded with a murmur. "Have you got *anything* I can use?"

Eric sighed and shook his head. He looked for a moment genuinely weary. "Nope. That's been the most bloody frustrating thing." Eric never normally swore and his tension was palpable. "We're dealing with the original invisible man, or woman, for that matter."

"No-one is invisible, Eric. The killer must have a calling card. I need *something* to go on."

"Well, here's the rub. There are no finger or palm prints on the bodies, no fibres in situ, no DNA for sampling...nothing. And I mean...absolutely nothing. The perpetrator is either using techniques I have never even heard of in over thirty years of investigating scenes of crime, or we are dealing with some sort of ghost."

"Which is, quite frankly, ridiculous." Chris blew out his breath and leant back against the sink, forgetting for a moment about its unsavoury contents. "I'm not questioning you, Eric, I know how good you are, but surely you must have missed something?"

Eric threw down his cleaning cloth and turned back to the

male body. "Unless he can speak, which I somehow doubt, then you'll not get anything more than what I've just told you. The bodies are clean, as I said."

"Sorry."

"Forgiven. I suppose."

Chris gave him a wry smile. "Let me have the toxicology results, as soon as?"

"Of course."

"Thanks. I owe you one."

"You owe me loads and you never even buy me a drink."

" Okay, I promise I will, Eric. Pinky promise." Chris tapped his fingers on the table where Katie lay, motionless, indicating his frustration. He didn't even want to look at her, he already felt such a failure. It didn't help that her hair was dark, like Kirsty's, and her fragile figure was reminiscent of a porcelain doll, delicate and barely able to withstand breathing, let alone the onslaught of a carefully planned acid bath on her face.

Swallowing a lump in his throat, Chris pursed his lips and, with a nod to Eric in genuine appreciation, pushed his way through the double doors and back to his car. He needed to get his head around everything before self-pity began to set in again.

Chapter 7

"You can't fire me!" Paul backed into the corner of the bar and folded his arms across his chest, defensively. His reflection in the large mirror behind the bar gave him the appearance of being older than his thirty-two years, owing to his balding head and tattoo on the back of his flabby neck.

Painter leant over him in contempt. He was not even tempted to take the young manager's soul; it gave him such a sick taste in his mouth. "I think you will find that I can, Paul. As of now. You have been in dereliction of your duties."

Paul's small eyes screwed up even smaller in anger, and he moved backwards, trying to fit himself even further into the security of the wooden bar surface behind him. " Dereliction of...God, what sort of a word is that? Why do you have to talk so heavy all the time? I turn up, I do my job...ask anyone here..."

Painter breathed down hard on the man, thinking just how easy it would be to snap his neck like a dry twig in hot sunshine. "I no longer need you as a manager. Get your things and get out. You have been here for a month. Your probation period is over and you have failed. I am quite within my rights to terminate your employment. And one other thing..."

"What?" Paul leant his head to one side, cockily, but his lower lip was already trembling. His body was automatically trying to slink away from Painter's heavy breathing and intense stare, but his bulk could not manage it. He was trapped like a mouse in a lion's den.

"Steal from my cellars again and I will personally string you up by your intestines and lower you into one of my barrels until you can't drink any more of the contents. Do you get my drift?"

"You're so fucking weird. Leave me alone! There's laws against people like you."

"I think you will find the law is on my side on this one, Paul. Unless, of course, you would like me to call our friends at Murray Road Station and ask them to explain personally to you that stealing from an employer is an offence?"

"You've got no proof..." Paul started to say and then abruptly seemed to think the better of it. His mouth snapped shut as he was compelled to stare into Painter's ice blue eyes. "You'd better pay me what you owe...I want my money."

Painter sighed and took a step back. He wanted to say that it was nothing to do with money. That it had never been about the money. He lifted his gloved, slender finger and gently brought it down over Paul's stubbly cheek. Paul flinched. "You will be paid in full and think yourself lucky that you can sleep at night."

"And...what's that...supposed to... mean..." Paul choked on his own burgeoning tears, unable to turn his eyes away. "You don't scare me," he lied, but as Painter grabbed hold of his jaw in a vice-like grip, Paul immediately acquiesced. "Okay...alright, just let...me go, yeah?"

Painter drew back his lips is a smile. "There now, that's

better. I would rather we parted as friends. You will have your money. I am not out to ruin you. You are doing a very good job of that by yourself." He drew back, as Kevin ambled in to start his shift. "Now get out. I never want to see your face in my nightclub again."

Paul let out a huge outburst of breath and backed his way quickly away out of Painter's overwhelming presence. He was red in the face and unsteady on his feet, but above all, he looked terrified. With the pulse in his throat visibly pounding, he picked up his leather jacket hurriedly from the bar stool and left the Nightshade Club as fast as possible.

With his manager gone, Painter closed his weary, sore eyes in a moment of meditation. His mind longed for the darkness again, just for a moment, to encase him in its black negativity and soothe his furious blood. It was time to feast again, to find another soul to extract and consign to oblivion whilst he fortified himself with the pure essence of human desperation. Not the scumbag Paul, who wouldn't know purity if he fell over it in the street, but a tender and sweet, vulnerable soul, another female perhaps, who would offer herself to him and then let him take everything she possessed in her sad little existence.

"Mr P....erm....what are we gonna do now? I can't work Paul's shift as well. I can't do everythin'." Kevin came over across the dancefloor and put down his damp tea towel on the wooden bar surface. "Are we gonna get another manager or do I have to stick a broom up me arse an' do all his stuff as well?"

"Kevin, you constantly delight me with your eloquence. Don't worry yourself unduly. I shall advertise immediately. I may need you to cover for a few days but I will pay you double for it."

Kevin grinned and then wiped his chin with the back of his head. "Cool, alright then. You got yerself a deal."

"Oh, that *is* a relief. I am so glad. Now, if you would excuse me, I need to run some errands. Can I leave you with the responsibility of running the Club for a few hours?"

"Course!" Kevin gave Painter a wide, gappy grin and whipped up the tea towel again. He looked around the bar area and tutted. "Does that mean I can make a few changes, then?"

"No, Kevin, it does not. Just ensure that the place doesn't burn down in my absence."

Closing his eyes, momentarily, Painter felt an intense heat begin to rise in his body, flooding into his blood vessels and bulging the veins in the pale white skin of his temples. He needed to feast again; his very essence and the urging of the Dark Ones demanded it. He couldn't hold on for much longer. As much as he wanted to destroy every bone in Kevin's body from sheer annoyance, he couldn't waste valuable energy on the wrong person. Killing Kevin would be satisfying for a moment but it would serve no long-term purpose.

"Hey, Mr P, yer don't look well..." Kevin flipped the tea towel over his shoulder and moved to get a glass from the rack above. " Can I get you a drink?"

"No!" Painter held up his hand and barely disguised the fact that it was shaking. "No," he continued, his voice softer," you carry on with your work. I shall go and lie down. I'm not to be disturbed."

"Sure, okay, whatever you need." Kevin dropped his hand,

meekly. "I'll hold the fort. You should get some kip. You look knackered."

Painter waved Kevin's comment away as if he were an irritating fly stuck in ointment. "You have no idea. I need to rest. I shall leave you in charge. For now."

"Cool." Kevin grinned widely and Painter resisted the urge to say anything in return. He was too tired.

Making a side line for his office, Painter coughed and reached to pull out his handkerchief. It was stained with blood and Painter knew what that meant. His energy was running dangerously low. Despite the delicious life essence of Katie McGlynn, or whatever name she was, Painter had barely had enough to last. It was beginning to become a problem. He needed something stronger. Something greater to satiate his hunger and slake his never-ending lust for souls. It was out of pure desperation that he sought out his next victim and he knew just where to go to get it.

Chapter 8

Lars held Tia's copy of the Psychic Times aloft in his left hand as he dug into his spaghetti bolognese with his fork in the other, grinning at Tia across the dining room table. He swallowed a mouthful and then sighed, before continuing to read aloud. "*There are countless stories of spirits who walk abroad, revisiting their earthly homes in sombre state, trying to convey the agonies of their unfinished business to any mortal soul sensitive enough to perceive them. The paranormal world is indeed a strange place. It is inhabited by more spirits and beings than we can possibly imagine, and, every so often, when the time and place is right, one will slip through from their world into ours.*" He dropped the magazine onto the table with a sarcastic laugh. "What a load of old bollocks! I can't believe that you actually read this stuff. No wonder you're away with the fairies most of the time. This is not healthy."

Tia sipped her wine and smiled back at him. "And how was *your* day, *Dear*?" She felt calm for a change and his sarcasm wasn't bothering her. "How were things at the office?"

Lars wiped his mouth with his napkin and Tia found her eyes were involuntarily fixed on the trace of tomato sauce left on its white surface.

"Fine. Why shouldn't they be?" Lars picked up his wine and sipped it, looking at Tia over the rim.

"Just asking, that's all. Any new clients?"

"One or two. I need to go in early tomorrow. We're working with our London office on a new corporate deal. The acquisition of a chain of hotels. Spin off work for our real estate teams, employment team with TUPE issues and so on. You know the score. I don't need to explain."

"No, I know. I just thought that you might want to discuss your day with me. I still remember what it is like to work in the firm, Lars. I haven't been away that long."

Lars shrugged his shoulders. " A few weeks might as well be a lifetime. You have to be at the top of the game to survive, or you might as well not bother."

"You don't think I am at the top of my game now, then? "

"I didn't say that. You're still damn sexy when you want to be. That's good enough for me. You can be on the top of me any time you like."

Tia smiled and looked down into her glass. At one time, Lars' words would have fired her up; made the dessert course much more exciting, but now - now it just felt cheap. And she still didn't quite feel he was being genuine. "Maybe," she replied, swilling the remainder of the wine around her glass. "But I have some good news as well."

"And?"

" I applied for a job this morning. It went really well. Some guy called Kevin called me back very quickly and, to be honest, I think they need somebody pretty desperately. So, I've got an interview tomorrow. Isn't that great?"

Lars put down his fork and stretched back in his chair. The low thudding clunk click of the grandfather clock in the hallway seemed to be the only sound penetrating the sudden silence surrounding them both. He sighed and turned his head towards her.

"You kept that quiet. I thought you would have at least texted me. Anyway, I thought we had discussed this?"

Tia tucked a strand of loose auburn hair behind her ear, nervously. She knew the signs when Lars was about to kick off. "Well, we didn't agree on anything, did we?"

"I thought we did," replied Lars, pushing back his chair, abruptly. "You were going to stay home. Give this place some tlc. Give *me* some tlc..."

"Oh, honestly, Lars...what century are you in?" Tia felt her blood begin to boil. "And I do give you tlc! What makes you think I don't?"

"So where is this job then?" Lars wasn't listening. He was going straight for the kill. "I should know where my wife will be working."

"It's a...it's at The Nightshade."

"What's that? A bloody hair salon? Or what?"

"A bar. It's a bar. A nightclub."

Lars threw down his napkin onto the table and pushed a hand through his hair. He turned and leant back against the chair, almost addressing the ether. " Well, this keep on getting better and better, doesn't it? A fucking nightclub? There's no way any wife of mine is going to work in a fucking nightclub."

"You don't have to swear, Lars." Tears were starting in Tia's eyes and she felt stupid again. Perhaps it had been a bad idea.

"I can swear all I like. For God's sake, Tia. How can you be such a moron? What will you be doing? Serving drinks and washing up?

"No, *no... actually*. It is an office role. When I spoke to him over the phone, he said the owner needs someone to manage the club during the daytime...help with the accounts and supervising. I don't have to work late. That's for the bar staff, apparently. It's just normal office hours."

Lars shook his head and walked around to Tia. He knelt down in front of her and took her hands. "Sweetheart, you don't need to do this. We have enough money from the flat sale. Why don't you wait until this place is finished and then get something better?"

Tia looked down at his imploring face and almost gave in, but something inside of her made her feel strong. "Lars, I know you mean well but I need to do this for me. I can still help get this place in shape but I need to be out in the real world as well."

"So, you call doing some crap accounts for a crap club is the way to do it? I must admit, Tia, I thought you had more ambition than that."

Tia couldn't stop the tears from spilling over onto her cheeks as his words punctured her solar plexus, shattering her last vestiges of courage. She brushed them away with the back of her hand, angrily. "Oh Lars, that's not fair. I thought you would understand..."

Lars rested back on his haunches, impatiently, and then stood up. "Oh, trust me, I have tried to understand you. Many times. But you make it hard for me, Tia. You just go off on a tangent all the time. You're not consistent. If you ask me, you are completely bonkers and this time, I'm not agreeing with you."

"Fine!" Tia pushed back her chair and began clearing the plates into a pile. As she vehemently scraped the remains of the spaghetti bolognese and salad into the bowl, she struggled to calm down again. Lars had crossed the floor and was pointedly turning up the music on his sound system. She knew he didn't want to argue anymore. He didn't even want to speak to her about anything. She was on her own and that was becoming normal. She didn't want to tell Lars that she was starting to feel more and more on edge being in the house on her own.

Taking herself off into the kitchen, Tia wiped away the remains of her tears and began washing up, throwing herself into the normally boring task with renewed vigour. The activity was soothing and sufficiently grounding enough, with its combination of water and rhythmic motion, that Tia soon found her mind calming down. As she brushed away at the plates with the dishmop, Tia sighed and squirted out the last of the washing up liquid in irritation. The bubbles tried to revive but fell flat, leaving the water full of gunk and orange scum.

"Lars, did you put the box of cleaning products in the cellar?" she called out, hoping that Lars would change his mind and start behaving more civilly to her again. When he didn't reply, she blew out her breath and turned around, looking for anything that looked remotely like washing up liquid.

Glancing towards the far end of the kitchen, Tia noticed the door that led down to the cellar. She hadn't even been down to the cellar yet, and didn't particularly want to go either, but Lars was ignoring her so there was nothing else to be done but check for herself.

Peeling off her rubber gloves, Tia went over to the cellar door. The wood had been painted in thick white gloss at one time, but now it was shabby, with flakes of missing paint that revealed the original door underneath was dark wood. Tia turned the door knob but it rattled, loosely. When she tried to pull the door open, to shake it, the door wouldn't budge.

"Damn!" she breathed, wondering where the key was. Surely there must be a key somewhere, and hopefully some electricity. Turning back towards the worktops and cupboards, Tia pulled open some of the kitchen drawers. They were still lined with old flowery paper and smelt of polish and mothballs. She wrinkled up her nose and picked through some of the old utensils: a set of nutcrackers, a tea strainer, a pair of sugar tongs…Tia leant back on the kitchen worktop and looked around more carefully. Where would someone logically put a key to the cellar door?

Scrabbling around the cupboards, Tia's eyes fell on an old canister marked 'Sugar', lurking in the back of the cupboard near the pantry. Something; a hunch; made her lift it out and wrench open the tin lid. With a smile, Tia tipped out the contents. A couple of old spare metal hinges, some paper clips and a lone key. It was an old iron key, black with an ornate head. Just like the other features of Redfield Grange, even the cellar key had been crafted with Victorian style, carefully and with artistic flair. Tia turned it over in the palm of her hand. It had to be the cellar key. She just knew.

Within a few moments, Tia had turned the key in the cellar door lock and grinned as it opened. But her eagerness was slightly marred by the horrible musty smell which suddenly assaulted her nostrils. The light switch was the old type, bulbous and dusty, and when Tia flicked it on, there was a low buzzing sound, followed by a crackling and then the single light bulb at the foot of the steps, pinged into life. Easing her way down the steps carefully, Tia held onto the wooden handrail with her left hand, keeping her other hand free to brush away any cobwebs from her face. The lightbulb hung down from the ceiling literally by a thread, so ancient was the wire that Tia wondered if it was a fire risk.

She looked around. The cellar was not as big as she had thought, with just a small window full of cobwebs that must have been the old coal chute. There was some free-standing metal shelving with various boxes on, containing old bottles of iodine and disinfectant. A couple of jars of dried up paint with the brushes sticking out, encrusted with dust, and a large barrel-sized tin of old paint stripper. A garden fork and a battered looking metal bucket with a single gardening glove left hanging over the brim. Over in the corner was an old biscuit tin with a label, yellow with age and curled at the edges.

Intrigued, Tia went over and picked it up. Instantly, she felt sick. A wave of nausea flooded her stomach and she retched. Slamming down the tin, Tia bent almost double. The cellar swam in front of her and she staggered over to the staircase, falling to the bottom step and grabbing on to the hand rail as she did so. She literally felt like she had been punched in the stomach.

Tia groaned and closed her eyes. Instantly, she saw a blackness, a presence which filled all of her senses. It pulsed and vibrated for a moment. As if it stood in the same room as her and was watching. She felt its intensity, its negative energy and felt it move towards her like some evil octopus with tentacles of pure pain. Tia held back a cry as then, as quickly as the vision had appeared, it disappeared, and she was once again aware of her surroundings in the cellar. Shaking violently, Tia took in some deep breaths and tried to steady herself. The vision had been so real, as real as the step she was now sitting on, but now the nausea had subsided and she felt vaguely normal again.

Completely floored, Tia managed to pull herself up against the hand rail and steady herself. It took all the strength and effort she possessed to pull herself back up the stairs and go back into the kitchen to get a glass of water.

Eventually, shakily, Tia sat on the kitchen stool, sipping gratefully at the water, feeling it cooling and soothing her throat and her senses. Tia felt the tears come, reactionary and unwanted. She choked and sipped some more water, not wanting to feel weak and pathetic. But the vision had been so strong, much clearer than any vision she had ever had before. and for a moment, Tia doubted her own sanity. She rested her hand in her hands and could have sobbed. Maybe Lars was right. Maybe she *was* unstable. Maybe her senses were warning her that she was overdoing things, thinking too hard and torturing herself. Everything has got worse since the sale of the flat, since her world had crumbled around her. Perhaps she was having a nervous breakdown.

Tia's first thought was to tell Lars all about it but then she stopped herself. He had been in a foul mood and she found herself getting anxious again at the thought of his reaction. Trying to keep things light and less stressful, Tia arranged a smile of her face and went out of the kitchen but stopped in her tracks outside the living room door.

Lars was talking on his phone and clearly trying to keep his voice down. Something within Tia stopped her from going inside and she found herself doing the worst of all things: eaves-dropping on her own husband. He was talking in a low, murmuring voice but every so often his voice rose and she could make out a few words.

"...*of course* I do...sure..."

And then he laughed. It wasn't his normal laugh. It sounded, well, seedy. Smutty.

Tia's stomach lurched in response. Lars didn't sound like he was on the phone to one of his clients. Her heart hammering, Tia leant as much as she dared into the doorway and felt the blood start to pound her ears.

"...you know I would..." He laughed again and then his voice dropped to such a whisper that Tia couldn't hear any further. Panicking and not knowing if Lars would suddenly wrench open the door on her at any moment, Tia made a bolt for it and ran upstairs as quietly as she could, not wanting to draw attention to her footsteps. With her mind threatening to go into overdrive, she fell onto the side of the bed and felt the tears come again. This time, there was no stopping them.

The Affair wasn't over and she knew. Deep down with every

fibre of her being, Tia felt the betrayal as fresh and as agonising as if it had been yesterday. There were still three of them within her marriage, whether she liked it or not.

Tia picked up her fleecy dressing gown from the end of the bed frame and hugged it against her, as the rage and anger boiled up within her again. Part of her wanted to run downstairs and confront him; to punch his arrogant, lying face and hurt him for hurting her. The other part of her, the sadder, oldest, wisest part, knew that, in reality, there was nothing she could do. Lars had made his choice and it wasn't her.

Sobbing, Tia curled up into a protective ball and leant back into the pillows, cuddling the warm, comforting material like it was a teddy bear. But what little comfort it gave Tia paled into insignificance as images of Lars and Sophie flooded her mind. She remembered seeing them together at work, going off together for meetings, saying they had a lunch meeting when they were going out in his car and doing God knows what.

Throwing off the dressing gown, Tia pulled her deck of Tarot cards from the top drawer of her bedside cabinet and angrily began to shuffle them.

"Come on, cards, *tell me*. Tell me what I need to know about Lars and Sophie." Wiping away her tears with the back of her hand, Tia continued to shuffle the cards. She withdrew a card and placed it, face-down, on the bed.

She turned the card over. It was the Tower card. "Great," she murmured, "tell me something that I *didn't* know." The tower in the card was depicted as crashing down in a rush of cracked stone, rubble and flames. It was a card of war between lies and truth. When everything you ever believed to be true came crashing down as a lie. The end of everything you had ever taken for granted. The end of an era.

  Tia felt the familiar punch of knowing. She tried not to let her thoughts go back to when she had first suspected Lars and Sophie of having an affair. The late nights, the constant demanding clients who suddenly needed his attention after hours. It had all been obvious but she hadn't wanted to see, to face reality until it had hit her in the face. Now it was impossible to ignore and what was even worse, she felt utterly trapped and unable to do anything about it.

Chapter 9

"So, what have you got? Katie McGlynn. Poor kid..." Chris bent over and watched the CCTV footage, frowning. His eyes followed her as she walked down the road. She looked fragile, vulnerable, and much younger even than her teenage years. Suddenly, he turned away, unable to look anymore. Perhaps he was growing soft, but Katie McGlynn and her whole sorry story had gotten under his skin.

Chris went over to the window and looked out. Below, in the street, life went on as normal, and yet he felt distant, unconnected to it. And, dare he say it, utterly lonely. He had seen Kirsty on Facebook the previous night, looking like she had won the lottery with an old boyfriend on hers. Apparently, they had "rediscovered each other". What a crock of bullshit. Chris felt his blood run hot. He didn't even want to think about her rediscovering anybody. The more he thought about it, the more he didn't believe that the boyfriend, Dave, Sam, or whatever idiot name he was, had merely climbed out of the woodwork twenty years later. Did she really think everyone believed her bullshit lies?

"Hey Guv, you ready for this?"

Chris broke away from his stare into nothingness and raised an eyebrow at Ben. "What is it?" He went back over to Ben's desk and folded his arms in anticipation.

"I'm not completely sure..." Ben hit the rewind button and

the two of them watched Katie walking down the road again. But then Ben enhanced the audio. She was talking. Her mouth moved sporadically as if she were talking to someone next to her, but the audio sounded muffled, as if someone had put their hand over the microphone.

"Poor kid," mused Ben, shaking his head. "Out of her face, obviously."

"Rewind it again."

"Patience is a virtue, Guv."

"Cut the crap."

"Okay." Ben hurriedly did something to the video footage and paused it. "Here we go again," he motioned, as the time on the footage stopped. "…weird, though. It really does look like she's talking to someone. She looks completely coherent. Her inflections, her mannerisms, it's like she is really having a conversation. But who the hell is she talking to?" Completely frustrated, Ben tossed his pen into the nearby pile of papers. "How many times can I keep looking at this stuff…"

"We might be missing something…"

"She's clearly ill, Guv. Look at her. Anyone can see that."

"Wait..." Chris leaned forward, frowning, "…what's that?"

"What's what?" Ben sighed, slurping his, now cold, coffee.

Chris pressed his finger on to the computer monitor, to the right of Katie's grainy, slim figure. A grey mist, a blurred shape had appeared and seemed to hang, as if suspended, next to her.

"Zoom in, Ben"

"*Okay…*" As Ben enhanced the visual as much as he could,

Chris leant in so close over Ben's shoulder, that Ben laughed. "Anyone would think you fancied me, Guv."

"You should be so lucky. Damn…" Chris shook his head in frustration, "it's gone."

Ben hit the rewind button yet again, but no matter what he did, the shape didn't reappear and both men were perplexed.

"I don't get it," murmured Chris. "You saw it, Ben. It was a shape, a…something…but how can it disappear from a *recording*?" A chill crept up his spine and he crossed his arms, defensively. A random thought ran through his mind. *Something is messing with us.*

"Shall I get the lab to clean it up even more?" Ben's voice broke through the strained silence.

"Yep, asap…" but in his own mind, Chris didn't feel convinced. He knew, on some deep level, that nothing would be found.

He sighed and went back to his desk, logging in to his own computer. Another load of emails had appeared in his inbox and he didn't feel like answering any of them. Somehow, he mustered the energy. "Let's see if there's any news on the other guy."

Chris searched through and clicked on the latest email from Eric. The news wasn't good. "Looks like the acid results are inconclusive. It wasn't sulphuric acid, apparently."

Ben lifted his eyebrows and swivelled around on his chair to face Chris. "Well, that's a surprise. I would have thought that would have been our weirdo friend's first port of call."

"Yeah, me, too. Eric says the ingredients were made up of a corrosive rat poison that you can't buy nowadays as it's banned, arsenic, and something else which the lab hasn't been able to identify. It doesn't match any known substance. Eric thinks it has an element of human-like blood but it doesn't match any known blood grouping."

"That's a bit bloody freaky. Excuse the pun."

Chris nodded in agreement. Eric had also sent through a list of known cases with similar attributes, as an attachment to his email. There were several names, spanning many years and he felt a sudden sense of dejection. If they were dealing with a copy-cat killer, then they had their work cut out. So far, there was little motive for the killings. No robbery, no sexual attack, nothing that would suggest the victims had anything worth being killed for. All known drug dealers in the area had been ruled out. So that left very little to go on. *Psychopath* seemed the best explanation, thus far.

"I'm sending these to you, Ben," said Chris as he forwarded the email and file attachments to Ben. "Eric has found similar cases. I want you to go through these and see if you can find any link. If we are looking at a copy-cat killer, then I would expect a common thread. Something that ties them altogether."

Ben blew out his breath as he clicked on the email which had just appeared in his inbox. "Blimey, Guv, this list goes back decades. And all over the UK. This is gonna take me ages…"

"Last time I looked, that was your job, Ben."

"*Okaaaaay*…" Ben clicked on Print and pushed back his chair. "I'll make a start, then. What are you going to do?"

"Back track."

"What do you mean?" Ben made a face but he had worked

with Chris long enough to know that his boss was up to something.

Chris smiled at him, but there was no humour in his eyes. "We need to go back to the start with this, Ben. Step by step. Sooner or later, this killer is going to slip up, make a mistake. And I'll be there, ready for him."

Chapter 10

Painter was reminiscing. He was thinking about the pretty, young Apothecary's assistant he had first purchased poison from in the East End of London. 1899. The end of a century and the dawn of a new age. Queen Victoria had been on the throne of England for many years when Painter first came into the world of human beings; the place they called Earth.

He did not fully remember his birthing into his first adult human form, nor did he care, for all he saw around him had been poor, disease-stricken unfortunates, scraping a miserable living with their wretched lives. And that had suited him perfectly. He had arrived on the Earth plane in the form of a fully grown man but as a Youngblood, and as such, his thirst for souls had been instant, as ingrained in him as hunger and thirst was in a human baby crying for milk. And Painter had been just as needy, consumed by his voracious appetite to feed on the life essence that only a human could provide. The Ancient Ones had always known where best to birth him. They had had millennia to watch humanity and decide where one of their own could be born with the most amount of food and the least amount of resistance.

His first victim had been rather pathetic. An old man, hanging over the ropes of the night shelter with hardly anything to his name, had been easy pickings. The life essence of the old man had slipped easily into Painter, as if the man had been glad, relieved that his harsh life was finally over and he had some form of release. But Purgatory was no release, as the old man would soon find out. Painter instantly went on to his next victim, for it had sharpened his abilities but not dulled his appetite. He had been impelled to move on, to feast on more and more souls. To spread the darkness that he carried even further into their filthy, disease-ridden world.

Painter remembered how the nights had drawn in early, made worse by the continual smog of the day. Now the nights, too, had also been blanketed in thick, unforgiving fog. Only a few lone street lamps, weakly shining a dim yellow gas arc through the swirling white mist, had given Painter any indication that he walked along streets lined with slum terraced housing, each building as decrepit and ruined as the next. Beneath the oppressive, choking air, the streets had been crowded with brick, dark doorways and just a few windows with tattered lace curtains and one or two lone candles etched through the dirt and grime of the glass. Less smoke had billowed out of these chimneys as the tenants were poor and had little means to provide fuel for the fires. From what Painter had initially gained from scouring the place, most people only had the rags they stood up in, and they had little else to throw on the fire. Painter had watched them from the shadows, seeing them eek out a futile day's pay, either from home or down at the dockyards. Some females made a few pence servicing the men, and then proceeded to obliterate their miserable existences in a drunken haze of cheap grog. Painter had watched them in detachment rather than any form of desire. He had felt nothing but loathing as he watched their diseased bodies being used and discarded like rags.

Painter had created a diversion to cover his tracks for his next victim. He had simply pushed a lone dock worker into the Thames river and watched the helpless man thrash about and drown, before anyone could reach him. Before the shouting and clamouring had died down, Painter slipped away, knowing that the crowd were too interested in what had happened to the dock worker, to follow him. It had been tremendous fun to watch them panic and scuttle about like little rats. That made is so easy to hide himself in the derelict old warehouse, wrecked by years of neglect and infested with river vermin and filth.

Throughout his time spent in the East End of London, Painter had realised that many of its inhabitants were neither clean nor law-abiding and that suited him. It had been easy to shadow their lives, seep into the background like a ghost and follow their every move. They were as predictable as the dead-eyed fish thrown daily onto the slabs at Billingsgate Market, and their language had been just as coarse. Their eyes, dull and clouded by poverty, alcohol and resignation, never made contact with his as they shuffled to whatever destination they had to get to. Even his height, which was unusual in an age of under-nourished and diseased men, gave little cause for interest or concern. He was just a shadow. No-one ever spoke a word to him and no-one hassled him. He was invisible and he couldn't have asked for more.

No-one had noticed him slip into the warehouse, and if they had, they would not have remained alive long enough to recognise him again.

The woman had been a mess of copper-coloured, matted hair and rags and she had smelt like a sewer. To Painter's refined tastes, she was like the mice and rats which scurried across the warehouse floor. As his boots crept quietly across the dusty, earthen floorboards, he saw that she lay propped up against a sack of flour. Rat prints left a trail from the hole in the sacking which had been gnawed through and went somewhere into the dark recesses. Painter had no doubt they would be back. It was the perfect opportunity for him to discard the body once he had finished with her. He stooped down in front of her, expecting some form of questioning, a pathetic attempt at resistance, but her half-opened eyes failed to register his presence. She looked through him, not even blinking and Painter knew that she was comatose. He sighed with a little disappointment as his eyes swept over her haggard body. How old was she, he thought? Twenty? Thirty, in human years? It was hard to tell from her filthy skin and tangled curls that fell from the untidy cap on her head. She wore a dress and apron, and perhaps she had run away from a life of service to the gentry, for it looked in slightly better condition than she did. He felt a rush of annoyance, as he had expected some fight from her, and as he took her in his arms and began the process of sucking in her soul, he felt let down, still hungry and instantly longing for more. Her soul gave itself to him readily and that was when Painter realised that he was actually doing her a favour. She had probably longed for death well before she had collapsed on that warehouse floor, unmissed by anyone and only noticed by himself. To Painter, it had been like taking a small morsel of food as an appetiser when he felt as hungry as a ravenous wolf.

He had been so disgusted, he had kicked her lifeless corpse over and left her to rot, face-down on the rat-infested floorboards.

Now in the present day of the old City of Edinburgh, in the macabre setting of Greyfriars Kirk and its sinister tombs, Painter slunk back into the decayed rubble of a disused old grave, waiting for the full darkness of night to immerse the old streets of Edinburgh. The old graveyard was perfect to hide in and watch those seeking out the paranormal or just wanting a scare. A couple of ghost tours were always happening at night, and the tourists hungry for tales of the old Covenanters imprisoned in the rear of the graveyard would provide easy pickings. A heart attack; a shock from being clawed at by the fabled McKenzie poltergeist; it all provided cover for him on a theatre stage of hauntings. People wanted horror, but in their little worlds of fantasy and schoolgirl giggling, they had no idea of the real evil that was stalking them, watching their every move and waiting to pounce on them with far worse consequences than they could ever imagine.

His eyes shone and his teeth gleamed in the moonlight, as Painter darted amongst the Gothic monuments and decayed epitaphs, splaying out his long fingers over the damp, cold stone and once again drinking in the air of death. Just like Hades at the Gates of Hell, he positioned himself in place, hiding amongst the tombs and almost reeling with hunger and anticipation. He was looking forward to the night ahead and he didn't have to wait long before the familiar tones of the usual tour guide echoed the path from the entrance into Greyfriars.

"The MacKenzie Poltergeist. No doubt you've heard of it or

you probably wouldn't be here…" The tour guide, resplendent in his theatrical long black coat and wide-brimmed black hat, raised his eyebrows and watched as the small group of tourists visibly shuddered.

One of them, a guy of about thirty, laughed even louder. "Yeah, well, that's why we're here, innit, mate? Ter test the theory. See if ghosts an' all that crap actually exist." Emboldened by the nervous group of tourists who giggled around him, he went further. "I've 'eard all about it. Some 'omeless bloke broke in ter the crypt and stirred it all up. Now it attacks people."

As the tour guide's torch wavered its beam across the young man's face, the tour guide suddenly switched it off. The group, their nerves already heightened by the creepy atmosphere and air of anticipation, gasped and one girl stifled a small scream and then giggled.

"Just so you know," leant in the tour guide, menacingly, "The MacKenzie ghoul doesn't like disrespect. If I were you, I would keep your thoughts on the *down low*. You don't want to be its next victim." The tour guide switched on his torch again.

"Yeah, well…" laughed the man in reply, looking around at the group, shaken, despite his bravado. "…bring it on. That's what I say."

"Be careful what you wish for." The tour guide lowered his voice as the wind suddenly whipped across the Greyfriars Kirk Kirkyard. "Edinburgh is a very haunted city, especially here in Greyfriars Kirkyard, and the Covenanters' Prison, where we will be going next, is the worst of all."

He turned and beckoned the group to follow him. As they trudged up the narrow path towards the church itself, one of the group edged forward. "So, what's the Prison all about, then? Who were the Covenanters?"

"Okay, well, the story goes back to King Charles 1, who wanted them to change their religion. I won't bore you with the politics but let's just say they said no. They wouldn't swear allegiance to the King, so they were rounded up and imprisoned in the Kirkyard here. They were kept out in the open through the harsh winter months with little food. Any who didn't perish in the inhumane and terrible conditions were executed or even sold into slavery."

"Pretty tough for them," went on the tourist, "but why MacKenzie? What has that got to do with it?"

The tour guide halted them all in front of the church. The darkened doorway was the only refuge from the wind, which was beginning to pick up strength. One or two of the group, a couple of teenage girls, looked frightened and huddled together.

"Bloody George MacKenzie. He was a Scottish lawyer and Lord Advocate. Judge and Executioner of the Covenanters. In 1679, around twelve hundred of the poor souls were rounded up and incarcerated here. Follow me. And let me warn you. As part of the disclaimer, once I unlock the gates of the Covenanters' Prison, I will not be responsible for anything that happens to you. Okay?"

"Bloody hell," said one of the teenage girls. "I don't think I like this."

"The Black Mausoleum, in the Prison, is where Bloody

George MacKenzie was laid to rest. Only, he isn't at rest. Not anymore."

He led them along the short path to the metal gates which were padlocked. As he flickered his torch beam through the metal, they could see the tombs within, embedded amongst the uneven grass. "When we enter the Black Mausoleum, be on your guard. Some people have experienced scratches, bruises, and fainting attacks. There is no knowing what might happen, and who might get singled out."

The group barely laughed this time as they went through the gates, one by one. The tour guide closed the gates behind them and went to the front of the group. "Oh, and one more thing that I didn't tell you. This area has been exorcised unsuccessfully."

"But that was a good thing. Surely?" asked the other teenage girl, her eyes as big as saucers. "Doing an exorcism, I mean?"

"Not for one of the exorcists," retorted the tour guide, with a shrug of his large shoulders. "He died a week later from a heart attack. Bloody MacKenzie had claimed another victim."

"Shit", she replied, and dug her hands further into her padded jacket. "That's really crap."

The small group waited with tangible fear as the tour guide led them down the macabre avenue of tombs, each one individually carved with the message of eternal hope and rest. As the torch light flickered across each one, the tour guide ramped up his narrative.

"There are those who think it might not be Bloody MacKenzie at all, but the spirits of the hundreds of plague victims buried in mounds beneath our feet. Perhaps they are the malevolent force which causes such misery around this place. Deprived of life, perhaps in death, they torment the living because they are angry and jealous because their own lives were snuffed out. You see the mounds in the Kirkyard, how uneven it is when you walk? That's the piles of bones which have mounted up over the centuries."

The whole group grew silent as the tour guide walked solemnly in front of them with his torch.

"That's weird," said a woman with glasses and an American twang in her voice, "have you noticed? There's no wind in here at all. It's as still as the grave. Sorry, bad joke," she laughed, nervously, looking round at the group.

"And quiet, too. Like you wouldn't think the traffic an' everything was going on outside..." Her husband squeezed his wife's hand reassuringly. "This is bizarre. Like a movie set or somethin'. Honey, stop breathing down my neck."

"I'm not, Hank. How can I be when I'm right over here?"

The man spun around like he was on fire and was visibly pale with fright as the tour guide's torch beam caught his face. His wife was standing over the other side of the group. "H...how...the hell..." he muttered, glancing around the group in horror. "I just touched you, Honey. I felt your hand..."

"Aye, it's begun," nodded the tour guide, gravely. "Be prepared. We are not alone, and it seems that MacKenzie may have already selected his next victim."

"That's it! I'm not staying another minute. Honey, we're going!" The American went to pull his wife away but the tour guide stopped him in his tracks.

"The gate is locked. We are in this together. Whatever you do, *don't show fear*. That's what it wants. It feeds off fear. Your energy will help it manifest. That's why you have to keep calm."

"But what the bloody hell did I just touch?"

"As I said," repeated the tour guide, evading the question, "just stay calm. We are about to enter the Black Mausoleum."

"Yeah, but you didn't answer me," muttered the man, following the rest of the group.

The tour guide stopped outside of the rotunda as one of the teenage girls threw up her hand to her mouth and gasped. "I'm gonna be sick. I can't stay here. Can't you smell it? It's like…like rotting meat."

"That's not uncommon," returned the guide, "but if you really feel bad, I suggest you wait outside."

"Yeah, okay…" She scuffed at the grass on the ground with her boot "Just don't be long…"

As the nervous group made its way hesitantly into the tomb, the young girl glanced around her in obvious fear. Painter started edging towards her. This time, there would be no seduction, no flattering conversation. He was rabid with hunger and her soul, gloriously naïve and unsuspecting, was like the whiff of the finest whiskey to an alcoholic. He had singled her out instantly as the weakest of the group and her rising fear was palpable. He waited until she moved away from the mausoleum with her nose muffled in her jacket sleeve unable to stand being so close to the stench. It was the stench of hundreds of years of suffering, torture and decay and nothing to do with him but he was pleased to use its effects to his own advantage.

He waited until the group were immersed in the mausoleum, hearing their inane giggling and gasping as the tour guide made good his word and continued his affray on their senses, with all the shock and horror his tales could muster. The young girl shook with cold and fear, her breath bright and swirling in the night air. She knew that something was there. Her already fledgling psychic qualities were heightened and she sensed his presence, moving in the dark, feeling his way along the walls. She did not know where he was but she could sense his movement. He knew that and it excited him even more.

Painter felt a flood of desire. Not human desire but something far deeper and more delicious. He was close to her now and as excited as a lion ready to leap on its prey. As she turned quickly around and saw him finally, her mouth opened in a whimper of a scream, lost within the noise of the nervous laughter of the group inside the tomb. Painter clutched her jaw in his gloved hand and bent over, as if to kiss her, drawing in the first vapours of her soul being squeezed from her human shell. He closed his eyes in rapture as she struggled for a moment and then fell lifeless against him, giving up her essence as easily as a feather to the wind.

He staggered for a moment under her weight and then hurriedly pulled her away into the darkest recesses of the Covenanters Prison where he could finish his meal and his task to annihilate her identity and her existence. As the surge of power and diabolism began to enrich his being again, he leant back his head to drink in every drop of ecstasy, feeling the tears trickling from his eyes and down his cheeks. Nothing could compare to the sensation of satisfaction forging through him, as it fed every pore, every cell of his human-like body and filtered into his etheric bodies and into the darkness of his being.

Rejuvenated, momentarily satiated, Painter plunged his hand into his cloak and took out the glass apothecary's phial, Laying the young girl's lifeless carcass on the grass, Painter began to drip the corrosive liquid onto her face. He watched, always fascinated, as the first drops hit her closed eyelids with deadly accuracy. The globules of mixed liquid and skin tissue hissed and bubbled, turning the air acrid with its own peculiar chemical stench. More droplets fell onto her nose, burning the bridge of her cartilage instantly and dissolving it like putty. As the acid continued its path of deathly destruction, Painter suddenly became acutely aware of the silence around him. He knew that the group would soon be finishing their vigil and he had to move fast.

Abruptly rolling her into a mound of grass clippings and garden tools, Painter swept up to his full height and flattened himself against the wall. The group was making its way out of the tomb, the myriad of torches casting cross beams of light around the ground and further towards the gates of the Covenanters Prison.

"I can't wait to get to the hotel, Hank," said the American woman, clutching hold of her husband's arm as if she would never let go again. "These ghost hunts might be alright for the youngsters, but I've had enough."

"Agree with that," retorted her husband, as they nodded in thanks to the tour guide and indicated that they would find their own way out of the Kirkyard.

As the couple moved off, still clinging to each other, the tour guide gratefully accepted his tips and smiled down at the teenage girl. "I'm not sure where your friend went, but it's a shame she didn't want to experience McKenzie's spirit for herself."

"I think the only spirit she would be interested in, is a bloody big vodka. "Don't worry, I know where she will be hanging out. Probably Frankenstein's bar. Cheers for that, though, the tour was great. *I* enjoyed it, anyway. It was good fun. Weird, but fun." The girl grinned and walked off, shining her torch steadily at the path in front of her.

Finally left alone, the tour guide finished locking up the gates, hurriedly, as he never liked to stay around the place on his own. For a moment, he thought he saw something move, a shadow, inching itself around the tombs. He peered again through the locked Covenanters gate, straining his eyes, but then turned away, quickly. He had enough experience to leave well alone, and he, for one, was not going to let McKenzie's spirit come out of the Covenanters Prison and torment him.

Jangling the keys back into his pocket, the tour guide turned and began his walk back to the entrance of Greyfriars Kirkyard, although all the while unable to fully shake off the unnerving feeling that something was watching him.

Chapter 11

Tia went into the Nightshade Club and caught a glimpse of herself in one of the mirrors on the wall that lined the corridor. She was dressed smartly, in a navy pencil skirt and jacket and open-necked pink blouse, but for a moment, she felt completely out of her comfort zone. It felt so alien to be in an underground nightclub, a world away from employment law and tribunals and everything that she had worked so closely around for the last few years. Tia's face was pale, despite her efforts to do her make-up really carefully. What was someone who worked in a nightclub office supposed to look like? Too stiff and formal and she might come across as very uncool. Too revealing and she would just feel uncomfortable.

After Lars had reluctantly agreed to drop her off in the car, he had been silent the whole way from Redfield Grange into the centre of Edinburgh. She had not got one word out of him. Grimly, he had let her get out of the car and was gone in a second. As she had glanced behind her, Tia knew he was really annoyed with her because she hadn't given in and changed her mind.

Tia sniffed and held up her head in her reflection. Her auburn hair, pulled back into a loose bun, looked burnished and shiny. It wasn't going to be the only thing about her that had any fire. Let him be angry. How was she supposed to feel after listening to *that* conversation? With her high heels clicking along the stone floor, Tia made her way to the Bar area, determined to give a good impression. She *needed* this job for her sanity.

When he eventually came out of the cellar to meet her, Kevin eyed Tia up appreciatively and she found herself almost squirming under his gaze. He indicated for them to sit down in the Brodie area and he immediately offered Tia a drink.

"You can have anything. Mr P has left me in charge. What d'you want? We have some new cocktails; The Body Snatcher? The Big O, that one is awesome, it lights up with blue sparks, or the Poor Monk if you just want flaming red water…it looks like bad piss, though…"

"Oh…no…I'm fine…thanks." Tia tried not to look rude by staring at her surroundings but it was hard as they were so beautiful. It was exquisitely designed and looked expensive. Most of all, Tia felt it was somewhere she could be herself. It wasn't corporate, or stuffy or over-bearing in any way. It felt perfect and Tia found herself hoping she would get the job.

"Sure? Okay, please yourself but yer missing a trick. I made the Big O and it nearly took me 'ead off. Can't wait to try it out on the old…clee…on…tell..." Kevin laughed and then realised, by Tia's stiff reaction, that he needed to tone it down and act more professional.

"So, who is Mr P? You said on the phone that you were the owner?" Tia sat forward to encourage the formality.

Kevin shifted in his seat and had the grace to look uncomfortable. "Well, no, not exactly. I mean I don't *own* the place," he laughed, scratching the gingery stubble on his chin. "Mr P is the owner. I'm managing it all, though. I can hire or fire."

"I see," replied Tia, trying hard not to smile. It was obvious that he had no more clout than she did, but if getting the job meant humouring him, then she was ready and willing to play along. "So," she smiled, leaning across more closely towards him. "What will my duties be? You said the role involves keeping things working smoothly…"

Kevin cleared his throat and took a big gulp of his beer. "Um, yeah, you can run the books, keep it all sweet, do the orders 'n' stuff. Mr P is only around at night. You'll probably never see 'im much during the day so you can do what yer like, really. Just turn up and…do your thing…anythin' has got to be better than the last arseh…I mean manager that we had. Pissface Paul."

"So…what happened?"

"Mr P fired him. And its cos *I* told him a few home truths. Like him never turnin' up for his shifts. So, as long as *you* do, you an' me are mates. Okay?"

"Sure. Sounds good to me." Tia continued to smile, good-naturedly, but inwardly she was starting to feel dejected. She didn't want to just "turn up". She wanted a proper job. A decent role.

Kevin slurped the rest of his beer and grinned. "Look, don't let me put you off. I'm alright an' this place is crackin'. Do you wanna start tomorrow?"

"Erm, yes, perfect. Do you want me to sign a contract or anything?"

"Oh, don't worry. Mr P'll put it all in the post. You can call this number…" Kevin took out a wad of yellow sticky notes from his jeans pocket and took the pen from behind his ear, scribbling down a few figures. "This is the payroll lady. Just give her your bank details an' she'll sort it all out. Mr P pays weekly. Where d'ya live, then? You ain't from round here. You sound like a Londoner. Like me but posher. I moved up here a few years back. Best thing I ever done, if you ask me. London was getting a bit…um…small."

Tia smiled again. "I'm from North London. Pinner originally, actually. My husband, Lars, comes from Kensington. He is a lot posher than I am. We live at Redfield Grange now, just outside the city. Do you know it?"

"Nah, don't think so," Kevin murmured, slurping the last of his drink. "Hey," he paused, wiping the last vestiges of foam from his full lips with the back of his hand, "wait, yeah, isn't that the big 'ouse, the one that's on its own in the middle of nowhere? The one that looks weird?"

"Yes, that's it." As Tia confirmed to him that it was, she felt another shudder, as if from nowhere. It was so strong and unexpected that she felt genuine goose bumps on her arms. It was as if someone had opened the door suddenly to let in a huge draught of air. Or that someone had walked over her grave. "How have you heard about it, then?"

"Oh, nothing major. Just that you get to know, with this club being in the caverns and everythin', all about the local legends. It was a right dive, back in the day. Everythin' dodgy went on, there. Rituals, animal sacrifices, kids buried in the garden…"

Tia opened her mouth in horror and then shut it again as Kevin burst out laughing.

"Just kiddin'. Gawd, you're easy to wind up, ain't yer? Better get used to the piss getting taken out of you. Loads more where that came from."

"Mmm...great. Can't wait." Tia stood up and smiled again, holding out her hand. "Well, thanks, Kevin. I'm looking forward to starting tomorrow. Where will my office be?"

Kevin stood up and pushed out his podgy stomach until the ACDC tee-shirt began rolling up his pale, freckled skin. "This is it, love," he gestured. "This is yer office. Pitch a tent anywhere you like, as long as it's not in front of the customers. That's what Mr P likes. But don't go backstage. He don't like anyone going backstage."

"Backstage?"

"Mr P's own personal office. The Moriarty Suite," Kevin indicated, by virtually flinging his chubby arm across her face. "He keeps it locked when he's not in. He hates anyone pokin' around."

"Where does Mr P live, then?" Tia picked up her shoulder bag and followed him across the floor back to the Bar entrance, glad that the so-called interview was finally over. "Is he local?"

"Yeah, well, I guess so. I dunno," he held the front door of the Nightshade open for her and hissed at the sound of traffic echoing down the stone passage as if he were a vampire being stung by a shot of sunlight. He shrugged his shoulders as Tia smiled back at him. "I s'pose he must be. Probably got a turret somewhere." He laughed at his own feeble joke and then finally gave her hand a quick shake. "Awesome. See you tomorrow then. An' don't be late."

Tia nodded her head in reply. "I won't."

As she finally walked up the road to the nearest taxi rank, Tia was already thinking of how she was going to relay the whole experience to Lars. He would have to get used to dropping her off before he went to the office, but the sooner she got a car of her own sorted out, the better.

She broke the news to him over dinner and waited for the attack. When it didn't come, and Lars merely lifted his shoulders and cut up his roast potato in silence, Tia felt even more hurt. The air of nonchalance around him only served to make her feel more vulnerable and yet more determined than ever to find a way through the situation.

"So, what do you think? Lars?"

He chewed slowly, deliberately, before answering. "What do you want me to think? You wanted a job; you've got a job. Great. What more do you want me to say?"

"Well done? That would be good. And the extra money will be handy, Lars. We can pay for a gardener to get the grounds into shape. They are really pretty…"

"On an extra five quid a week? Or do you get paid overtime? Sweetheart, why don't you just get real?"

Tia felt pain stab her heart. "I thought…hoped…you might be pleased."

"Pleased that my wife will be doing a school leaver's job in a seedy nightclub? Oh yeah, I'm over the moon. Wait until I tell everyone at work how well you're doing,"

"You're just a snob, Lars. If I got another role in a law firm then you wouldn't be acting like this."

Lars laid down his cutlery in a studied, careful manner and looked down at her. Not at her, but down at her, as though Tia was worthless.

"But you aren't in a law firm, are you, Tia? Not anymore. And you aren't exactly the best candidate now, are you? You're missing the boat. You should be going forwards, not backwards. It's a good job one of us at least cares about our career and is doing the right thing. You make me feel…"

"What? Tell me, Lars. Ashamed? Is that it?" She put down her glass of water, only just resisting the urge to throw it at him. "Am I just an embarrassment to you now?"

Lars leant forward and put his head in his hands. "You're a nightmare, Tia. Do you want to know the real reason why the firm made you redundant? Got rid of you, as you put it?"

"No, I don't, Lars. So, go on, why don't you tell me?"

"Because I bloody asked them to, that's why!"

Tia dropped the knife and fork fall onto her plate with a clang, staring at him for a moment in complete shock. "What do you mean", she managed to say, noticing that her hands had begun to tremble, "you *asked* them to…"

Lars got up abruptly from his chair and swung around, thrusting his hands on his hips, defensively. "Yes, I recommended that you were one of the redundancies. The firm didn't need you, Tia. It didn't need your role and I thought…I thought you would be better at home, here. That's why I thought Redfield Grange would be good for us."

Tia felt her whole body about to go into meltdown. For the

moment, all she could do was get away from him, to put as much physical distance between them as possible. Not only had he betrayed her with Sophie, he has also forced her out of her job. And lied about that as well.

    Pushing back her chair, Tia left the dining room with as much dignity as she could muster, pulled her coat off the peg in the hallway, and walked out, leaving the front door wide open. Despite the darkness, the isolation and the cold, Tia made her way to the gardens in a sea of rage. In that moment, she hated Lars more than she ever thought she could. He had betrayed her, belittled her and ground down every last vestige of self-esteem she had left. In that moment, she needed to get as much physical distance between them as possible and the night offered solace to her tortured soul. She wanted to meld with it, feel its cold embrace soothe her rage and will it to extinguish the flames of anger which threatened to consume her like fire lapping at the foot of a wooden stake, ready to consume it fully in an unrelenting surge of heat, pain and destruction.

Chapter 12

There were only so many tears you could cry when life became too much. That's what Chris's mother used to say to him when he was little. It was a phrase which never meant much to him as a boy. But it did now to the man he had become. So, he was apparently a laughing stock on social media and even Ben hadn't dare mention to his face that it was common knowledge that Kirsty was now engaged to the "love of her life". Everyone it seemed, except him, knew that Kirsty's engagement celebrations were now big news and she was partying in Paris with a rock on her finger the size of the Eiffel Tower. Chris had been de-friended, ghosted or whatever the stupid trendy phrase now was, and whilst he didn't give a stuff to the outside world, inwardly, he was shattered and devastated.

"Here," Ben held out a cup of coffee and Chris gave him a watery smile. Spurred on, Ben had the grace to look sympathetic, at least to his face. "Thought you could do with this. And I'm sorry."

"Sorry?" Chris stared at him, and then took the coffee in surprise. "About what?" He steeled himself that Ben was going to try and make some attempt to tell him not to worry about what people were saying about him and Kirsty and he dreaded it. He didn't want any explanations or sympathy. In fact, he didn't want anything at all.

"About getting rat-arsed and being an idiot the other night. Well, me and Sandra…put it this way, she's had enough…"

"No, you can't stay at my flat, Ben, but thanks for the apology."

"I wasn't going to ask. Well, I was, actually, but it doesn't matter. She can go to her mum's place. I don't care."

Chris sipped the coffee and winced as it burnt his gums. "Yes, you do, Ben. Take it from me, you should. Don't be a loser like me and end up with no-one because you gave up on working things out."

"Blimey." Ben blinked in disbelief. "That's heavy, coming from you."

"Well, I'm not a bloody police robot, despite what you think. I do have some feelings, you know." Chris gave Ben back the mug of coffee and attempted a smile. "Let's push on, shall we? Less Oprah and more real job, get my drift?"

"Yeah, 'course." Ben puffed out his lips in sudden appreciation at being let off the emotional hook. "I've been waiting to catch up with you. I've found some interesting facts about our killer which you need to be aware off."

"Really? Good. I'm all ears." Chris gestured for Ben to continue over at the large incident room table. As soon as the two men sat down, Ben pulled out a stream of paper from his laptop bag and unfurled the contents across its surface.

"Sorry for the whole library but it's all I've got with the situation at home..." He broke off suddenly, acutely aware that Chris was in no mood to discuss his marriage problems. "Anyway, first of all, our killer seems to fit the pattern of a spate of murders in the 1920s. All five victims were homeless, two were male and three were female. All of them had been disfigured after they died with some form of acid. The killer was never found."

Chris leant forward and nodded. "Okay. What else?"

"The bodies were unmarked, no sign of struggle, no other injuries. Nothing to suggest that they had been attacked at all. All the tests at the time for cause of death were inconclusive. The cases were never solved. They were never made public, either. It was decided that people would be too frightened, so the Press were never informed."

"So, what about the acid?"

Ben shook his head. "Again, not much to go on. The best they could come up with was rat poison mixed with some type of corrosive but the victims were entirely melted. Their faces, I mean."

"Where did the murders take place?"

"Bath, in Somerset. In the Sydney Gardens near Pultney Bridge. It was a favourite hangout for down and outs, apparently, at the time."

Chris sighed and locked his hands behind his head. "Not much to go on. Anything else?"

"Well, here's where it starts to get weird. So, fast forward to the 1950s and you have another spate of murders, but this time in Oxford. Some students, two from India and one British, all melted with no sign of struggle or cause of death. Trust me, Guv, I just put *acid* and *unsolved* into our force database and a whole new world opened up for me. There have been similar murders every decade for pretty much the entire twentieth century. Not one suspect has ever been charged. The usual scum were interviewed, drug dealers, mobsters, but no-one was ever convicted. Again, the public were never made aware, due to the alarming nature of the killings."

"So, we have a hundred year span. If it is the same killer, then he's positively dead. Or should be, at any rate."

"Yeah, but how do you explain the best of all? Victims, all prostitutes in the East End of London, all killed with no sign of obvious injury or struggle and all disfigured with acid. Just like Jack the Ripper, they never caught this guy, either. I guess they didn't want to alert an already terrified population that there was another psychopathic killer in the loose, so it was kept quiet."

"So, what's best about it?" Chris was testing Ben, bringing out all of his analytical qualities.

"If you add the date of *these* murders,1899 to be exact, then you get a killer who is heading upwards of one hundred and fifty years old. And that just isn't possible."

Despite his innate rationality, the hairs on Chris's arms prickled and he shivered, involuntarily. "So, we have a copycat. We *must* have. But how did he know the details? Unless he's got inside knowledge, which is a very serious ballgame for us. If we could get an identification on the acid composition, that would be something."

Ben dug around again in his laptop bag. "The guy found just before Katie McGlynn? We have a positive ID. His name's Danny Logan. A part-time tutor of Celtic studies at Edinburgh University. He didn't answer his phone one day and the staff got concerned about him. Apparently, he split up with his wife and started drinking heavily. Eric has confirmed there was a high level of alcohol in his blood." Ben handed the post-mortem report to Chris, who took it with a heavy heart.

"Poor guy. Another casualty of life's break-ups. Who said romance was dead, eh? So, he fell out of the mainstream and got targeted by our psycho killer. But why? One thing that ties all these victims together is that they were all had nothing to offer. There was no reason to kill them except that they were weak and unable to fight back."

"You've hit the nail on the head, Guv. No sign of a struggle on any of them. You would have thought at least one of them would have kicked, scratched, bitten their way out of the attack. But it looks like they virtually laid down and accepted it."

"Yeah, if they had been drugged first then it would make more sense. So how does a killer, especially a copycat with very limited access to any facts, learn techniques which can render someone virtually comatose?"

Ben rubbed his tired eyes and tapped the wad of paper in frustration. "Dunno. A high degree of trust, maybe? The victims must have felt safe, to some extent. At least for a moment. What the hell the killer did to them after that, God only knows. But you're right, Guv. They were all people who wouldn't be missed for a while. So, the killings weren't random and opportunist. They were targeted with thought and consideration. Buying the murderer some time before moving on to the next victim."

Chris nodded, seriously. "Good work, Ben. I want you to go up to the University and talk to the staff. See what else you can find out about Danny. I want to know what friends he had, who he hung around with. And talk to his ex-wife as well. She might know something."

"Sure. And what are you gonna do, Guv? You said you wanted to back track?"

"It's time I started getting my feet wet again. Get out on the streets and start watching. We need to catch this guy, Ben, whoever or *whatever* he is."

"Right. Yeah, you're right."

"And remember to keep a lid on the Press, okay? That would be the last thing we need right now."

Later on, at lunchtime, Chris bypassed the Station canteen and took a walk up to the Castle. He had always loved Edinburgh's old fortress and the view from the battlements across to the north. It helped to clear his head and streamline his thinking. Plus, ever since he was a kid and not even aware of what he wanted to do as a career, Chris had always felt it gave a sense of protection over the City. As though the Castle was in some way a sort of guardian, watching over the streets and its people going about their daily lives. He could imagine what it must have been like to have been a solider, centuries ago, part of the garrison defending the Castle and the old City against its enemies. It brought out his own fighting streak, his sense of roots and stability, and made him feel like he had a purpose.

He waited until the usual One O'clock Gun had been fired out from the battlement across to the Firth of Forth, and the small crowd of tourists had cleared away, before leaning on the stone wall and closing his eyes. The wind was refreshing, rather than bitter, but Chris knew, as most did in the City, that the clouds changed by the second, and the weather was notoriously fickle. Rain could follow bright sunshine in seconds and completely change the atmosphere. But today, Chris could enjoy its feeling of clarity and let the good Scottish air blow away the cobwebs of his mind. He needed to think straight. To start putting himself in the killer's shoes.

But it wasn't easy. It was like dealing with a supernatural being with no face or identity and Chris knew that Edinburgh was already full of ghosts and ghouls. It was a city which reeked of pain, death and torture, as much as it showcased its glorious architecture and fascinating history. So much of the City was built over ancient layers of the human story, much of it as dark as the granite stone from which it had been constructed. But it had also been the birthplace of enlightened and forward thinking and perhaps that was why he loved it so much. Peel away a layer and there would be a virtual cavern of unexplored history, atmosphere and stories to tell, even to someone like him who had lived there all his life. There was always something unexpected lurking in the shadows and Chris felt its presence every day. It made him tingle with anticipation.

But something different was brewing now. He just knew it. Something far sinister and darker. Primeval, even. He always felt something of that when watching the annual Beltane Fire Festival up on nearby Carlton Hill. It tapped into Scotland's pagan history and brought out feelings of continuation of a far older way of life, a system of belief that had never died and instead spoke to part of the ancient soul in all who witnessed it and took part. Whatever they were dealing with felt tied to that atmosphere of the old and unknown, but he just couldn't put his finger on what it was.

There was a strange atmosphere in the air and it put Chris on heightened alert, even more than usual. It wasn't just the fact that there was a killer loose on the streets of Edinburgh. It was the unseen menace, the sense that he was being toyed with, which was the worst thing about it. Surely the killer knew that he was being tracked by now? At some point, despite his best efforts, the murderer would soon make a mistake and Chris was ready for him. For the most part, he wanted to believe it was some chemistry nerd, sitting in his makeshift lab in a studio apartment, with nothing to do but research acid killers and try to wreak the same havoc just for kicks. But something wasn't sitting right. The CCTV footage still made him feel chilled and despite re-running it several times, he had not managed to see the misty shape again.

    Chris started trudging back to the Station, feeling invigorated and more determined than ever to find the killer. It pushed all his buttons, made him feel his old self again and gave him renewed strength to continue the search and prove to himself that he still had something worth fighting for. Kirsty was gone now. She had made her choice and he was no longer part of her life. Now he had to put his own life back together and make it stronger than ever. Like the Castle, like the hewn rock around him, Chris knew he needed to emerge from his self-pity and forced isolation like a warrior, battle-scarred and re-born. No longer weary and wallowing in his own despair, Chris felt ready to fight and do whatever it would take to dig out the faceless enemy who now seemed so close.

Chapter 13

All the clues had been there for a long time and Tia knew it. Ever since the day of the office Christmas party, two years ago, Tia had known, *felt*, that something was up. Something had been going on behind her back. But she never thought Lars would be so callous that he would actually have instigated her redundancy. Now it was clear, crystal clear, that Sophie was far more influential that Tia had imagined. This was as serious as it could get.

Tia sat on the low stone wall of the fountain. The water had long since dried up, but she could visualise how elegant it must have been in the summer, in its heyday. Now the garden was dark and quiet, except for the low hoot of a distant owl, somewhere in the surrounding trees. For once, Redfield Grange didn't feel oppressive, it felt...as if it somehow knew what she was feeling. As if, it too, had been through its own troubles and now empathised with her, trying to console Tia through its sighing walls. Or was that just the wind?

She looked around her as the chill night air wrapped itself around her body, trailing its cold fingers across her face. Crouched over, Tia couldn't even cry. The pain and hurt was so deep that it was like a void, an endless chasm which stretched out beneath her. Only her strength and sanity stopped her from toppling in completely. The worst part, the very worst thing about all of it, was the betrayal. That Lars was not her best friend at all. Real, genuine friends, especially lovers and married partners, didn't betray each other like that.

"Are you coming in? It's cold out here. Tia…we need to talk…" Lars stood a short distance away.

Tia realised she hadn't heard him come outside, nor even registered that the light from the hallway shone out over the ground, casting part of it in shadow, the remainder of the stick-like rose bushes beginning to grow frost over their spindly branches. Even the hedges glimmered with a dusting of white, but Tia didn't feel the cold. She couldn't feel anything. As Lars sat down next to her and sat forward with his hands clenched together in his lap, Tia watched as though from afar. Disjointed and unemotional.

"I…think…" he began, hesitantly, twisting his fingers around and not looking at her, "that we…"

"It's not over, is it, Lars? You and Sophie."

Lars sighed and pulled at his hair. His breath blew out in a long, white curl in front of both of them. It was as if a piece of his soul had been exhaled into the air. He shook his head. "No. Believe me, I wanted it to be. I wanted it to work, and… I know that you don't believe me, but I really thought this could be a fresh start for both of us."

Tia looked at him, miserably. "I've known for a long time, Lars. This whole move thing was just papering over the cracks. Now we've sold everything and taken on Redfield Grange…you've been a complete bastard."

"I know."

"You should have told me before that we really were over.

Why did you even let it get this far? I wish I could hate you, Lars, but right now…" Tia leant forward to stop the crippling pain in her stomach. "… I just don't feel anything…"

Lars tried to take her hand but Tia flinched and pulled it away. "No, Lars. No more pretence. Let's be honest with each other from now on. And I mean, *really* honest. Tell me the truth. What are you and Sophie going to do?"

"We…hadn't…"

"Tell me, Lars! Stop playing games with me for once in your life."

Lars swivelled around to look at her, his long legs brushing the grass. "We thought that…you might like to move into the centre of Edinburgh, take on an apartment? I could pay… help set you up. I wouldn't leave you high and dry."

Tia stared at him, incredulously. "You mean, move out of Redfield Grange? Our home? What, so that Sophie can move in?"

"Well, yes…" Lars had the grace to look embarrassed. Even coming from his own mouth, Tia could tell that he knew he was being a complete and utter bastard.

Tia was lost for words. As if it couldn't get any worse. Everything had been a lie, every hope she had clung on to in order to save her marriage, had been a pathetic attempt to gloss over a stinking mess of betrayal and deceit.

"Did you ever love me, Lars? Really?"

Of course I did. I'm still…fond of you. It's just that, well, you *are* hard to manage, Tia. What with you blowing hot and cold, the nightmares, visions, crazy stuff like that. We're just too different now. We've grown apart."

Despite her hardest efforts to stay strong, Tia felt the tears begin to come but stopped them immediately with her fingers. "And what does Sophie offer you then that I can't?" She didn't want to know but was compelled to ask, despite knowing that she was going to hate the answer.

Lars sighed. "She's ambitious. She wants to get ahead, Tia. She knows what it takes and isn't afraid to do it."

Tia found herself letting out a laugh. "So, sleeping with a partner in a law firm is *ambitious,* is it? I call it sleeping your way up the ladder. No, Lars, I'm not going anywhere, especially for *her*. She's stolen my husband but she isn't getting my home as well. And trust me, Lars, I'll fight you every step of the way. You can't just throw me out of the marital home, especially when *you're* the one having the affair. I have rights and I'll make sure they are protected."

Lars looked at her again, as if studying her afresh. "So, what do you suggest?"

Tia felt suddenly, momentarily, crushed again by the void that was opening up beneath her. The enormity of what Lars had proposed stabbed at every cell in her body. It would be so easy to give in, to go along with him and just curl up and die, but Tia was aware of a growing strength inside her. On a psychic level, she had known for months that the marriage was as good as over and although she had not realised how far Sophie was prepared to go to get rid of her, Tia knew that her gift had, in fact, protected her from knowing the worst until she could deal with it.

"Okay, Lars. Here's what *I* suggest. *You* move out of

Redfield Grange. After all, as you keep reminding me, you earn more than me now so that should be easy enough. I'll speak to my friend Rachel, remember who works in family law? She'll get the ball rolling with the divorce."

"Div...?" Lars cleared his throat "I hadn't even thought that far, to be honest. Seems a big step."

"Why not? What did you expect, Lars? Did you think I would let Sophie just barge her way into my life and destroy everything? I can't change the fact that you've fallen in love with her, but I won't be trodden down and thrown away like rubbish. If she wants a fight...if *you* want a fight, then you've got one."

Lars almost smiled. "More like the feisty Tia I remember, eh? I just wish things could have worked out differently."

"Well they didn't, did they. You went for the flawless, fake-tanned legs and tight skirts of Sophie Martin and now you've got what you wanted. Great, winners all round, then, I reckon..." Tia trailed off, all of a sudden devoid of any more emotional energy.

"Tia..." Lars suddenly grabbed hold of Tia's hand before she had the chance to stand up, "I really am sorry. I never meant for it to turn out like this. Everything has just snowballed. I thought starting in the new office would be a fresh start."

"Save it, Lars. I'm really not interested in your lies anymore. The affair I can deal with, the moving out I can deal with, the fact that you helped push me out of my job...mmm...somehow I just can't get over that."

Tia brushed away her tears of anger and hurt and looked down at Lars. At least he appeared downcast but, in that moment, it was as though the rose-tinted glasses had been snatched from her vision and she saw him afresh, for what he really was. "You're pathetic and weak, Lars. And all this time, you kept telling me *I'm* unstable and there is something wrong with me. Well I don't go stabbing people in the back. I'm not callous like you."

"You're right, I am. But I love her, Tia. I can't help it."

"Oh, stop it! I've heard enough!" Tia pulled away from him abruptly and ran back inside the house, feeling a new and almost animal-like sob threaten to burst from her throat.

"Tia, wait!" Lars shot up and was attempting to follow her but Tia had had enough. Running up the stairs, she ran into the bedroom and slammed the door behind her, fumbling with the lock. She wanted to keep Lars out. He was no longer welcome in her world. He had violated everything they had built up, torn away her ground and left her hanging by a thread.

Instead, Tia fell down on the bed and looked around her through a haze of tears. She didn't have a single ounce of energy left with which to even pull out all of Lars's clothes and begin stuffing them in a suitcase. She didn't even want to touch his clothes. Everything about him now made her feel sick, contaminated, and she climbed instead beneath the duvet. When that also smelt like the remnants of his aftershave, the expensive one he always wore, Tia finally allowed herself to cry intensely, feeling the waves of misery fully engulf her.

Chapter 14

Painter dipped his brush into the vivid purple colour and swept it masterly over the brick, watching with a new satisfaction and wonder as the droplets of paint sank into the porous surface and began to coagulate into the first outline of an image. He leant in closer, smelling the paint, and breathed deeply over it. As he did so, the paint thickened instantly and bubbled, interacting with his breath and transforming into something deeper, darker, until there appeared on the surface the beginnings of a face. As Painter continued to breathe and paint over the image, it gradually became the likeness of the girl in the graveyard. All except her expression, which was no longer full of hope and positivity for the future. Now it was racked with pain and shock; a disturbing caricature of what was once a young woman with everything to live for.

He stood back proudly and assessed his work. It reminded him somewhat of The Scream by Edvard Munch, which he had seen once before. The same cry of a soul which has found itself trapped in the horror or its own world, whether by its own making or not. Painter didn't care for art critics but during his time on earth, he had found the art form to be the perfect way to express his darkness, and that was satisfying enough.

Painter found himself laughing. No art expert would ever dare to criticise his work, even if they ever had the chance. Surely the whole purpose of art was to convey the innermost thoughts, feelings and desires of the artist. To bring to life people whom the artist observed and capture their likeness in a way which mirrored the world in which they found themselves. He was a true artist and his work carried more purity than any of the quaintly titled Old Masters. If anyone was a genius at portraying the despair and pain of humanity, it was he. No-one else could reflect the hopelessness of a soul in Purgatory as superbly, as painfully.

His eyes moved over the other faces, each one now blurring into the other, becoming a mass of purple and vivid yellow, a wall spread with horrified, hazy features. It looked as though some of them were crying – how many were there now? Ten, twenty, a hundred? Painter had lost count and soon it wouldn't matter anyway. All the wretched faces would soon be forgotten by him once he was fully immortal. Their faces no longer needed as a reminder of what he had carried out so despicably to attain his food. It would just take one final, special soul and his hunger would be satiated forever. He felt a new stirring in his depths, a growing, animalistic need. That time was drawing close. He could feel it, sense it in every fibre of his being. The time of reckoning was close. So close.

Painter walked over to his mirror. He could see into the glass, into the darkness beyond and felt the age-old sensation of homelessness tear at his own soul. His true world and everything he belonged to, was just out of reach. He put his long, white fingers to the glass and imagined for a moment that he could step inside, fully immerse himself it its delicious blackness, and then pressed his fingers to his lips. Soon he would be fully accepted by the Dark

Ones as one of their own. Comprised of pure evil, able to move amongst them all and hold his head high. They would have to acknowledge him then, to feel his power and recognise his ability to cause sweet chaos and destruction. Invincibility, immortality. For now, these thoughts sustained Painter and kept him strong. It helped ease his own pain to inflict pain on others, and whilst he was feasting, he could forget for a moment just what he was being driven to. He resented not being an Ancient One, forced to scrabble around in the pathetic human world for any morsel he could muster, scraping by on the foul-smelling carcasses of down-and-outs, listening to the moaning and groaning of the human story, pretending to smile and offer comfort as they poured out their annoying problems to him. He was better than that. He was powerful, strong and able to wield such despicable slaughter on the human world that the Ancient Ones would be forever in his debt.

For now, though, he was tired and needed to retain his strength. The chaise longue would give him respite and rest, and he yearned to close his eyes and forget his existence, even for a short while. As Painter eased himself onto the sofa and rested his weary head against the black velvet cushions, he had only just closed his sore eyelids when he became aware of a hammering on the door.

"Hey, Mr P! You in there?"

Painter sighed and tried to lift his eyelids open again but they were too heavy, and the call of the darkness was too strong to ignore. "What is it, Kevin? I am resting. I am not to be disturbed!"

"Fine. That's fine. Of course. I just wanted ter say we've got a new manager startin' today. Do you want to meet her?"

"No!" Painter's voice was sharp and abrupt. "I've already told you. I am resting. What part of resting don't you understand?"

"Sorry, Mr P. Okay, I'll sort it…"

"You do what you need to. Just make sure I don't need to replace you as well."

"That won't be necessary, Mr P. Promise!" Kevin's voice was rushed and desperate through the door. "I'll leave you alone, then."

Painter's mouth pulled back in a sneer as Kevin eventually gave up and went away. He was tired of the little idiot but he didn't have the energy to care much more for the shenanigans of running a nightclub. Once he was immortal, the Club could go to rack and ruin for all he cared. It would no longer be a cover for him and any concern he had to fake for the moment would no longer be necessary. Blood, his blood, trickled into his mouth and his was aware that he had bitten his own lip. The taste was sweet and hot, and it reminded Painter for a moment how much of his bodily shell was human. Human just enough to carry his essence through the Earth plane, whilst disguising his true nature. Time was running out now for any further disguise, any pretence at blending into the human world. As his bodily shell weakened, his resolve to achieve full immortality and greatness pushed him to the limits of endurance and he fought to stay focused.

But eventually, the call of his true nature and the sanctity of black nothingness pulled the last vestiges of awareness from him and Painter sank into a sea of darkness, feeling its cold embrace enfold him like some kind of diabolical Mother, holding her son to her venomous breast whilst ready to throw him once again to the wolves if he did not prove his worthiness.

Chapter 15

"Sorry 'bout that. Mr P is a funny one. You can just dump your things here an' I'll show you round."

"Thanks." Tia put down her shoulder bag on the bar and smiled, although she felt sick and didn't feel much like smiling.

"Are you okay? You look pretty rough." Kevin scrubbed at a wet washing up stain on his blue tee shirt, scowling to himself when it didn't come off. "Sorry, luv, but you do."

"Yes, no, I mean, you're right…I didn't get much sleep last night. I'm not feeling great, to be honest."

"You sure you should be in? I don't want you throwin' up everywhere or anythin'…"

"No, I'm fine. I will be fine, honestly." Tia dismissed his look with a deflective smile but inwardly she felt terrible. Lars had dropped her off sheepishly, even trying to be nice and wishing her good luck on her first day, but they both knew that the damage had been done and there was now no way back. They hadn't yet talked about it properly, but Tia knew the next step would be to set a date for Lars to move out. He had been surprisingly acquiescent about everything, not even arguing about her questions that morning regarding how they would unravel their financial situation into a workable monthly arrangement. It was as if all the fight had gone out of him, but whether that was only temporary, Tia had no idea. Her feeling was that he was just relieved that the situation had come out and things were now in the open.

Tia was suddenly glad she had decided just to wear jeans and a hoodie, as Kevin threw a tea towel over at her.

He grinned, pulling a face. "Just cos you're doing orders, an' stuff, don't think you're beneath doin' the glasses. It's a team effort, see?" He groaned and stooped down to pick up one of the heavy crates of beer glasses to wash up and his jeans pulled down low enough for Tia to swiftly avert her eyes before she felt even more sick.

"Okay, no problem." Dutifully, she followed him out of the bar area and along a passageway towards the small galley kitchen. Stacks of other crates with clean glasses were loaded up already by the door.

"Give these a wash," he ordered, sweating heavily as he half-dragged the crate over to the draining board. "Then we can go through the orders. I'll show you what we're runnin' low on an' stuff like that."

"Yeah, okay, great." Tia felt a sense of relief that she could just be left alone for a while and Kevin was already walking off down the passageway back towards the bar area, when she began to pick the glasses out of the crate. So many thoughts and emotions were tumbling around inside of her, all vying for attention, that she wouldn't have been able to properly focus on anything that involved paperwork anyway. It was soothing to her raging nerves to just turn on the hand washer and begin to clean the glasses with soapy water.

As she washed, rinsed and stacked the glasses, Tia looked

around more carefully at her new surroundings. The kitchen was small, and opened out into a pantry, with various cardboard boxes and tubs full of dry food. Two large fridge-freezers held the rest of the fresh food, and some ready meals, but the Nightshade Club, as Kevin had already reminded her, was more about drinking than eating, and apart from light snacks like sandwiches or rolls, nothing more was offered to the regulars and that seemed to suit everyone. If you wanted a four-course meal, said Kevin, you buggered off into town and went to a proper restaurant. Cooking was time and time cost money. He wasn't paid to slave over a cooker and neither was she.

Tia tried to calm the churning sensation in her stomach as she picked up another glass and sprayed it with the washer. It suddenly occurred to her how the whole family would soon need to know about their breakup. Her mum and dad, who liked Lars and thought he was a decent guy, but in reality didn't like confrontation and just wanted to live their lives quietly without any bother, and then there were Lars' parents; Brian, the self-made businessman who was a sweetheart who had never lost his working class roots, and Bridget, who was the snob of the two and never referred to their humble beginnings. As far as Bridget was concerned, Sophie would be much better accepted as a partner for her precious son. Tia had always felt tolerated, rather than liked, by Bridget, and now, perhaps all the true feelings would begin to surface. Perhaps it could actually be liberating to be free of it all, rather than something only to be dreaded.

There was no going back now anyway, and in the present

moment, Tia felt it best not to try and deal with any potential outcome. No news was good news as far as the wider family were concerned. For the moment, the best thing she could do was deal with her own feelings and then tell them when the heat had died down and she was feeling emotionally stronger.

She could hear Kevin singing to himself down the passageway and her mouth lifted slightly. He didn't seem a bad guy, just someone who you wanted to keep at arm's length. There was no way she was going to confide in him and let him know that she would soon be single, judging by the way he kept occasionally looking her up and down when he thought she wasn't watching. Tia sighed and let the rhythmic motion of the spray lull her into a day-dreaming state, imagining how it was going to feel living at Redfield Grange by herself. It wouldn't probably be forever; she couldn't afford the upkeep by herself but at least it was some sort of refuge whilst her personal life was in turmoil. It was strange how the house was becoming a friend, rather than an enemy, although she still couldn't put her finger on why the house felt odd. Perhaps it was unloved, just as she was.

Tears smarted in Tia's eyes and she wiped them away with the back of her sleeve, hurriedly. It wasn't healthy to dwell on things, and besides, she had a job to do. A new job which she needed for both the money and for her sanity. Even if it *was* an odd job, but beggars couldn't be choosers and right now she was grateful. Grateful to Kevin and even to the enigmatic Mr P who had agreed to hire her, whenever she would get to meet him. There still hadn't been a contract through the post, and Kevin hadn't even mentioned it, but that could be sorted out later and for now, Tia was glad to at least have a reason to get up in the mornings.

"So," smiled Tia, when she handed Kevin a freshly made coffee a couple of hours later, "when does Mr P do his rounds, then?" She climbed onto the bar stool and rested her elbows on the counter. The coffee tasted good, and she was glad of a break as the constant washing of glasses at the low-level sink had started to make her back ache. "Will I see him at all today?"

"Nope, doubt it." Kevin pulled a chewed pencil from behind his ear and scribbled onto a piece of paper. "I can do the beer order; you can do the crisps n; stuff." He paused and then decided to fully enjoy his coffee. "As I said, Mr P don't come out much in the day, actually never."

"Never?" Tia raised her eyebrows. "It would be good to meet my new employer but I understand, I guess he has long nights, every night. This place is really amazing. I love the décor. It is beautiful."

"Yeah, not bad, eh? I like it, too, although it can get really busy, heavin', to be honest, but Mr P 'andles it well. He just takes it all in his stride and I guess he just sleeps it off durin' the day."

"Why not, I guess." Tia smiled and sipped her coffee. "It's an owner's prerogative. I'm glad I won't have to work late shifts. I'm definitely more of a morning person."

"Well, yer husband won't be sorry that he'll have you in the evenings, "Kevin, grinned, leaning just a little bit closer, eyeing up Tia's chest. "He's a lucky man."

Tia felt herself burn up inside her skin and swiftly looked away. Jumping down from the bar stool, she faced him again, professionally. "I doubt he will agree with you. Now, what about this crisp order? Salt and vinegar or cheese and onion?"

Chapter 16

"So, how did you get on? How was your first day?" Lars made a point of turning down the background music in the Audi, as he watched Tia silently do up her seatbelt and settle back into the passenger seat before he indicated and drove away from the kerb-side. "Was it as good as you hoped?"

"Yeah. It was good. Thanks." Tia stared straight ahead whilst he aimed his questions, aware that he was purposely keeping his voice steady and light. "No complaints. I've sorted out a lease-hire car, though. I can go and collect it at lunchtime tomorrow, so you won't need to pick me up after work."

"Good. I mean, that's good that you have got a car. Now you won't have to wait around for me if you just want to go off somewhere."

"Yep."

"Good."

The Audi swung down the hill and out along the roads that led to Redfield Grange; all the while neither of them spoke. The headlights shone ahead of them, the trees now almost bare of their leaves, as the nights had drawn in early. There were very few other cars on the back roads leading out of Edinburgh and Tia was glad. Her nerves were jangled with the energies from the day and her own internal turmoil.

Lars said nothing further until the car turned into the long driveway that led up to Redfield. As the house loomed up like a huge black shadow, Tia felt suddenly relieved that Redfield Grange was so commanding with its presence. Once it had seemed threatening, intimidating, but now it reared over her like a guardian, a protector of her world. She was relieved to get home. A long, soothing bath with some home-made lavender bath salts and a hot water bottle was a comforting option, compared to facing Lars over the dinner table.

"I'm going to grab a sandwich for dinner." She gave Lars a strained smile as she walked past him into the open hallway. "You don't mind, do you?"

"No, of course not." Lars shook his head and pulled off his coat. He put down his laptop bag with a sigh and ran his fingers through his hair. "I've got some work to do anyway. More on that acquisition deal. Did I tell you…"

"I'm going for a bath first." Tia cut him dead, taking her things upstairs and leaving him standing in the hallway. For a split second, she felt a bit guilty but not enough to warrant going back downstairs. The best option was to keep some space between them. Then she couldn't get caught up in his drama with Sophie and all the fallout that it would inevitably entail.

"Do you want a coffee?" Lars called upstairs after her, but Tia had already gone into their bedroom. The first thing she wanted to do was clean away all of the day's events and soak in her bath, but Lars soon appeared in the bedroom doorway after her.

"I know you're angry with me, Tia. I don't know what to do to make it better…" He stared miserably around the bedroom. "I've already thought about moving my stuff into one of the spare bedrooms. There's my old camping sleeping bag in our stuff. I'll use that for now."

"No worries." Tia pulled out her phone and studied it. There were some spam texts and a couple from friends, but nothing major. She tried to quell the growing sense of loneliness in her stomach; soon Lars would be gone from her life and she still couldn't get her head around it, let alone her heart. "It's for the best," she managed to say, tossing her phone on the bed and brushing past him, wishing, just for a moment, that he would take her into his arms and tell her he was sorry and that Sophie had been a terrible mistake.

But he stood there with his arms rigidly down by his sides, looking dejectedly at the floor, and Tia couldn't bear to look any longer at him. Going into the bathroom, she pulled on the light and turned on the bath taps so that the sound of the water would drown out her rising anxiety and calm her nerves.

"I'll leave you to it, then," she heard Lars call after her. Pouring in her bath salts, Tia drew in the healing, calming aroma into her nostrils. She tipped some into the water and swished it around with her hand.

"Yep." She retorted, and then closed and locked the door. In a few moments, she had stripped off her clothes and climbed into the comforting warm water, feeling its embrace wrap itself around her hurting senses. It was then that the tears finally came and she couldn't stop them.

Sometime later, Tia crept back down into the library and lit the fire, aware that Lars had gone to bed. Neither of them had exchanged a word for the rest of the evening, even when Tia had made a sandwich for herself in the kitchen whilst Lars made himself an omelette. The room was cosy and warm, once the flames flickered gently in the hearth and Tia snuggled up on the sofa with her blanket. She closed her eyes for a moment, feeling its soft wool caress her skin. It was like being a child again, when things were simple and life had not yet become painful and hard to navigate. It was a time when fairy tales were real, romantic heroines always got their man, or at the very least were always rescued by knights on horseback, and life stretched out before childlike eyes as something to look forward to, when anything could be achieved and happiness was taken as a right.

  The flames crackled and spat slightly, bringing Tia back to reality. She sighed and took up her cup of chamomile tea, sipping it and feeling the soothing sensation of its mild taste ease her throat. Crying in the bath had been cathartic but now she needed some comfort to ease the soreness. Tia was glad that she had had the foresight to bring along her herbal teas and home-made remedies; it was something that had been an interest all of her life, and now it was part of the natural green path which she tried to follow. It was an old path, with ancient knowledge and as deep seated within Tia's DNA as her skin and eye colour. It was another aspect of her that Lars had often ridiculed but at least she had intercepted him when he had almost thrown out her home-made soaps, lotions and jars of herbs before they had packed up to move.

  Taking up the organza bag which held her Tarot cards, Tia withdrew the pack and shuffled them, carefully. Moving forward, she laid them on the coffee table in front of her and closed her eyes.

"Please, show me what I need to know. I am not afraid of seeing anymore. I know it is for the greatest good..." Respectfully, Tia cut the cards and placed the two piles, face-down, next to each other. Her fingers were tingling and she could already feel the magic and energy flowing through them. All of her senses began to focus her intention; to find out what she should do in the situation with Lars, to work to a conclusion that would be for the highest good of both of them.

Intuitively, Tia turned over the card on top of the first pile that she had been drawn to and raised her eyebrows in surprise. It was the Empress card. A card which depicted abundance, growth, development and...*fertility*. Tia gasped in shock. Of course! Why hadn't she seen it before. The Empress card signified pregnancy, and as that didn't include Tia, it meant only one thing. *Sophie was pregnant*.

Chapter 17

"You aren't going to believe this, Chris. Another murder. There's been another murder and the acid freak has struck again." Ben shook his head and sat down at his desk. He stared, unblinking at Chris, who looked up instantly from his computer. "I don't get it. What are we missing?" The bags under Ben's eyes were evident as he sighed heavily and rested his face in his hands.

"Tell me," ordered Chris, getting up and going over to Ben. He folded his arms and looked down at his colleague. "When? Where?" He felt the anger begin to rise up in him. They were being toyed with, laughed at and they might as well be blind in a ring with an opponent clearly capable of punching them right in the face without seeing who it was. "When did this come through?"

"An hour ago. Some maintenance guy was clearing up around Greyfriars and spotted an arm coming out of a pile of grass. I don't think he is well enough to be questioned yet. He's in A&E at the moment. He passed out a couple of times in the ambulance. Eric and his crew are already down there. It's sealed off."

"Don't tell me, she had no face."

"Yeah, pretty much. The poor old boy only helps out to keep busy during his retirement. He's been through the War, seen a lot of crap but he cried like a baby and I don't blame him."

"This has got to stop, and stop now." Chris marched over to

his desk and pulled his jacket off the back of his chair. "Get the engine running, Ben, we're going down to Greyfriars."

"Right o', Guv…" Ben quickly shut down his computer and spun around on his chair, watching as his boss pulled on his jacket. "Another young girl. This bastard seems to like young girls, particularly."

"I don't think he likes anybody, Ben," returned Chris, picking up his keys and phone. "This is a psychopath who doesn't give a crap about any living thing."

A short time later, they were both in the car and Chris was driving them along the roads towards Greyfriars. The traffic lights and sheer number of people and tourists hindered their progress and Chris felt himself getting even more wound up. This was all getting out of hand and he despised the fact that he hadn't yet made any real progress.

"This is getting personal, Ben," he said, as he swerved the car around a bus. "Have you put a lid on the Press?"

"Yep, as always. Blimey, watch you don't run anyone over…" He turned and mouthed an apology at an angry and shocked Japanese couple who had been getting off the bus and on trying to cross the road, had to flatten themselves against the bus in order to avoid being knocked down by Chris.

"Sorry. Sorry…" Chris instantly took his foot off the accelerator and took a deep breath. "This is what the bastard wants. For us to get wound up, angry and to make mistakes." He looked grimly in his rear-view mirror. The Japanese couple were okay and had safely crossed the road. He, on the other hand, looked weary, lined and hassled. "I just want to catch him."

"I know, so do I, Guv. The worst thing about it is we can't protect everyone, can we. We can't be everywhere at all times. We have to be lucky all the time. He only has to be lucky once."

"Yeah, don't I know it. Now we have another family we will have to break the news to, that their daughter is dead. Not just dead, but mutilated as well. As if killing her wasn't enough. I swear when I get hold of him, he'll wish he hadn't been born."

Ben stared at Chris for a moment. "That's a bit strong. You seem to be taking this a bit, well, personally."

Chris threw him a look and Ben was surprised to see that Chris's blue eyes were moist. "It has become personal. I'm sick of people suffering because of evil bastards like this. What has all these been for, the career, police, everything, if we can't stop someone like this?"

Ben pursed his lips and nodded. He opened the passenger side window to let in some much-needed fresh air, despite the fact that it has started to spit rain, in true Edinburgh fashion. As they swung into the small parking area in front of Greyfriars, both men could see that it had already been cordoned off, cones put out and any crowds of tourists gently dispersed. For all intents and purposes, it just looked like workmen needed to do some repairs.

Chris got out of the car first and eased himself underneath the cordon. All officers had been told to wear plain clothes and keep low-key. As part of the instruction, Eric was equipped with a yellow high-viz vest, and he was already hard at work when Chris and Ben walked around the Kirk to the back of the Covenanters Prison.

"What's going on, Eric? What's the latest?" Chris went as close as he was allowed to before Eric finally turned around faced him. He looked serious and not his usual, sarcastic self.

"Hard to say at the moment. The killer disposed of the girl's body here…" he indicated to the pile of grass cuttings and twigs. "Strange thing was, though, that he didn't even try to cover it up properly, almost done in a rush, I would say."

"Good, that indicates he was under pressure, and considering that this is not your usual tourist haunt, excuse the pun, I would say that there had to be other activity going on at a similar time. More possible potential witnesses."

Ben came over. He had been talking to one of the uniforms, surreptitiously dressed in electrical engineer overalls, and was taking notes. "There are ghost tours here every night in the week, so I'll start with the tour organiser, first. We also have a witness, the girl's friend, who said she never turned back up to the B&B they were both staying at. She's been taken down to the Station for questioning."

"Good. Go and talk to the tour guide now, Ben. Trace all those who have been on the tour in the last week."

"On it, Guv." Ben nodded and walked off, leaving Eric watching after him.

"Looks like Matey-Boy's had a rough few nights. What happened? Split up with his missus?"

Chris looked down at the stripped area where Forensics were going through their searches. "Sort of. What a mess, Eric. Talk about needle in a haystack. This is going to take your team a while."

"We'll find something, don't doubt it. We want this lunatic as much as you do."

Chris lifted his shoulders and put his hands on his hips, surveying the area. "What I don't understand is, if all the keys are accounted for, the maintenance company, tour guide, et cetera, how the hell does anyone get in here? And you certainly can't drag a body over those gates."

"Like I said, we'll find something. Sooner or later, our acid-loving buddy will slip up and make a mistake."

"I hope you're right, Eric. I trust your judgement as always, but I can't help feeling that we're up against something really strange here. So many things just don't make sense."

Eric grinned. "Well, that's why we're here, isn't it? To put sense back into the madness. Otherwise, what's it all about? What *would* we be here for?"

"That's true." Chris sighed and stood up. "I'm going for a look around the Kirkyard. Back in a tick."

"Sure. Okay. No probs. I'm not exactly going anywhere."

Chris gave Eric a half-smile and walked back over to the grass to the gates of the Covenanters Prison. As he continued to walk around the Kirkyard, he looked at all the macabre monuments, the decayed angels and crumbling effigies and felt his mood dropping. The whole place was morbid and sad and he wanted to get the job done quickly and get back out into the real world. He paused and then crouched down in front of a darkened tombstone and tried to read the inscription but the words had faded so much that he couldn't make out the lettering properly.

Chris gave up, got to his feet again and moved on. So, you lived your life and ended up as a couple of words on a rain-worn grave, your name eventually eroded by the weather and any long dead flowers blown away from the pot. What was the point, he thought, if you have nothing to show for your life but a memorial that no-one even cared about? Surely there had to be more to everything, to life, than that. He looked up and around him. The brown and grey stone buildings that edged around the Kirkyard with their square-paned sash windows belonged to another era, with their dormer windows eking out a stern view from their grey slate eaves. They had probably witnessed more gloom than Chris would want to see in his own lifetime, and if walls could talk then no doubt whole libraries would be filled with tales of what they had witnessed through the centuries. Religious dissention, plague, hangings, mob lynching, murder...all the loveliness of humanity at its best.

A sting of cold air suddenly whipped up against Chris's cheek, as if someone had pinged elastic on his skin. He looked up abruptly and shivered. He was used to the weather but this was different. As if someone had suddenly brushed past him, given him a preview of his own doom and then left him to process the consequences. Chris shuddered and turned up the collar of his Barbour jacket, shoving his hands in his pockets and staring around at the cold graves in renewed dislike. It was easy in such an environment for the imagination to play tricks, to subtly lift the veil, blow a whisper and then drop it again to run away, and he wasn't falling for it. He had a job to do.

Crunching over the dried leaves, Chris made his way back

towards the Kirk of Greyfriars and along the path back to his car. Just before he reached the gate, he stopped and turned around. A thought had suddenly occurred to him that they had only been looking at one level for evidence. The obvious level, which all officers had been trained to do. But this wasn't obvious. Something was happening on a different level and Chris felt it in his bones. He couldn't explain it either, but it was a strong hunch and he needed to act upon it. He fumbled in his jacket pocket and got Ben on speed dial.

"Yes, Guv?" Ben's voice came over the speaker, slightly crackly but responsive and enthusiastic.

"Ben, I want you to get me maps."

"Maps?"

"Yep. I want maps of all the underground vaults, everything beneath the city. The famous ones and the not-so-famous ones. I want to see tunnels that go somewhere. Where they lead, who opened them up and when. I especially want to see what's beneath Greyfriars."

"Sure. No problem. Leave it to me. By the way, I've got some interesting information for you already. And it's not what you might think. It looks like our acid freak buddy may have finally left a calling card."

Chapter 18

"Are you going to tell me what's wrong, Tia? I know you're pissed off with me, and I don't blame you, but you've hardly slept and you keep looking at me daggers."

Tia put down her toast as the piece in her mouth, despite being covered in marmalade, scratched her throat and stuck there. She took a large gulp of lukewarm coffee and swallowed it down but it still felt stuck, like a rock in her stomach. Lars was right about one thing. She had barely slept for an hour and not even the nightmare coming back again had been able to turn her thoughts away from what she needed to confront him with.

"Why didn't you tell me, Lars? I would have thought that, after all of our years together, you could have at least been honest with me."

"Tia, it's too early in the morning. We need to go to work. Can't this wait?" Lars' face darkened as he got up in irritation and threw the unfinished contents of his own coffee into the sink. He ran the cold tap hard to swill the tepid beige liquid into the plughole. "I thought this had been sorted. We both know what we have to do."

"About the house, yes. But what about the baby?"

"The bab…" Lars swung around and stared at her. "What baby? Tia, are you, surely you're not…pregnant?"

Tia let out a sarcastic laugh. "Let me think, now I wonder

when *that* could have happened? No, Lars," she got up and stood in front of him, glaring up into his eyes without blinking or flinching, "don't be stupid. I mean *Sophie*."

Lars let out a small half-laugh but his complexion flushed, instantly. "Don't be ridiculous. Of course she isn't pregnant. She would have told me."

"Would she? Are you sure? I mean, let's look at the facts. She's nearly got you, and she nearly had Redfield. What would seal the deal? Be the icing on the cake? Oh Lars, I could actually nearly feel sorry for you. That you could be that thick and not see what she's up to."

Tia swung around and went to pick up her coat and bag. "Come on, cherub, don't just stand there gawping, we need to get to work. Your office needs you, remember?"

Lars followed Tia dutifully to the car without saying a word. He put his laptop on the back seat and put on his seatbelt. It wasn't until he had put on his driving glasses and started the engine, that he finally turned to Tia.

"So how do you know? How the hell do you know something that I don't?"

Tia rested her head back into the seat. Her heart was thudding but with every word, she was feeling stronger, less afraid of the future, and more certain of her growing abilities. "I just do."

"You *just do*." Lars smacked the steering wheel with his hand and once the gesture would have alerted Tia and made her feel anxious but now it just made her smirk. "What's that supposed to mean. *You just do*."

"Like I said. I know she's pregnant, and judging by your immature behaviour, I take it that you didn't have a clue."

"Well, no, actually. I thought it was all fine. I didn't want any accidents, not until we were sorted..." Lars trailed off in mid-sentence and Tia felt her blood start to boil.

"I don't care how many weeks she is, Lars, because then I would have to work it back. I would have to remember just what you were saying to *me* when you were sleeping with *her*. I would have to remember the lies you were telling me, how everything was going to be fine, how it would be a new start. How we could spend *our* money on a fresh start. And you both really thought that I would give everything up without a fight? *You* thought I would give up, didn't you?"

Blind-sided, Lars didn't reply for a further ten full minutes, before hitting the street into Edinburgh at more than the regulatory speed limit.

"You're a nasty cow."

"Just telling the truth, Lars. One of us has to. And one other thing, pregnancy, adultery, whatever you want to call it, will look even better in my favour in front of a divorce judge. Better get used to relying on half your salary. Oh gosh, Sophie might have to contribute to your new lifestyle. I hope her ambitions can afford it."

"Get the hell out of my car! And if you're lying to me..." He stopped the car a couple of streets away from the Nightshade Club's entrance and Tia opened the door. "Walk the rest of the way. Better still, why don't you fuck off and don't come back."

Tia felt all her muscles contract in defence and she stared at him, icily. It was as if he sat in front of her stripped of any decency he had ever possessed. A half man, no longer the husband who had made her go weak at the knees, but a low-life scumbag who had lied to her and torn up their marriage like the pages of an unloved and unwanted book. Pain engulfed her but rage also pacified her. It was a stone-cold rage, born of survival. And from now on, it was her survival that mattered. She had to take care of herself and there was no-one else who was going to do that for her.

"Thanks for the lift, Lars. I appreciate it. I can pick up my own car at lunchtime. When you get to work, you can speak to Sophie about moving in with her. The sooner the better, don't you think?"

Closing the passenger door before he could get another chance to speak, Tia hauled her rucksack onto her shoulder and began to plod up the hill towards the street entrance which led down to the Nightshade. She didn't look back as Lars turned the Audi around and sped off with a screech of tyres.

A short time later, Tia let herself into the entrance which Kevin had given her a spare key for and went down the narrow, dimly lit stairs to another door at the bottom. Opening it, she became instantly aware of the familiar draught of cool air as it led downwards through a tunnel and to the bar area of the Nightshade Club. There were other tunnels leading off but Tia had been told by Kevin that they were blocked off. They were part of Edinburgh's underground vault system, once a haven for thieves and vagabonds, but although some of the vaults were now part of the Edinburgh tourist trail and subject to ghost tours, some had never been reopened. Odd tales of hauntings soon spread that the tenants of the vaults had never actually departed and roamed the tunnels still, over a hundred years later or even longer, but Tia shook off any unwanted vibes. She had learned to shut down her extra sensory perception when she didn't want to use it, and that control was vital to maintaining a balanced and healthy life in the day to day world of the living.

When she eventually made it towards the bar and dropped her rucksack into one of the cubicles, Kevin was already sweating. He had been loading the kegs and dragging boxes and his armpits and chest were damp.

"Hey Tia, how's it goin'?"

"Great," she lied, putting on a grin and going over to him. "You want me to carry on stocking up?"

"Yeah, if you can. I need ter finish off in the cellar." He brushed an imaginary cobweb from his face and then caught a glimpse of himself in the bar mirror. He groaned in response. "God, I look like shit. Already. An' it's not even nine o'clock."

"Well," laughed Tia, "I would offer to help but I can't even budge one of those things. I did try yesterday and nearly crippled myself."

"Sod's law that Mr P won't get another bar assistant, he's got no clue what I 'ave to do on my own. Every day. Mind you, "he laughed and lowered his voice, conspiratorially. "That's gonna change."

"Oh?" Tia raised her eyebrows in surprise. "Am I doing okay? I hope…Mr P isn't going to sack me already?"

Kevin blew out his lips in a laugh. "Nah, you're alright, mate. Like I said, *I* do the hirin' n firin'. What I mean is, I've *borrowed* my cousin Mikaela, for a while. Just as an extra pair of 'ands. I'll just bung her a tenner of my cash. She's dropped out of Uni and needs some work. Mr P said it was fine. Well, he didn't say it *wasn't* fine. Actually, I haven't told him yet. But we need the staff. People don't stay, see. It's the nature of bar work. They get a better offer up the road and they're gone."

"I didn't realise…that people don't stay, I mean." Tia heard the buzz of her phone in her bag and her attention was momentarily averted "Sorry, I'd better see who this is. I'm supposed to be picking up my car at lunchtime. I hope there are no problems with the garage. I really need it."

"No worries. Just keep it on the down low, luv. Mr P must be poorly. He didn't come out at all last night 'n' the regulars really missed him. Not like him to stay away, neither. Somethin' must be up. He don't look the picture of health most of the time…mind you…God knows what he's on…" Kevin sighed and heaved another box up into his arms. "None of our business, but just keep it all quiet, eh?"

Tia nodded but she was already scrolling down and reading Lars' text. *"You were right. Don't bloody know how. I've spoken to her. I'll be late home."* Tia didn't bother to text back and just stuffed her phone back into her bag. She felt vindicated, and it gave her courage. Her gift was nothing to fear, it was helping her, guiding her and she felt buoyed up, emboldened and strengthened. Whatever happened now, whatever Lars threw at her, Tia knew she would be able to handle it.

"You okay?" Kevin threw her a questioning look as he staggered backwards towards the passageway.

"Never better. Thanks." Tia grinned at him and she really meant it. She felt relieved, lighter, and everything she had ever experienced now seemed justified. It had taken a leap of faith to really get this far but now there was definitely no going back. "I'll go and wash up the glasses..."

"Cheers, mate." Kevin struggled off and Tia made her way after him, remembering to try and be quiet in case the infamous Mr P should be suffering from a migraine.

Tia strode down the passageway, stopping just as the passage branched off to the right-hand side where a connecting short corridor led down to the Moriarty Suite, situated at the far end. Tia paused and looked with renewed interest. She hadn't really noticed the other passageway before now. A red light bulb lit the area around the door and there were no pictures, posters or photographs on the wall, just a long red curtain on the left of the door which slightly moved in the draught. Tia felt her curiosity grow. A draught meant there was a gap somewhere and she found herself tip-toeing down towards the door. Her trainers trod carefully over the stone floor and she felt oddly scared that Mr P might all of a sudden throw open the door and tell her off for being too noisy. The curtain quivered again, and there was a strange hum in the air, although Tia soon realised that it was the noise of the antiquated light bulb. Tia pressed her ear to the door of the Moriarty Suite but couldn't hear anything inside. The door looked heavy and well insulated. It made sense considering that the noise of the nightclub would permeate down the corridors and easily echo around the stone walls, being a natural amphitheatre. But today, Kevin had turned off the sound system so no music could find its way to disturbing his boss, and Tia could only hear the sound of her own heartbeat.

The curtain fluttered again and she edged closer to it, all the while her senses on high alert for the door of the Moriarty Suite suddenly opening on her. Tia didn't even know why she felt so nervous but she definitely didn't want to get told off or sacked so early on in her new job. Her fingers reached out, hesitantly, gently pulling away the curtain. The soft breeze lifted up the wisps of hair around her face and Tia smelt old, musty air. It assailed her nostrils. It was a peculiar odour, a pungent combination of wet stone, mouldy wood, earth and dank water. She wrinkled up her nose in response. Slowly drawing aside the curtain a little further, she could see the outline of an older, wooden door, rustic and devoid of any paint. There was an old-fashioned iron ring handle and a key hole and Tia almost tried to turn the handle. It was only the sound of Kevin panting back up the passageway, that stopped her.

Quickly, Tia spun guiltily around and made her way back into the kitchen, which luckily Kevin had by-passed as he headed straight for the toilet. She heard the door creak as he went in and relaxed, turning on the washer. Pouring in the washing up liquid, Tia was intrigued about the hidden door but decided against asking Kevin straight away in case he thought she was snooping. She would make to make do with dropping it into the conversation. For the moment, she just wanted to get the glasses done and move on to stack of letters and bills which Kevin had passed to her earlier in a box. It looked like Mr P was not someone who bothered with his mail.

Later that afternoon, once Tia had picked up her new car, sorted out the paperwork and taken ownership of the keys, she climbed into the Peugeot and adjusted the rear-view mirror. The car seats still had their plastic protective covers on and paper mats over the carpet. All in all, the deal had been affordable and the car was only a couple of years old, an ex-demo car which the garage had put out on their showroom as a lease-hire car. Tia felt glad she had only had to shell out a small deposit and signed up for a monthly direct debit, rather than dig further into her savings. She had a feeling she was going to need all the money she had for the fight with Lars in front of her.

Just as she was about to pull away from the roadside, Tia's phone buzzed again and for an instant she dreaded looking at it. If it was Lars, she wasn't in the mood to fight him. It had been a long day and she was tired.

However, Kevin's number flickered up on her voicemail. Tia dialled 121 to listen to her message, suddenly feeling irritated that she had given Kevin her number. It was only supposed to be for emergencies. Like the burglar alarm going off, or lost keys.

"Come back t'night and meet Mikaela. She's doin' 'er first shift. Starts at 8." Kevin's voice had sounded as breathless as he normally was and Tia smiled. He was harmless enough but she didn't know if she had the energy to come back later.

Pulling away and heading off in the direction of Redfield, Tia relaxed back and began to enjoy her first proper sense of freedom in months. Lars had been right about one thing at least, now she didn't need him at all. And it felt good.

Chapter 19

Painter vomited, bending over double as his fingernails scraped at the tomb wall. He could see the police cordon through the gap in the crumbling stone and anger seared through him. His last meal had not agreed with him. Either that, or he was growing weaker. He struggled up, leaning back in the dark, dankness of the tunnel and closed his eyes. The pain inside him was expanding by the day, even by the hour and he knew that time was running out. If he didn't become immortal soon then he would fail and be consigned to…what? Oblivion? He knew enough of what was expected of him by the Ancient Ones to know that failure was not an option. He either existed, or he didn't. It was as simple as that.

Severe dryness etched his throat and he gasped. The human shell was a pitiful, weak vessel and he was beginning to feel old, like parched and cracked leather. There was nothing he could do to halt the effects until he found the one who could turn the tide of his inevitable destruction. Pain racked through him again and Painter slid down the wall, groaning as the searing sensation pierced his veins and shot up his neck. The force of the assault made blood start to trickle from his ears and nose and he slid his long white fingers under his nostrils, staring down at the smeared, sticky substance in disgust. He put his bloodied fingers up to his neck and felt the faint human pulse throbbing from his artery. He hated the prison which the human body had constructed around him. He was oppressed by it, kept down and forced to exist within its strait jacket of tissue, blood and cells.

The sound of activity outside in the Kirkyard and its immediate surroundings finally alerted him to move, as quickly as the remaining vestiges of his energy would allow it. He staggered back into the roughly hewn tunnel and made his way through the dark vaults and chambers, until he reached the small stone steps that led up to the secret door into the Nightshade Club.

As Painter peered carefully through the keyhole, he saw that the passageway was dark still; it was early in the morning and no-one, not even Kevin was around yet. He unlocked the door with his shaking, bloodied hands and closed the red curtain carefully behind him. With just enough strength left to unlock the door to the Moriarty Suite, Painter almost fell inside his room, bolting the door shut and collapsing in exhaustion onto his chaise longue.

The darkness came for him at once, but this time it wasn't the same. It was a threatening blackness, intimidating and cruel. All Painter could see behind his eyes was pain, his pain, and he knew that he was being accused. He was betraying them and he felt their contempt as clearly as if he stood in front of them, his head hanging in shame and despair. He knew what he needed to do and now he was becoming acutely aware that if he didn't succeed soon, then he would be doomed forever. His eyelids flickered open again, narrow with renewed determination.

In the far corner of the room, beneath the crimson curtain of his painted Wall of Purgatory, the faces and images seemed to howl cross the divide. He could hear their wailing and tortured groans and that consoled him. Why couldn't the Ancient Ones reward him for what he had already done; for the souls he had already consigned to Purgatory? What more did he have to do to extract one iota of recognition for his travails? Painter grinned as their cries became more urgent, insistent and pain-racked. It was what humans termed music to the ears. They wanted freedom, they wanted to move into the Light and he was doing everything the Ancient Ones demanded by acting as their Gatekeeper. To keep them enslaved. Whilst he remained alive, they could never be free.

Painter lifted himself with difficulty from the chaise longue and pulled aside the crimson curtain with a trembling hand. The Wall pulsated with life; he could see fingers moving inside the stone, scratching and tearing at the wall of their prison. And there was nothing they could do but scream for mercy. He had none to give. Painter cried out in ecstasy and felt wet tears on his skin. Were they his tears or theirs? It was no matter. They were bonded together with him, joined for all eternity and that gave him some small morsel of pleasure and satisfaction. Disdainfully, he let the curtain fall back roughly and raked away the tears from his face. There was no room for weakness and pathetic displays. It would achieve nothing and would never extract any ounce of pity, either from him or the Ancient Ones.

Lifting his head proudly, elegantly, Painter moved over to his mirror and picked up the make-up artist's sponge. He thrust it into the pot of white theatrical makeup and wiped it thickly across his skin. Carefully lifting off his white wig, Painter then sponged the thick masking cream into his bald scalp. It camouflaged the blue throbbing veins and rivulets of sweat until he looked icily perfect, as if hewn from an exquisite piece of marble. Rather like Hell's version of Michelangelo's 'David'. Painter smiled as he turned and viewed his reflection from different angles. Why had he never seen before how perfect he actually was? He could surely have been an artist's Muse. The idea made him almost laugh out loud. He was the Supreme Artist, not an artist's servant. No Muse had ever had inspired such beautiful artwork as he had created and never could.

Chapter 20

Chris stood in front of the body and felt sick to his stomach. She lay there on the metal table, naked and featureless where her face once was and he had an almost overwhelming urge to throw up in the sink.

"Jessica Barker. Aged nineteen. On holiday with her friend, currently a student at London's University of the Arts. According to her friend, she wanted to experience some of Edinburgh's architecture. I don't think she bargained on this..." He put a hand to his mouth as Eric came over dressed in his surgical gown and gloves. "Did she die before the acid was applied?"

Eric nodded, solemnly. "Y'know, you look at me sometimes as if I'm okay with all this...but it doesn't get any easier. Especially when I can't find the cause and I have to admit, I'm stumped." He sighed and began rinsing his hands. "Don't go near her face, by the way, it's still working. I've no doubt it is the same composition."

Chris turned up his head, picking on his lower lip. "So again, no sign of struggle, no indication of assault? Same as before?"

"Seems so, yes. The results will no doubt come back inconclusive again on the acid. Don't worry, the lab's going through everything. There must be *something*..." Eric sighed and scratched the back of his head through his scrubs. "Normally we can run the DNA through our database for any potential matches. What can you do when there is *no* DNA?"

"She was on the ghost tour," went on Chris, turning away from her lifeless body for a moment. "Apparently she left early as she was scared. Between the time that the group went into the Black Mausoleum and the discovery of her body by the maintenance guy the following morning, she was murdered."

"Well, that *is* something I can tell you." Eric picked up his flip chart from the side and flicked through the papers. "Time of death, according to the tests, was between 22:30 hrs and midnight."

"All the tour party had disbursed by 23:00 hrs, according to the tour guide. He locked up and went straight back home to his apartment. His girlfriend confirmed it."

"Primary cause of death, natural causes. I'm afraid. It must have been very quick. In all the acid victims, there was no time to struggle or fight off their attacker."

"You know, and I know, that she didn't die conveniently before being disfigured."

"Well, there were no toxic substances or alcohol in her blood. No underlying conditions..." he pointed to the neatly sewn lesion below her breast. "Heart and lungs were healthy. No signs of disease..." Eric put back his chart and pursed his lips in a defeated grimace. "Just a normal young woman with her whole life ahead of her."

"Thanks, Eric. You've done your best."

"Not good enough though, is it? To be honest, I've never seen anything like this in all my thirty years' experience."

"If anyone can be blamed, it's me. I've let another victim slip through my fingers. It's happening on my watch, Eric. But let's not have a pity party, eh? I'm going back to the office. There must be something, *one* thing, that pulls all of these victims together."

"Sure, good luck." Eric lifted his shoulders in resignation. "I'll sort out the paperwork for her next of kin. I take it they've been informed already?"

"Yep," Chris responded, as he went through the double doors without a backward glance. And the less he dwelt on that, the better.

"So," said Ben, as Chris sat back down at his desk a short time later, "Nothing further Eric can tell us, I take it?"

"Nope, apart from the time of death, which is what we had pretty much ascertained already. "Now what's this calling card that you wanted to tell me about?" He leant back and took gratefully took a mug of coffee from another colleague who wielded a tray of fresh drinks. "What have you got?"

Ben got up and walked over with a digitally enhanced photograph. He laid it down on the desk in front of Chris and put his index finger on the image. "Katie McGlynn's ring. Do you remember it?"

"Of course." Chris leaned in closer. "The pagan one. A pentagram. There are hundreds of rings like that out there. Anyone can get one online."

"It's not the ring, it's the fact that she was into Wicca, or Paganism, or whatever." Ben grinned and took out his notebook. He looked fired up and immediately held Chris's interest. "Danny Logan, apparently his ex-wife said he had started to hang out with group of students into Wicca, or psychic phenomenon. He did a couple of paranormal investigations. She said he got into it really heavily after they split up. He used to frequent the local bars and clubs and sometimes a group of them would meet up in the woods. Not far from where his body was found."

"Interesting," mused Chris, leaning forward and staring with fresh eyes at the pentagram. "Very interesting."

"Jessica Barker's friend told me that she was also interested in the paranormal – hence the ghost tour. In fact, I went back further into the older cases and virtually all of the acid victims, even those recorded initially, were either Spiritualists, fortune-tellers, psychics or into some sort of alternative spiritual path."

"Ben, I think you might have actually redeemed yourself."

"Yeah, I thought so too."

"But not enough yet to warrant staying at my place. I want as much data as you can find on all local paranormal groups, Pagan websites, anything that would fit. Find out if any of them knew our victims. Good work, Ben."

"Cheers, Guv."

"Keep me on speed-dial, Ben. By the way, did you get the maps for me?"

"Sent to your inbox, Guv. You'll be amazed just how many of the vaults have been used by paranormal and other groups. Super creepy. Rather you than me if you wanna go down there."

Chris gave Ben a sarcastic smirk. That was exactly what he was going to do, but first he needed to figure out where to start.

Chapter 21

The woodland around Redfield Grange seemed darker than normal, as Tia negotiated her car along the driveway which led up to the house, her eyes looking at the trees with a growing familiarity. Sometimes it was easy to forget how much she had disliked the parkland upon her arrival. Now its isolation gave her protection, from life, even from her feelings, which still jumped out in front of her and smacked her in the face when they caught her off-guard. She was already beginning to dread having to sell the house, but it was going to happen. There was no doubt about that. It was inevitable. Tia sighed and switched off the radio. She didn't want to hear any doom and gloom news about world events or the financial markets. She would soon have enough financial battles of her own.

Despite her growing fondness for Redfield, the road was still annoyingly rutted and pitted and Tia suddenly thought about having to explain any chips in the paintwork to the lease hire company. She pursed her lips. Why did the mind, *her* mind, always throw up things she hadn't even thought of? Like flies in the ointment or spanners in the machinery…

Tia felt the lump of familiar anxiety begin to grow in her throat. She knew that, if they hadn't done so already, tonight Lars and Sophie would be having That Talk. Their future, the baby…Despite her anger, Tia had to bite her lip in sudden pain. Lars had always said he wasn't ready for kids, that he wanted to become a partner in his law firm, and buy a fabulous home in which to raise a family. Well now he had, but it had been with someone else in mind all along. It was the ultimate betrayal and Tia didn't think she would ever be able to forgive him. He thought he had trapped her into living at Redfield Grange, unaware of what his true plans really were and, like an old film unravelling before her mind's eye, she could see the whole sorry story being played out. She squirmed as she thought just how gullible she had been.

An owl hooted up in trees and Tia brought the car to a gentle stop for a moment. Opening the car window, she let the cold air embrace her, soothe her emotions and calm her soul. She could just about make out where the owl had flown to; it perched up in one of the trees over towards the dense woodland. There was solace in the peacefulness of the early evening, now that winter was drawing closer and the sky was cloudy and moody one moment and then clear and sprinkled with stars, the next. It was the time of the Holly King, who would reign during the dark months according to traditional folklore, or the coming of the Wild Hunt in Scandinavian mythology, when Odin and his army thundered across the sky amidst storms and ferocious winds sweeping across the land.

Tia breathed in deeply. There was no storm but instead a cleansing wind which came over the water from the Firth of Forth, from further away in the distant glens. It carried the smell of something older than any town or city or even any human being. It pulsated with its own magic and Tia could feel it in her own veins. It spoke to her in a way that London never had, with its constant noise and traffic and heavy population. Now she was truly free for the first time in her life and something was opening up in her that had been lying dormant for years.

Plunging the car back into gear, Tia continued her drive up to the house, feeling ready for something to eat and some hot soup. It suddenly occurred to her that she hadn't eaten all day and she was hungry. As she pulled up on the gravel sweep outside the front door, Tia shivered as the wind suddenly picked up and it fed through the car vent. It was going to be a cold night.

Tia eventually opened up the front door and hurriedly switched on the lights. The entrance hall brightened into life as she put down her bag and hung her jacket on the coat rack. Lars still had a couple of outdoor jackets hanging on it and for a moment, Tia felt a pang of sadness. It was easy to almost believe that nothing had happened and that Lars would walk in at any moment like he usually did.

Going into the kitchen, Tia switched on the radio and began to make a meal. She heated up some soup and buttered some toast, all the while wondering about Lars and Sophie. She felt humiliated about the whole thing, and the worst part was knowing that Sophie must have fallen pregnant whilst Lars had been promising Tia a new start.

Climbing onto the kitchen stool, Tia played with the spoon, stirring the tomato soup and watching as the steam curled up in front of her. The smell was nourishing and repellent in turn, causing her stomach to feel queasy. Lars must have thought she was an idiot not to find out eventually, but perhaps by then he assumed she would have given up any fight and just handed him, Redfield and what had been the most important part of her life for so many years, over to him and Sophie on a plate.

Tia sighed and sipped the rapidly cooling soup as much as she could. Redfield Grange was a big house to be alone in and she felt a creep of anxiety twist up her spine. The nightmare was bound to come back and she dreaded falling asleep. Even though she felt tired and ready to curl up on the sofa, Tia decided to get some housework done. Maybe some cleaning and vacuuming would take the edge of the black dog of melancholy that was tapping on Tia's shoulder with increasing urgency and she was doing her best to ignore it.

It was a couple of days before Tia managed to go back for a late evening at the Nightshade and it was only after Kevin had kept pestering her that she finally agreed. When she got back into the Club, he was visibly pleased to see her and grinned at her from the bar. He gestured towards a young, dark-haired woman who was cleaning down some spilt beer from the table in the Jekyll and Hyde cubicle. Some of the beer had stained the red velvet sofa cushions and she was frantically trying to sponge it out. All around her, men and women were laughing and trying to flick the washing up liquid water over each other from the bowl.

Tia pushed her way through and tapped Mikaela on the shoulder. The girl spun around, ready to punch her unknown assailant in defence but, luckily, she paused.

"Hi," Tia shouted over the music and raucous laugher, "I'm Tia. You look like you could use some help?"

"Hi…er…yeah, thanks, that would be brill!" Mikaela grinned apologetically and looked down at the now almost empty bowl of water. It had ended up being dispersed over the crowds around her, or found its way out by seeping into the stone floor. "I guess I can try and dry it off. It's the best I can do while all this lot are here."

"Leave it, I can finish it off tomorrow and arrange for a proper cleaning." Tia moved out of the way as a couple of men pushed their past her and into the cubicle, where they collapsed together holding their bottles of lager. "It's wet, guys. You should move."

"We ain't goin' nowhere, luv. You should join us…" One of them lifted the bottle to his lips and tapped on the wet cushion beside him. "Come an' give us a cuddle…"

"No thanks, and if you want a wet arse, it's up to you." Tia pushed his hand away and motioned for Mikaela to leave them alone.

Mikaela laughed as they both went into the kitchen to wring out the sponge and cloths. "Well said, Tia, and thanks for sorting this out."

"No worries." Tia smiled and switched on the washer, swilling the soapy bowl and then putting it on the draining board to drip dry. "Kevin has been desperate for us to meet. Now he can stop texting me," she laughed.

"Oh, don't worry, he will. I'll make sure of it. He can be a bit of a stalker sometimes." Mikaela took up the tea towel and dried her hands. They were red and rough. "He's been good to me, though. He's always there for me, you know?"

Tia nodded. "That's good. Everyone needs a good mate. And Kevin tells me you are his cousin? That's cool you're so close."

Mikaela hung the tea towel back up on its peg and adjusted the ball bearing piercing in her lower lip. It was still crusty from only being pierced a few days ago.

"Ouch, that looks sore," stated Tia, standing up close to Mikaela and looking at the wound. "You need to put some aloe vera ointment on that. Who did it for you?"

"Erm, me, actually, I did it myself," Mikaela replied, sheepishly. "*I know,* it's my own fault, but I'm hard up for cash."

"Well, I can understand that but it probably isn't worth losing your lip over. Warm salt water should be a good start. There's some catering salt in here, somewhere, which is better than nothing. Ah, here it is," Tia indicated over to the shelf behind Mikaela.

"Thanks. That's really neat of you. I appreciate it. Kev said you were nice."

"Oh, he did, did he? I might need to have words with him about that," Tia laughed, quickly mixing up the salty concoction and then drying her hands. "Now, dab some of this on and I'll bring you in some ointment with me tomorrow. I'll leave it with Kevin for you. I'll just have to make sure he doesn't eat it first."

Mikaela laughed in response. "I'd...better get back out there or Mr P will be on the warpath. Kev told me that he likes to come out around midnight, make his entrance with the crowds, and it's eleven thirty now."

"I still haven't met him, the *infamous Mr P*," replied Tia, giving a half-smile as she followed Mikaela out of the kitchen. "He doesn't seem to be around much. Not in the day, at any rate."

"Haven't you heard? He's a real-life vampire, or so the regulars here think," giggled Mikaela, as they walked back down the passageway. "Apparently he would melt if he comes out in the daytime. Although I think he just hams it up really, as Kev has sometimes spoken to him in the daytime actually, once or twice."

"Oh well, it obviously brings in the custom. It's good marketing. The club seems to attract people who are into that sort of thing, from the looks of it."

"Yeah, well its partly that but people love the vaults as well. I mean, they're well-haunted. Not all of them are accessible but the famous ones are. Hey, we should go on a ghost tour together. That would be really cool."

"Yes, it would," laughed Tia, "but I'd better get going now. I've got a long shift tomorrow. Some of the supplier payments are due and I have to speak to the accountants, apparently. Kevin gives me the low down, to be honest, as if it were left to Mr P, I wouldn't get any instructions at all. A bit odd, but I'm just going with the flow...."

"It's been so great to finally meet you, Tia. Let's get together soon. I think we have lots in common."

"I'd like that, definitely." Tia gave Mikaela's arm a friendly gentle squeeze. "Will you be okay now if I go?" Tia couldn't explain why but she felt quite protective, even motherly towards Mikaela. There was something about her that was vulnerable, child-like and innocent. She felt guilty for leaving her alone but she couldn't do a night shift as well without making herself exhausted.

"I'll be great, honestly," Mikaela smiled back at Tia and her large brown eyes were soft. "It's just a shame we won't meet more often at work. What with the different shifts an' all that."

"Well, from what Kevin tells me about Mr P, that could change anyway," Tia laughed. "I'm beginning to learn that no job is guaranteed in this club. At least it keeps me on my toes."

When Tia finally got back home again to Redfield, Lars was fast asleep on the sofa in the lounge, and he had clearly been drinking as the room smelt like a brewery. She crept past him in distaste and made her way upstairs. She felt exhausted but it had been good to meet Mikaela and remind herself that she still had a life outside of her disintegrating marriage.

Taking a warm shower, Tia felt herself begin to relax as the water ran over her face and splash away down the plughole. Her hand-made, rose scented shower gel was uplifting and soft, giving Tia the sense of love and protection. It was the best she could do in all the circumstances but she knew how important it was to stay strong. Lars and Sophie would soon go their own way and she would be alone. It was crucial that she did not allow the thoughts and emotions to grind her down and make her feel less worthy and able to cope. Closing her eyes, Tia forced the thoughts of Lars out of her mind and instead deliberately imagined white sparkles coming out of the shower and over her body. Visualisation was powerful and would help to balance her on many levels.

Eventually, after rubbing herself down with a soft towel and putting on some clean pyjamas, Tia made her way to bed. It had been a long day but worth it. Mikaela was such a nice girl and it felt good to have a new friend. Without a further thought for Lars downstairs, Tia made a point of sleeping on the other side of the bed. She would have to get used to it and it felt good; liberating somehow. Although she missed his physical touch, Tia didn't want to go through anything like it again. To know that she was being used when all the time he had been thinking about Sophie. Forcefully, Tia thumped the pillow into shape, taking out all impression of Lars, and closed her eyes. Within an instant, worn out and yet fortified, Tia fell asleep.

Neither of them spoke to each other the following morning, and when Tia left the kitchen to go to the Nightshade Club, she saw him emerge from the lounge looking terrible. He hadn't shaved and silvery stubble was already evident on his face. It looked like he had slept in his shirt, it was so creased. Tia almost said something, as part of her still wanted to make sure he was okay, but she thought better of it. Whatever Lars went through now, he wasn't her problem anymore. He was Sophie's problem. They had both made that evident enough and she couldn't afford the emotional energy of getting caught up in it.

Chapter 22

"The Southbridge Vaults. You already know these," said Chris, spreading out the paper map onto the huge pin board at the back of the Incident Room. He was speaking to his team, who were sitting in chairs in front of him, and he felt suddenly irritated by them. He put a hand on his chest, aware that in his blue tee shirt and jeans, he was getting slightly more interest than the map behind him. A couple of the younger women eyes him up appreciatively. All he could do was call them out. "And whilst I'm obviously Brad Pitt," he went on pointedly and with sarcasm, "if you could concentrate on what I'm saying, the quicker we can get this over with?"

Ben sniggered and caught the eye of one of the women. She had the decency to lower her eyes and make a renewed attempt to stop staring at Chris but, even Ben had to admit from time to time, Chris was still a good-looking guy.

Chris sighed inwardly. It was going to be a long morning. "Right, as this map and the smaller maps on your individual handouts show, the vaults and the tunnels are marked out so you can see which are open to the public and which ones are closed. I want to narrow down our search to this area, here." He pointed to the section highlighted in yellow. "I'm interested in the connection between all of these victims," he then pointed to the various photographs pinned up alongside the map, "and these tunnels. I believe we are dealing with a copycat killer who may be involved in the local Pagan community."

Ben also stood up and walked to the front of the group. He held up the enhanced photograph of Katie McGlynn's ring. Chris took it and pinned it to the board.

"Cheers, Ben. As all of you already know from some of our previous investigations over the years, some of the vaults have been the focus of Satanic worship, witchcraft covens and that sort of thing. What we don't know yet is whether the killer is an active participant in these rituals or whether he is hiding behind the Pagan community and using it as a front for his activities. Either way, I believe the killer is targeting those in the Pagan community. What I'm not sure yet is whether these killings are in some way ritualistic."

Chris gave them each a sheet of paper with a list of names and addresses typed out. "I'm splitting you up into teams; each team will be allocated a local group to contact. You can see from this list who is going where. Ben and I will take some back up and start with these tunnels."

Ben gave the group a pained expression. "I think you guys are getting the better end of the deal," he joked, and the group laughed.

"Enough said, Ben." Chris indicated that the session was over and the group began filtering back to their respective desks. "We need to move fast. This is happening right under our noses now and one thing I detest is being played with."

"I know that, Guv. And I'm on it."

"How's things with Sandra, by the way?" Chris flopped his pile of papers onto his desk and turned up his head "I might act like a complete bastard sometimes, but I do care, you know."

"It's okay, thanks. Sandra has decided to take some time out, see her sister n' stuff like that. So I'm back in the house. Feels weird being alone."

"You'll get used to it." Chris kicked himself, inwardly. "I mean, it's not so bad after a while. And I'm sure it's only temporary. You are making good progress, Ben. Just keep at it."

"It's not like you to be so…open, Guv. What's brought all this on?"

Chris sighed and sat down in his chair, wearily. "I just don't want you to end up like me, Ben. And I really mean that. Look at all this…" He gestured around him and the office and their various colleagues hard at work. "this is my world. And the highlight of my life at the moment is a murderer who delights in mutilating his victims. Maybe I'm just getting too old for this."

Ben smiled down at his boss. "You're the best, Guv. It's because of you that we don't have more scumbags like that out there. You've given everything to keep this city as clean as possible. Without you, it would be so much worse."

"Maybe." Chris looked up. "Thanks for the vote of confidence, Ben. Now, let's get on, shall we?"

Ben nodded and went back over to his own desk, still looking at Chris as he did so. He eventually switched on his computer and began trawling through his emails. For a moment, he paused and then moved his computer backwards and forwards.

"What's up, Ben?" Chris, always acutely aware of his surroundings, turned his head towards him. "What is it?"

"D'you remember the CCTV footage of Katie McGlynn? We've had a local paranormal investigation group take a look at it. They checked for EVPs, that's electronic voice phenomena, and looped it. They've got something."

"Well, can we hear it?" Chris got up and went over to Ben's desk. "Have you got it now?"

"We need to go down to their office. They've got everything set up for us. They want to talk to us. They wouldn't say anything more over their email."

"Get them on the phone, Ben. Tell them we're on our way."

Within a half an hour, Chris and Ben had reached the flat which served as the base for the Edinburgh paranormal group known as ESIP, headed up by Lucas Frain, who met them at the door.

Once all of the introductions had been completed and Chris and Ben had been given mugs of tea, Lucas sat down on his sofa where he had all of his equipment set up on a low coffee table in front of him. Putting on his headphones, Lucas used his laptop keyboard to pause at the place on the recording that he wanted them to listen to. The computer screen showed the electronic graph of the recording. The rhythms on the screen varied in size and speed and when he got to the correct place, he paused it.

"So, what we basically did was take the footage and try to debunk the usual things that aren't paranormal at all. We tried to focus in on that shape that your lab tells us you saw. I'll come to that in a minute. But first, I want you to listen to this." He handed the headphones to Chris, who sat forward in the armchair. "You'll hear the girl talking. She says she's grateful for his help and then asks him a question. There's a pause and then you hear it. I've put it on a loop so that you will be able to hear it constantly for a few moments."

"Okay," Chris nodded, watching the screen carefully. "Play it." He listened intently so that he could hear Katie's voice, just as Lucas had said, and then he strained his ears. Sure enough, there was another voice. It was slightly raspy and harsh. "*Stop…here…*" Chris repeated, with a frown. "It sounds like someone's saying s*top here.*" He gestured for Lucas to repeat the loop. The voice was there again and he felt a sick feeling in his stomach. "It's strange. It doesn't sound…human. Sort of tin-like. Distant."

"Can I hear it, Guv?"

Chris nodded and passed him the headphones in silence. He watched with concern as Ben listened, frowned and then handed back the headphones to Lucas.

"That's actually as creepy as hell," said Ben, looking visibly shaken. "How can you get a voice like that when there's no-one next to her?"

Lucas clicked on another image on his computer. "Take a look at this. I think this is what you thought you saw?"

Chris moved in closer and saw again the misty shape. "Yep, that's it! What *is* it and why did it disappear?"

Lucas rewound the image and played it a couple of more times. "Well, what you have is a Class A voice phenomenon. It's responsive to the girl and it's intelligent. Watch how she interacts with it and then look at the time of the corresponding voice…"

All three of them watched again, as the voice came in at exactly the same time after Katie had asked a question and the shape appeared.

"So, the girl says, or asks, *where are we going?*" Lucas re-looped the whole thing again for them. "Then you get the voice responding, *stop here.*"

"But what would explain the image, Lucas?" Chris was growing increasingly unnerved. "Do you think they're connected?"

"Yeah. Definitely. No offence but your average CCTV can't always pick up stuff like this. You need specialist equipment and your average crim-catching camera won't be sensitive enough. That's why your lab guys couldn't pick it up fully. It was always there, but you needed to be able to see it properly, if that makes sense."

"It does." Chris sighed and sat back down on the chair, stretching his hands out on his knees. "So, what you are basically saying is that we aren't dealing with a human being at all? We're dealing with a ghost?"

"Well, entity, I would say. Ghost are usually residual energy, replays if you like. They don't interact with the living as they aren't aware of space and time. They just go on repeating the same pattern, walking the same path or doing the same thing, that they always did in life."

"What's the difference between ghosts and spirits, then?" Ben was intrigued. "Why do you get hauntings?"

Lucas sipped some of his coffee, which was growing cold. "It makes better sense if you think of it in terms of vibrations. Humans, that is all of us here, exist on one vibration. Spirits, earth-bound ones particularly, are, like, here..." he held out his arm just away from his chest. "They can be stuck for various reasons and some humans are sensitive enough to sense them, and then there's the nice Granny in the Spirit World spirits, who come through mediums which messages up *here*. And then..." Lucas stopped and winced as he drank the rest of his cold coffee."

"And then?" Chris looked at him intently. "What else is there?"

Lucas blew out a deep breath and rolled his eyes. "Well, I'm afraid you're into a different league and way out of mine."

"What do you mean, *a different league*?"

"Demonic, I'm afraid."

"Demonic?" Ben looked around the flat as if he thought someone would overhear them.

"Yeah, sorry to say. I mean, it's rare, thankfully, but we have done some investigations in the past where something darker and more evil was at the root of it. Well, we've only done two, actually, and both times we've had to leave it to the exorcists to sort out. There's seeking proof and there's being an idiot. None of my team are emotionally able to deal with the fall out of things like that. We are searchers for evidence of the paranormal, but we're not going to end up in a psycho ward to prove it."

"Then why set yourself up for it?" Chris was beginning to get irritated. "You can't call yourself an expert and then back out of it, can you. What about the poor people left behind trying to live with something like that?"

Lucas flushed under the intense questioning. "We just try and capture the evidence, that's all. We don't have answers for everything."

Chris was quiet for a moment. He was thinking hard and trying to piece together every aspect of the case. "If these...*demons*...do exist, how old are they? I mean, are they as old as us?"

"Oh, older. Much older. As long as evil has been in the world, I should think. You have to remember that outside of this world, the earth-plane, there *is* no time. Any non-human entity that exists on a different vibration can travel through time and space. It's when they decide to interact with our world, that we have a problem."

"But why do entities like that target certain people? What draws them to some human beings, and not to others?"

Lucas shook his head and picked up a couple of books from beneath his coffee table. "Take these and read them. They may help. They are true accounts of what people have encountered. I don't know for sure, but it may be something to do with the occult."

"What makes you say that?" Chris looked at the front and back cover of one of the books. It added to the growing distaste in his mouth and the unsettling sensation that the acid murder case was no longer about a copycat human killer but something entirely more unworldly. And he didn't know how he was going to deal with it.

"Well, it stands to reason that anyone messing around, with Ouija boards, for example, may open a portal to spirits. The problem is, what they are essentially doing is opening a door for any old passing spirit to come and play with them. The same thing happens with inexperienced practitioners of magic, rituals, stuff like that. A lot of the time, people think after doing a weekend course in Wicca that they are somehow all-knowledgeable but it takes years to understand how energies work. Unfortunately, a lot of things have been summoned when they shouldn't have been. Think of it this way, if *you* were summoned by someone and then told to get lost because they were no longer interested, you would get pretty pissed off as well."

"So, they just…hang around? Waiting for what?" Ben was visibly nervous and kept looking around him as if expecting something to come out of the shadows to confirm its existence.

"Get a grip, Ben," ordered Chris, but in reality, he didn't feel much better. He hadn't expected to be told that he could be dealing with a demon. And worse still, that it couldn't easily be sent back to Hell. "You clearly know a lot about this type of thing. Would you say that an entity like you describe can *physically* harm people? Have you come across this, in your investigations?"

Lucas shifted on his sofa. He looked uneasy. "I don't normally like talking about it, but if you want, I can show you?"

"You have some footage?" Chris pulled in his breath and got himself ready for whatever it was he needed to see. He felt more out of his comfort zone than he had ever been and unsure how to really proceed. It was only the need for the truth that compelled him to continue. "Yes, I want to see." He didn't, but that wasn't going to stop him.

Lucas brought up the footage and pressed the Play button. "I hope you're ready for this as it isn't easy viewing...."

Ben was scrolling down his phone, as it bleeped and made him visibly jump. "I'll get this, Guv..." He walked off into the entrance passageway, leaving Chris to watch the video footage alone.

The video was shot mostly in the dark, with night vision cameras and various pieces of equipment. Chris recognised Lucas and saw other members of ESIP, identified by the white letters on their black tee shirts. Lucas fast forwarded several frames and then stopped. "You can see clearly see the three scratches on the man's back?"

Chris winced. "Yep. So, an entity did that to him?" The red scratches were clear and large on the man's white skin. He was holding up his shirt. The camera had captured it in full definition and Chris felt his irritation grow again. "Are you positive he didn't do that to himself? Or anyone else around him?"

"Can tell *you're* a copper," Lucas mused, and fast-forwarded the tape again. "Nope, no-one did that to him. No-one *living*, anyway..." He stopped and blew up another frame. "The mocking of the Trinity."

"Sorry, what?"

"That's why there are three scratches, It's a traditional mocking of the Trinity. Another sign that the haunting is demonic."

Chris frowned. It was chilling stuff but still didn't answer his questions. He was dealing with something that acted like a human killer but appeared to be an entity of some description. It didn't fit anything that Lucas was showing him so far. "Okay, so it can scratch people, but can it act as a real human? I mean, masquerade in some way as a living person? So that no-one could tell. Until it was too late?"

Lucas looked up at him, intently. "I…dunno…I mean, has something happened?"

Chris sighed and kicked himself. "I just need to know if you have ever come across something like this before?"

"Nope, but like I said, I'm not in the realms of the exorcists. If you asked them, I expect they'll say it's possible."

"How do you get rid of them? Kill them, or send them back to where they come from?"

"No idea. I'm just a paranormal investigator. I'm not a psychic or anything like that. If I could sense half the stuff I try and document, I'd be in the loony bin by now."

"Well, thanks for all your help. I really appreciate it. I'll need a copy of your CCTV footage. Can you get that to me?"

"Sure. Hey, it hasn't got anything to do with what's been going on down in the vaults, has it? Rituals an' shit like that?"

"Can't say, Lucas. But thanks, you've been really helpful. I'll be in touch if we need anything else."

"Sure…" Lucas went to get up but Chris indicated for him not to bother. "Okay. Anytime…"

When Chris got to the front door, Ben was already standing outside.

"Everything alright?" Chris bleeped his car alarm and they both got in the car.

"Not really." Ben shook his head and looked again at his

phone.

"What's up?"

"It's Sandra. Apparently, she's taken an overdose. I need to get to the hospital."

"Consider it done, Ben…"

Chris started the ignition immediately, threw up the emergency blue light on to the roof and they sped away, leaving Lucas looking out of the flat window after them.

Chapter 23

"This is it, then." Lars took down the last of his bags and put them by the front door. He looked miserably at Tia. "How are you going to manage? This place and everything?" Lars held out his hands and looked around.

"Well enough," Tia replied. Emotions were running through her like a fire threatening to rage out of control but she was determined not to crumble into an emotional mess. "I'll be okay, Lars."

He looked crestfallen and almost sad. "Tia, I really wish ..."

"Wish what? Haven't you got what you have wished for, Lars?" Tia bit her lip to stop the hot tears but it was almost overwhelming. "You've got Sophie, and a new baby on the way. Isn't this your dream?"

"Yes, no, I don't know. I thought I did but...well now I'm not so sure." Lars put his hands on his hips and then wiped his mouth with the back of his hand. "You seem different."

"Different?" Tia stared at him, her green eyes burning. "What do you mean?" She studied him as he sighed and then glanced at his watch.

"Stronger. More...independent. More like the old Tia, I guess."

"You mean, before I was ground down by you and our

marriage? Before you tried to turn me into some sort of *thing* you could control?"

"No! I never tried to do that. *You* wanted it that way, Tia. You could have changed it at any time."

"I did try, at first. But then you became more overbearing and used to getting your own way. You wanted *everything* your own way. I just gave in, in the end, as it was easier. But yeah, I am definitely blaming myself for not getting out of this marriage sooner."

"Do you really mean that?"

Lars looked crushed, and once, a long time ago it seemed, Tia would have thrown herself into his arms and said she was sorry but she couldn't do it now.

"You betrayed me, Lars, at the most human, deep, level possible." She steadied her voice, carefully, "I thought you were my best friend. That we would face life together. I really did love you, Lars, and I wanted it to work. But I couldn't compete with Sophie in the end."

"Tia, you and Sophie are just very different. Both beautiful in different ways. I suppose I thought," he laughed, more at himself, "that I could have both of you. Have the best of both worlds. I realise now how unfair I was to both of you. I had to make a choice in the end."

Tia felt her heart constrict and she folded her arms, looking up at the ceiling and then back at him. "Whatever you say to me now, Lars, the damage is done. I could say that I've given you the best years of my life, that I am left with debt, a house I won't be able to afford for much longer, a job washing up dirty glasses, and thanks to your wishes, also childless. There, hopefully that makes you feel better about having made the right choice."

"I've been a real bastard to you, haven't I?"

"Yep, you said it. But it's done. I'm moving on, Lars. The best you can expect from me now, is an amicable divorce with as little legal cost as possible. Because as you once said, what's the point of having you as a solicitor if I can't get *some* use out of you?"

"Okay, well," Lars stooped down and picked up his large sports bag which was stuffed full of clothes. "I'd better be going. I'll put these in the car…" He tried to smile at her but Tia was having none of it.

Everything that she had ever wanted to say about his treatment and betrayal of her raged through her body and she could no longer control it. Tears finally spilled over onto her cheeks and she felt them run down, hot and unwanted. The man who stood before her was no longer the same man she made her vows with. All of that now seemed like a terrible lie and she could barely speak.

"I do still love you, Tia. It's just that I'm not *in* love with you anymore. I can't, I couldn't be expected to stay in a marriage on that basis. Sophie can give me what I need."

"Oh good. You deserve each other, Lars. You're both scheming, manipulative, selfish and only care about yourselves. I think you make a great couple. I'm just glad to be rid of you now. So why don't *you* now fuck off and don't come back?"

"Yep, okay. I'm going." Lars opened the front door and stepped outside into the cold. He opened the Audi boot with his key fob and began to thrown in his bags. "Oh, by the way," he called, "I meant to say. You have some paintwork chips on your car. You might want to be more careful."

"Lars, if I thought you were genuine, I might take your advice. But as it is, I don't and I won't. Thanks."

Lars shrugged his shoulders. "Up to you, I guess. I was only trying to help."

"Bit late for that now. I think you should hurry up. Sophie will be waiting for you. No doubt she's cooked you a nice shepherd's pie or something nice and warm and cosy."

"I'm taking her out for dinner actually. She doesn't cook." Lars got in the car and slammed his door.

As he switched on the engine and headlights, Tia brought up her hand to shield her eyes from the dazzling light. Why was she even on the doorstep watching him go? She closed the door with as much grace as she could summon, but it was very hard once his car had completely disappeared down the drive and she was faced with the cold harsh reality of being alone. Tia stood for a moment in the hall just trying to digest what happened. The enormity of Lars leaving was almost a kind of blur. She felt numb, in shock and all the rage that had pounded furiously around her body had now dissipated.

The tears finally dried when Tia made her way calmly upstairs, ran herself a nice hot bath and sank into it, a short time later. There was nothing she could do except let the lavender-scented water soothe her and form a balm to her soul. She needed to keep strong and not let herself fall into any kind of despair. She needed to survive, to keep any sort of roof over her head and plan carefully for the future.

Soaping her skin carefully, Tia leant back and closed her eyes. Images of Lars and Sophie flooded her mind, torturing her, but she refused to let the feelings take over. It would be easy to fall into a pit of depression and let herself sink to the lowest depths of misery, but Lars wasn't worth it, and Sophie certainly wasn't. Of all the times that had been good with Lars, there had equally been dark moments when he had belittled her, laughed at her interest in psychic matters and his ultimate betrayal was enough to turn anyone against their husband.

After her bath, Tia forced herself to make a sandwich even though she had no real appetite, and settled down in the library. As she drew her knees up under her on the sofa, she bit into the bread and cheese, feeling glad she had put on some incense earlier. The smell of frankincense and myrrh still lingered and it took the edge of the remaining musty odour which was the result of years of being closed up. Tia felt herself begin to relax. It was warm and quiet and with the rain softly beginning to beat against the windows outside, she felt safe and removed from all the hurt that Lars had caused. The house was protecting her, making her feel that she could deal with anything, and for a moment, she could have cried. Suddenly, losing Redfield seemed heartless, callous. The final hurtful blow that Lars could inflict on her. Tia struggled against her mind as it threw up images of having to give the house up and put it back on the market. It filled her with sadness and her stomach churned at the thought of having to move somewhere else, probably into another apartment. But for the moment, Tia sank back into the sofa and made herself focus on the positive events that were happening. She had a new job, and who knew where it might eventually lead? Mikaela was nice, even Kevin was okay, and there would be good things to look forward to in the future. If she kept telling herself that, sooner or later she would believe it.

The clock ticked and the rain grew louder in its intensity. As she managed to finish one half of the sandwich, Tia's eyelids flickered and she turned over onto her back. Looking up at the ceiling, with its ornate ceiling rose and beautiful plastered architrave, it was like going back in time, to when Redfield Grange was at the height of its wealth. She could imagine the house parties, the sound of carriages coming up the drive, perhaps the music of a piano and singing. At some point in its history, Redfield Grange had been much loved and Tia felt a sudden surge of protection over it. It wasn't the house's fault that it had been reduced to a dilapidated state and thrown into an auction with no-one to love it anymore. Perhaps it was fate in some way that had brought them together. Tia liked the thought of that. As much as she felt unloved, the house must have felt it, too, and she wanted to restore it, to bring life back within its walls again, to fill it with love, music and laughter.

Tia leant her head on her folded arm and closed her eyes. One thing she had learned over the years about her ability, it was to trust it. To go with the flow, as the saying went. What was meant to happen, would happen, and she needed to remind herself that when one door closed, another one always opened. It was a cliché, perhaps, but hopefully a true one.

Chapter 24

"So, what happened? With her landlord?" Tia lifted her head up from the cubicle table and paused, her finger over the calculator. "Sorry, Kev, I need to get these figures done. What were you saying?"

Kevin came over with a couple of glasses of cola. He sat down opposite her and rested his elbows on the table. "She got thrown out. Apparently, he tried it on with her, the slimy shit, and when she told him ter…fuc…I mean, get lost, he threw her out, clothes 'an everythin'."

"But that's disgusting! Poor Mikaela. Where is she now?" Tia moved the pile of receipts out of harm's way as Kevin took a long gulp of his drink.

He wiped his sweaty forehead and withheld a burp. "She's at mine fer now but there's no space. She's having ter kip on the floor. You're legal, ain't yer? 'As she got any rights or what?"

Tia sighed and picked up her glass. "Cheers for the drink. Well, it depends, I would think, on her tenancy agreement. Does she have one?"

Kevin shrugged his shoulders. "No idea. Nah, actually, I don't think so. He was a friend of a friend, so ter speak."

"Well, that makes things harder. I can ask some of my ex-colleagues who work in real estate and litigation. I'm still in touch with a couple of them." Tia stopped short of telling him that she was already getting help on her separation and forthcoming divorce. "It's really unfair for her, but I don't know how else to help. I worked in employment law, which is a bit different, so I would need to double check."

"I was wonderin'… *we*…were wonderin'…"

"If she could stay with me?"

Kevin slurped his drink and wiped his mouth. "Well, yeah, … how the 'ell do you always know what I'm gonna say? Are you psychic or summat?"

"Erm, well, yes, I am." Tia smiled at him. There was no point in beating around the bush and she wasn't going to hide her light under one anymore. "I…don't…it's hard at the moment."

"Your 'usband? Will he say no? Is that it?"

Tia sighed and knew she needed to be honest with him. "It's a difficult time for us at the moment."

"Okay, well, I get it. Not your fault. I said I would ask, anyhow." Kevin drained his drink and gave Tia a grimace. He stood up and gestured down at the paperwork. "How's this goin? Makin' sense?"

"Yeah, kind of. I don't understand why Mr P lets it get in such a mess, to be honest. I guess accounts aren't his thing?"

"Nah, he's not fussed about stuff like that."

"Where is he today?"

"About somewhere. No idea. I knocked on 'is door but no answer. He could be dead, fer all we know."

Tia shivered. "Best not say things like that."

"Wooh, Tia's scared," laughed Kevin, giving her a grin. "I'll just give Mikky a call."

Tia looked up at him. She felt suddenly bad that Mikaela was in a bad situation and was torn between going with her head and her heart. Her head told her that she didn't want to get involved, but her heart felt sorry for Mikaela. Perhaps they needed to stick together. Perhaps having some company might do her some good, as well.

"Maybe, just for a while? Until she gets herself straight?" Tia saw the relief cross Kevin's face and knew she had made the right decision. Whatever Lars would think about it, he couldn't really talk, considering the mess she was in now. "She can pay towards the food if she can. I know she won't have any money for rent."

"Ah, man, that's so cool, mate. I really appreciate it, 'an…well, Mikky will be so grateful."

"That's okay," Tia gestured towards her glass. "You can get me a coffee, if you like?"

"Sure, no worries." Kevin grinned widely at her and took the glass away. When he returned a short time later, he had his phone in his hand. "Mikky says thanks so much. She's comin' in now with her stuff. Don't worry, she 'asn't got much."

"Okay, fine, I can take it back home with me when I finish later."

"Awesome. 'An don't worry about lifts 'an stuff like that. If she comes in early with you an' hangs around, I can take her back to yours at night. Drop 'er off."

"Okay, that's fine." Tia pushed the calculator back on. She was aware that they had spent nearly half an hour talking and she didn't want Mr P to think she was slacking. She wondered where he was and why she hadn't yet seen him. He seemed very elusive. Tia began to total up her numeric figures. It wasn't her place to worry about him and if he was happy with her, then that was all that mattered for the moment. She needed the money and the stability of having a job, especially if it meant taking in Mikaela for a while.

"Oh, by the way," said Kevin, coming back over with a box of crisps, "just ter let you know, the kebabs are on me, just ter say thanks."

When Mikaela came in a while later, Tia smiled kindly at her. The young girl looked a mess; she had been crying and makeup was streaked down her face. She walked in with two black bin bags and was dressed in the same clothes she had been wearing when Tia had previously met her.

"How are you doing, Mikaela?" Tia went over and gave her an instant hug. "It sounds like you've had a bad time?"

Mikaela nodded and was on the verge of crying. "Tia, I'm so grateful to you. I don't know what to say. I…"

"Don't worry, you don't have to say anything. Let's get you a coffee and a sandwich."

"Thanks, that'll be great…" Mikaela sniffed back her tears and dragged the bags along with her. She put them in the kitchen as Tia busied herself getting Mikaela something to eat.

"Kevin told me what happened. Are you okay? Or is that a stupid question?" Tia passed her a plateful of chicken, bread and a few crisps.

"No," Mikaela shook her head and began eating the bread,

ravenously. "It's okay..." With a mouthful of food, she leant backwards over the draining board of the sink and quickly swallowed. "He was a total bastard. Just because I wouldn't sleep with him, he said I should have thought of that before he offered me the place."

"Men like that should be prosecuted, Mikaela. He can't do that to you."

"Let's be honest, Tia, what else have I got? No money and no real proper job. He can do what he likes."

"It doesn't make it right, though."

"I know. This is good, thanks, Tia."

"No problem. I doubt Mr P will miss a couple of slices of bread and the chicken is Kev's. I'll buy some more," Tia laughed, wiping the crumbs from the side and brushing them into the waste bin.

Mikaela wiped her mouth with the proffered napkin and took the fresh cup of coffee from Tia. She blew on it, desperate to drink it before it had even cooled down. "Are you sure your husband won't mind me staying?"

"He's not at home at the moment." Tia wasn't sure yet how much she wanted to confide in Mikaela so determined to keep things as light as possible. "It's fine, I promise."

"I'll help with the chores. I can make myself useful."

"Well that's a good bargain, then," laughed Tia. "You should see the size of the place. It needs some work but it isn't falling down. Not yet, anyway."

"You're so lucky, having such an amazing place. I'd love

something like that. Even if it looks creepy. It was up for sale for ages, wasn't it?"

"Yeah. It's a proper fixer-upper. It does look a bit intimidating, I must admit. When we first moved in, I thought it was probably haunted."

"No way!" Mikaela's large brown eyes grew even bigger. She seemed revived after having some decent food to eat. "That's so cool! Have you seen anything? Any ghosts?"

"No, not yet. But even if there is something there, I think it would probably be a good spirit. I'm more afraid of people than of ghosts."

"I wish I was that brave. I've seen…things…but then I guess it comes with the territory."

"Territory?"

"Being a Wiccan." Mikaela rolled her eyes and went over to one of the bin bags. She undid it and pulled out a fresh but crumpled black shirt. She took off her checked shirt and stuffed it into the bag. "People think it's all about doing spells 'an stuff, but really it's more about a way of life. Trying to save the environment, psychic development, things like that."

"Oh, if you've vegetarian, I'm sorry about the chicken…"

"Don't worry, I haven't got that far yet. I only started a while ago. Well," she turned and looked guilty, "to be honest, it was more because I wanted to get that creepy sod off my back."

"Your landlord?"

"Yeah. He was coming on too strong right from the word go, but I thought he would pack it in once I moved in. It got worse.

Doing a spell was all I could think of in the end to keep him away from me."

"And did it work?"

"No. Obviously." Mikaela frowned. "I must have done it wrong, or maybe I didn't put enough intent into it. Either way, he got worse. If anything, I think he thought my *alternative* personality was a turn on. Urgh," she stuck her fingers in her throat in mock sickness, "as if I would have ever let him *near* me."

"Unfortunately, you always get men like that, Mikaela. I doubt doing a spell would have stopped him. Men like that think they are unstoppable and powerful. Like they can get away with anything."

"Your husband sounds like he's decent, though. You must think yourself lucky having a bloke like that. I wish *I* had a husband like that."

Tia quickly finished washing up the plate and sighed. "Karma will sort him out, Mikaela, and as for wishing you had a husband like mine, well, you should be careful what you wish for."

"Oh. I'm sorry. Have I said something wrong?"

"No, of course not, but, well, Lars and I are in the process of separating."

"Oh my God, no way? I'm so sorry, Tia. I really am. I didn't mean to offend you."

"You haven't, I promise. I guess you might as well know now, before you come over to the house. Just one thing though…"

"What's that?"

"Please don't tell Kevin."

Mikaela laughed. "Because he fancies you?"

"No, well, I don't know, but I don't think he needs much encouragement, put it that way. I'd just rather he didn't find out."

"Your secret's safe with me, Tia." Mikaela rubbed Tia's arm in moral support. "I've got a long shift tonight. Better psyche myself up for it, I guess."

"Kevin knows the directions to Redfield. He can drop you off after your shift. I'll give you a spare front door key. Just head upstairs and turn left. The spare bedroom is first on your left. I'll get it made up for you."

"Great. Thanks, Tia. You've really saved my life." They walked out and Mikaela then stopped and looked in the reflection of the bar mirror. "I look so crap. Look at the state of me."

"You look like you always do," shouted Kevin, from the other side of the floor. He had a mop and bucket and a stressed look on his face. "An' you can give me an' hand with this."

Chapter 25

Mikaela smiled at Tia over their fish and chips. "This is great, thanks so much, Tia." She wiped her mouth on her napkin and looked around the dining room of Redfield Grange. "This place is actually incredible. I love it here."

Tia reached over to the middle of the large dining table and picked up some bread. The table was too big for them really but it had been nice to set it with a tablecloth and lay the fire in the elaborate fireplace. The room looked out onto the rear gardens and Tia found it peaceful. Although the wallpaper was now faded, it had once been a soft duck egg blue colour, with tiny birds, in a Chinoiserie pattern and the blue damask curtains hung from a finely carved Victorian pelmet. The windows were long, four of them, and the middle two windows opened up into French doors that led out onto the small stone terrace.

"I'm really glad you like it. I think this is where the original family would probably have taken afternoon tea. The sun comes in during the late afternoon. It lights everything up. It's really pretty."

"Oh, to have money back in those days, "mused Mikaela. "What wouldn't I give for that. Sometimes I think I was born in the wrong century. Today's world is pretty harsh."

"I think you're right about having money back then. It probably wasn't great if you didn't. What with the workhouses and orphanages. That's probably where most people actually ended up if they weren't careful."

"So, tell me about your psychic stuff, Tia." Mikaela sat forward, eagerly, and rested her arms on the table. "What sort of things have you been doing?" Hey, this would actually be a great place to hold a séance."

Tia laughed. "I think you have been watching too many movies. Besides, I don't really do anything like that. Just Tarot and that sort of thing. Most of the time, things just happen, if you know what I mean. I don't really go looking for it. I'm not sure I always want to encourage it, to be honest."

"But that's the best way to be, Tia. If you have strong ability then you know it's there. It's just controlling it and using it for the right reasons. I realised that when my stupid spell didn't work."

"It wasn't stupid. You meant well. I think there is more to it, though. Intent is one thing but there are other factors involved. You know about the Law of Three?"

"Of course. What you give out comes back to you threefold. That's part of the Wiccan belief."

"It's cause and effect though, isn't it? What you give out is bound to come back eventually. That's how you learn lessons. And once the lesson has been learned, then perhaps the circumstances don't need to manifest anymore."

"Do you think I deserved what happened in some way?" Mikaela looked upset, momentarily. She sniffed and picked up her drink, draining it dry.

"No, not at all. I think, if anything, you have been attracting these people into your life to help you to be a stronger person."

"So how do I know when I've passed the test? It's not exactly clear, is it? Do I just stop attracting nutters?"

Laughing, Tia, topped up Mikaela's glass with cider. "I guess so. I think we choose our path and our lessons, on a higher level. Perhaps before we even come into this present life."

"Heavy stuff. But it does make sense. I believe in reincarnation. I know I definitely don't want to come back again, that's for sure. This world is horrible."

"Yeah. Sometimes I agree with that. But whatever we do, I think we have to look on our sensitivity in some way as a gift. I think we need to use it to help others, not try to manifest money and power and all that."

"So, you think doing that is a bad thing?"

"I don't think we are supposed to use it for our own gain. Perhaps I'm wrong, but maybe that's why people very rarely predict lottery numbers. If it is part of your path to experience lots of money then you will, but there is always a lesson to be learned from it."

"Cool. Shall we get the cards out? We can read for each other."

Tia put down her napkin. "Yeah, okay. I'm full now. I bought dessert for us. We can have that later if you like, with some hot chocolate."

"Yummy, yes please. I'm going to be as fat as a house with you looking after me, Tia."

They moved into the library and settled down. Mikaela sat down on the rug in front of the fire and watched as Tia got out her

Tarot cards and sat down opposite her, cross-legged. Tia could sense how excited Mikaela was and it was hard to dislodge the sense of foreboding she already had about reading the cards. One thing she had always known about the cards, is that they weren't a parlour game, a party trick for wasting away time in boredom. They were a tool which could sometimes bring to the fore things which were unexpected and sometimes unwanted. Tia had a feeling that Mikaela was not going to like her reading.

Shuffling them, Tia let her mind relax and focus. It wasn't long before she knew that Mikaela had some secrets about her childhood that the young woman wanted to stay hidden.

Mikaela rubbed her hands together. "So, what can you tell me, Tia? What gorgeous man am I going to meet?"

Her heart thudding, Tia turned over the first card. "This is The Lovers card. I know this is what you want, Mikaela, a long-lasting romantic relationship. All of your life, you have felt unloved and you want a knight in shining armour to save you. But it won't. It can't."

"Blimey, Tia. You're tough. Don't pull any punches, eh?"

"Your path is about learning to be strong and rely on yourself. To love yourself and accept all aspects of yourself, even those you find disgusting."

Mikaela shifted on the floor, uncomfortably. "What do you mean?"

"Well, I can see that things haven't always been easy for you. Men, even those you have trusted, family, have treated you badly. You have had to put up with abusive behaviour from those who you thought were on your side." Tia slowly over the next card. "The Chariot. This shows that you have all the confidence and perseverance you need to overcome all of the difficult challenges you are having to face. You have all the resources you need within you to cope and to win. To stop having to repeat those lessons," she added, smiling softly at Mikaela.

"What's the third card, Tia? Gosh, you're good. Tell me there is a happy ending? Please?"

"The Devil card."

"Oh, *great*."

"It doesn't mean literally, it means that you are feeling trapped in your life at the moment, and it's not surprising with all of the problems you have had to deal with. You need to be strong, get through this and look to making a better and brighter future for yourself."

Tia smiled and moved to get up. "Now shall I get us some hot chocolate?" She paused at the silence and looked down at Mikaela. The young woman was sitting motionless, staring over somewhere in the other corner of the room. Looking but not focused on anything in particular. "Mikaela, are you alright?"

"I…yeah…" Mikaela almost jumped and her eyes came back into focus. "How weird is that? You were talking but I wasn't hearing you. It was like I was somewhere else."

"Okay. What were you feeling?"

"Sort of, like there was no time or place. But something was there."

Tia's face drained and she sat back down. "What did you see,

Mikaela?"

"I don't know. A kind of black presence. Does that make sense? It probably doesn't. I'm just stupid."

"No." Tia pressed her arm. "You're not. This does make sense. Could you see what it looked like?"

Mikaela shook her head. "No, it was just there, watching. Waiting."

Tia shivered. She was aware of a different vibration in the room. A tense atmosphere that hadn't been around them before. It was like something had gate-crashed their cosy, enjoyable time together and stood in the wings, in their peripheral vision, waiting for them. A horrible, churning feeling turned like a knife in her stomach. She knew that Mikaela had seen the same presence that was haunting her in her nightmare.

"I... haven't been sleeping well. There is this figure. A black figure always chasing me. It's beginning to creep into my life in the day time as well. I can't explain it. I just know it's getting worse."

Mikaela got up and gave Tia an impromptu hug. "You know what I think, Tia? I think you have been scared of your gift for too long. You need to turn around and *face* this thing."

"But what if this is something real? A real dark force which is getting stronger. And now that we are both aware of it, what will happen now?"

"I don't know but there must be a reason. As your reading said, *I* need to be a stronger person and *you* need to be more accepting. Perhaps then this figure will disappear from your dreams and visions."

"Like some sort of shadow self?"

"Possibly. I really don't know but when I turned to Wicca, it felt like a *calling*. And I realised that this was being given to me as a friend. A way to get through life. And I didn't feel so alone anymore. I felt like I belonged to something."

"Like what?"

Mikaela shrugged her shoulders. "It's difficult to put into words, really. Like I was part of something older than any organised religion, that spoke to me through nature, the elements and the energy all around us. It spoke to me. I think it speaks to you, too, but you are afraid to listen to it. You are afraid of its power because you don't know where it will lead you."

"You are probably right, Mikaela. I have been afraid. Lars, well, he laughed at me about it."

"But *you* let him, Tia. You had to outgrow your relationship in the same way I had to get rid of my sleazy landlord. These men were trying to hold us back. From being our true selves."

"You know a lot about this, Mikaela. I really admire you for being who you truly are. And not being afraid to tell people."

"It's as natural as breathing, Tia. Just think, when we were back in the caveman times, our psychic senses were a lot stronger. We needed them for survival. We ran with the air, the best hunting grounds, the seasons. We knew when the other members of our tribe were in danger. We've just…switched off the antennae over the centuries. Learned to dumb it down."

When Tia lay in bed that night, she thought about what Mikaela had said. It made a lot of sense, considering that all her life she had not wanted to fully face herself. There was courage and bravery in daring to stand apart and not be a part of the crowd. People with psychic gifts had dealt with that problem for centuries, from being venerated Oracles to being horrifically persecuted for witchcraft. Depending on the position of people in power at the time, sensitives had been honoured or hanged. Now was a safer time to live, when it was more accepted to be different, and it was a good, comforting feeling.

Chapter 26

The music thumped around the Club loudly, as Painter grimaced and made his way from his office to the main dance floor, aware that shortly he would be swamped by sweating, odorous bodies and people generally getting up too close and personal with him. They always hoped to get a free drink out of him and usually he made it his purpose to oblige, to keep them drunk and stupid, but tonight he had other plans. His tall figure, clad in his usual customary black, passed by the bar and along to the far end, where he was immediately assailed by Kevin, wanting to know about further bar staff arrangements.

"But Kevin," he smiled, as loudly as he could in Kevin's ear, "you seem to have worked out the arrangements commendably. And this, I take it, is the divine Miss Stone?" He lifted up her hand as she giggled and kissed it. The act almost made him retch; she smelt like a mixture of soap and cheap perfume that stung his eyes and irritated his delicate nervous system. He was growing steadily weaker by the hour and the music pounded in his ears. He was careful not to drop her hand too quickly, despite the growing nausea rising up inside him.

"Mr P, thank you so much for giving me this job. I'm so grateful. More grateful than you will ever know."

"I'm happy to assist, my dear. I must say, you are very pretty.

You will be an asset to my Club. Now, if you will excuse me?"

"Yes, yes of course," Mikaela beamed, and then grinned over at Kevin. "Thanks for making me so welcome!"

Painter smiled again at her, drinking in her young energy and ploughing her mind with his own senses. Despite his increasing weakness, he delved into her psychic vibration and saw her expanding crown chakra within his own mind. She had ability and had clearly done some psychic development. Gorge and stomach bile rose in his throat, seeping through his teeth as he felt the familiar murderous urge to devour her, to suck in her soul and squeeze every drop of life essence she possessed. Like a ravenous wolf, panting over the bloodied stench of its prey, he moved away from her with difficulty, feeling her pulse within his own pulse. His tapered white fingers felt his throat, the blood pumping from the veins in his neck and he felt hot. Hot for blood, for her soul and the potential end to his searing pain.

As he smiled benevolently and nodded gracefully at his regulars, who were just a chaotic scrum of noise, inane shouts and gesticulations, his eyes watched Mikaela carefully, as she rubbed a glass with a tea towel, clearly in animated conversation with a young customer at the bar. She was listening to him, nodding occasionally and then handed him a drink. She took his money and rang it into the cash register, all proper and correct. But as Painter scanned her aura, he saw the darkness there. The abuse she had suffered as a child and told no-one, not even her mother. Not even Kevin. And then the boy who had lived in her neighbourhood, whom she had trusted. He had made her do things to him that she was ashamed of, but at ten years old she had been coerced, believing him when he told her that it was normal and it was something all girls did. Painter dug deeper, seeing in his third eye a vision of her landlord preying on her and then throwing her out when she resisted his sexual demands. He saw her first foray into Wicca, her juvenile attempts at spell-casting to try and empower herself. She was ripe for plucking and he couldn't wait to ravage her soul and drain her of every living drop of the fighting spirit she had so desperately tried to retain all of her young life.

All throughout the midnight hours, right up until the last stragglers had sung their way back up the tunnel and sprawled out into the cobbled, damp streets of the old City, hailed taxi cabs or staggered home, Painter had waited patiently. He had observed how she had interacted with the customers, how she had occasionally tugged at the silver pentagram which hung on a leather shoestring around her neck as if seeking comfort and strength from it. Her vulnerability and inherent innocence delighted and aroused him to the point of agony. He was desperate to imprison her in his arms and devour her, but in the last few moments amongst the chaos and pushing and shoving of the revellers, to his utter dismay, she had disappeared. Gone.

Painter screamed inside, almost running up the passageway towards the exit. He saw her getting into Kevin's car, watching her haul her bag into the seat beside her. He watched in frustration as Mikaela mischievously dangled the keys at Kevin. The two of them shouted something incoherent at each other, laughing, and when the car sped away, Painter felt the rage threaten to exit his throat in a howl.

Slamming the door after Kevin, Painter locked it, feeling the droplets of sweat run down his pale skin and dampen the collar of his cloak. In a surge of desperation and temper, he let out a low growl and headed for the door to his tunnel. The little bitch had evaded him and now he had to wait for another opportunity to feast on her. But the waiting was becoming unbearable and his physical human body was breaking up under the strain.

Gasping for breath in the stale air that now reeked of body odour and alcohol, Painter went into his tunnel and staggered along, dragging his hands along the walls to steady himself. He knew where to go for a quick meal. There were enough homeless people in the city who wouldn't be missed and he no longer cared about prolonging his pleasure over his victims with acid. He took out the almost empty bottle and threw it hard, smashing it against the wall. It shattered into pieces of glass and any droplets of acid left in the bottle now began to corrode the stone. Painter ground the glass down still further with his boot. The acid had no effect on him but his hunger did. It was driving him to utter despair and if he did not find the one soul who could save him soon, it would be too late.

He headed out of the tunnel and into the night, making his way down to the park area known as Princes Gardens. There were few around at that time of the morning, just some homeless people who were trying to stay warm and dry. Painter spotted a man who was sleeping in the area by the bushes near to the bottom of the steep staircase that fed into the Gardens. The man was bundled up in plastic bags and a sleeping bag. Empty cans of lager lay around him. Painter felt no pity. He was desperate for a meal and anyone would be better than nothing. Hot blood coursed around Painter's veins as his sight easily sliced through the darkness and onto his target. The man was huddled up well enough away from any streetlights but Painter took no chances. He swept easily along the wall, like a shadow cast upon the ground from the moonlight; there for an instant and then gone the next.

Now he breathed hard against the cold night air, watching as his breath curled out in front of him. Painter rose up on the man, who slept fitfully on his bags. The man turned his head and tried to open his eyes but he was half comatose and couldn't speak. For a moment, his heavy, blood-shot eyes seemed to flicker with some sort of recognition. He struggled inside his sleeping bag. Perhaps there was a weapon in it. Painter grinned, maliciously. No weapon could stop him when he was ravenous.

The man opened his mouth as Painter lifted the man's head and looked deep into his eyes. The man tried to turn away but the compulsion to freeze, like a rabbit in a fox's mouth, was too strong. He went rigid with fear as Painter sighed, smoothing away the few greasy tendrils of the man's hair away from his face.

"Hush," smiled Painter, "I am here to save you."

There was a struggle of sorts, as the man tried to turn his head away but it was too late.

Painter grinned down at him. "No-one will miss you. But at least you will have been useful to me."

With that, Painter inhaled the first vestiges of the man's poor, pitiful soul and the darkness for the victim came quick this time.

Chapter 27

"Sandra's been discharged now," stated Ben, as he got into Chris's car. "Thanks for coming to pick me up."

"That's okay." Chris looked over at him and smiled. "You look better. It must be a big relief. What's going to happen now? With Sandra, I mean?"

Ben buckled up as Chris negotiated around the hospital car park and back out onto the main road. "She's going to carry on staying with her mum for a month and then we're going to have another shot at everything. I just feel so bad. It's all my fault."

"Well, you have another chance to make things right, now. You have a good marriage, Ben, you just lost sight of it for a while."

"Thanks for sticking with me, Guv. I've been a right idiot."

"Yep, that's true. But time to put it behind you, Ben. We've got a fun job to do tonight."

Ben groaned. "Oh no, don't tell me…"

Chris grinned. "Yep, your favourite place in all the world."

"The vaults."

"Yep."

"Can I get off now? I don't like this ride." Ben buttoned up his coat and lifted up the collar around his neck.

"Scaredy-cat. This is the man who once told me he could take on anyone."

"Yeah, but I think I was drunk at the time."

"Let's see how brave you are sober, then."

Ben sighed and rested his head on his elbow. "I was beginning to like you, Guv. Why are we going back down the vaults anyway? We've looked at this already."

"Not completely. We're missing something. I want to see what links up beneath Greyfriars."

Ben turned up the radio. "Nothing. We know that."

"I'm not convinced. I was thinking back to the film footage that Lucas Frain showed us. I just don't think we are dealing with a normal suspect."

"So, what *do* you think it is? A demon? Come on, Guv, you have to admit, it does sound a bit far-fetched. A bit ridiculous."

Chris looked in his rear-view mirror as they drove along, mindful of the busy commuter traffic. It was already dark and people were beginning to make their way home after working all day. Rain spat on the windows of the car and he put on the demister so that the glass of the car windows wouldn't fog up. "I just don't know, but how else do you explain it?"

"Not a clue. I've no idea. But a *demon*, in this day and age? I mean, maybe ghosts and things exist, but the rest of it is like something out of a teenage fantasy."

"Perhaps we need to be more open minded, then. We can't explain everything in this world. Even now, with all the science and forensic knowledge, we still don't know what the composition of that acid is. The one component, which *should* be human blood, isn't human. So, what the hell is it?"

Ben looked over at Chris, uneasily. "What if we do find something down there? In the vaults? Should we stop off and get some holy water, just in case?"

Chris almost laughed at the suggestion but he was beginning to feel more serious about the idea than he ever had before. "That's not a bad thought. Let's see what we can come up with first. And hit the exorcist next if we run out of answers?"

"You *are* kidding? Ben looked over at him and raised his eyebrows.

"Of course," muttered Chris is reply, but they both knew that he wasn't.

When Chris eventually parked the car and they walked down the Royal Mile towards the Cathedral of St Giles, he couldn't help but glance at all the posters offering ghost tours of the vaults. There were still people around, hurrying home in the rain now that the business and shops were closing for the day. No-one gave them a further glance when they entered the vaults from the usual street entrance and made their way down the staircase with a couple of torches.

"At least we know where to get a drink afterwards, if this goes badly," Ben made a joke as they entered the dark vaults. He looked quickly at Chris. "Just kidding. I've turned over a new leaf."

"We aren't going near any clubs. We're going in the direction of Greyfriars."

"Oh great. Even better. I love creepy graveyards even more than I like creepy vaults. Brilliant."

Chris held up his phone. "Some of the vaults were bricked up many years ago and not all of them have been re-opened. I think the killer has found a way of accessing one of the tunnels and might be using it."

"But most of the tunnels are already known, Guv. He would have to be super-human to get past the ghost tours, at least."

"Or blend into the background? Think about it. You have groups of people already frightened, ready to see anything in the shadows."

Ben caught his foot in a small depression on the stone floor and moaned. He flashed the torch down. "Oww. Bloody hole. Yeah, okay, I get that, but people take photos, don't they? Of orbs and lights and things that can't be explained."

"What better way for someone, or something, to hide then. If you are expecting to see a ghost, then you'll probably see a ghost. But whether it is actually real or just a figment of the imagination or paranoia, then no-one can prove otherwise."

"Yeah…maybe…but I'm still not really not liking this," Ben replied, as he and Chris continued to follow their torchlight along the dark tunnels. "There's a reason why I've never come down here."

"No point in being scared of what you can't see, Ben," Chris retorted, following the torch beams and trying to follow the map on his phone at the same time. "People are worse than ghosts, any day."

"Hmm, not sure about that…" Ben made a face and brushed a spider off his shoulder. "They're haunted as hell, if you ask me. I don't believe you can get all the scumbags and criminals down here and not have some of their spirits hanging around."

"Apparently in the Great Fire of Edinburgh in 1824, people

sheltered down here in the hope they would survive. If they didn't suffocate, then they baked to death in the heat. Poor souls. No-wonder they just walled everything up."

"You're not making me feel any better. This is grim. I'd rather take on…"

"And there's also Damnation Alley." Chris pointed to his phone. He squinted as the light hurt his eyes. "That's what they called the worst part. And there's always the body snatchers as well."

"Will you shut up, Guv? I'm really not enjoying this."

"So you keep saying, Ben. Well, if it's any consolation, we are under the streets of Edinburgh now. Our phones might run out of battery and no-one might ever find us again."

"You're such a sod."

Chris chuckled to himself as they moved further along. Since entering the underground vault, all they had encountered were spiders and damp and dripping water. He could hardly imagine what it must have been like for the poor men, women and children who had ended up having to live down in the vaults. Not that all of them were law-abiding; in fact, most of them weren't, but it seemed cruel and inhuman to reduce people to such a terrible environment and expect them to thrive. Survival would have been the name of the game and he would have been no different. He felt an unexpected surge of compassion and empathy for them. This was why he continued to do his job. To try and rid the city of all those who preyed on the helpless.

"If you were attacking people, where would you hang out?"

Chris flicked the torch as they came to one of the chambers, long since deserted. He wrinkled his nose at the dank air and shivered. "This sort of place is tailor-made for an acid freak to spend the daytime."

"Maybe we should have brought some back up," Ben looked around him, visibly uncomfortable. "I don't fancy struggling with something like that. We're at a disadvantage, aren't we? If this is his territory, his home ground, then he could be lying in wait for us now."

"Perhaps, but I just don't think so."

"Why not? Why not attack us as well?"

"I don't know. I just don't think we are on this… *thing's*…radar, somehow. Look at the facts, all the victims were into psychic stuff, they were alone, vulnerable, *picked off…*"

"Then what are we supposed to do? Just wait for this thing to turn up?"

"We don't know when he, it, whatever this thing is, will strike again, but we can spread a net around it. I'm willing to bet that there is some sort of open tunnel which connects down here to Greyfriars."

"Why not just hang out in one of the graves, that would be easier…" murmured Ben, turning around carefully.

"What did you say?" Chris stared at him for a moment. He closed his eyes and thought back to where Eric had been examining the grass cuttings in the Kirkyard.

"I said… oh no, hang on a minute, before you say anything else, I am *not* rummaging around some rotten old graves and climbing in mausoleums and stuff like that."

Chris had to laugh at Ben's horrified expression. Ben looked more like a terrified boy than a grown man. "But you're on to something. Maybe, think about it… maybe we're starting at the wrong end. We're looking at this as human beings doing a jolly old ghost tour. We've got to stop thinking along the lines of normal, rational human beings."

"Meaning?"

"Meaning we need to go to Greyfriars and work backwards."

"Oh great. So now we have to find an open tomb, climb in, fish our way around some long dead corpse, hope to God we don't die from some disgusting disease and find a tunnel with a demon in it, probably picnic-ing on his latest victim for dinner."

Chris grinned and his eyes twinkled in the torchlight. "What's up, Ben? I thought you had turned over a new leaf? You should be up for the challenge. Ready to prove how good at your job you are."

"You're really enjoying this, aren't you?"

"Every minute, yep."

"Let's get back up for this one, Guv. Seriously. If anything happens to us, who the hell would know?"

"Don't worry, I'm not sending you in alone."

"Phew. Thanks."

"We're going to take Lucas Frain with us."

Chapter 28

"Would you like to see my paintings?" Painter took Mikaela by her arm and led her away from the thumping music and smiled at her, intently. He had managed to corner her in the kitchen as she was making some snacks for the customers.

"Oh, sure, but what about these?" Mikaela pointed down at the plates of food. "Kev will need these bringing out, or you'll have a riot on your hands."

Painter inwardly cursed Kevin but remained dignified. He didn't want to give her any cause for panic. She was sensitive enough and he had to work hard at concealing his true intentions. He could feel her delicious energy already seeping through to him and it excited him; but he had to tread carefully. He was aware that she had done work on her aura. She had learned how to expand and retract it. The best way to feast on her would be to reel her in gently, before breaking her on his shore. It had to be the right time and place, before she knew something was going to happen.

Standing back, Painter gracefully gestured for Mikaela to continue. "Of course. Please carry on. I'm sorry for getting in your way."

Mikaela giggled and blushed as she tipped some crisps out onto the plates of sandwiches. "That's okay. You're my boss. I don't want you to sack me."

Painter held up a hand to his mouth, delicately. Was she toying with him? He found it rather amusing. His ice blue eyes looked up and down Mikaela's body. "You are a very pretty girl. I hope the male guests aren't giving you any problems?"

"No. Not really. Well, you always get one or two morons. But Kev tells them where to go."

"He looks after you?"

"Yeah, he's great. What with him and Tia, I'm doing well at the moment."

"Ah yes, Tia. I haven't yet had the privilege to meet her. I've been rather…busy, lately."

Mikaela added some sachets of sauce and dressing to the plates and looked back up at him. "Do you mind me asking? Is that your real hair? You look amazing, by the way. It's a great way to get in the customers."

"You are very sweet. Yes, all this is real. Of course it is."

"Yeah, right. You're just saying that."

Painter laughed. He lifted up her hand and caressed it, looking down at her white skin and feeling her grow hot beneath his touch. "Do you think I am attractive, then?"

She giggled and stared up into his eyes. "Sure. Who wouldn't find you attractive? You must have loads of girls after you."

"Oh, I don't know about that. I am a very private person. I am very specific about whom I choose to become involved with."

Mikaela drew her gaze away and picked up the plates. "I'd better get these out."

Painter put a hand on her arm and she paused. "Come and see

my paintings after you finish."

"But I need to go home with Kev. I'm staying at Redfield Grange. With Tia. You know that big creepy house just outside the main drag that everyone thinks is haunted? It's so cool. Both me 'n' Tia are into psychic stuff so it's the perfect place to hang out."

"Ah yes, how fitting for a girl like you. And Tia, too? That *is* interesting. I won't keep you too long, and I can order you a taxi afterwards? I'm sure Kevin will understand."

"I don't know. I'd like to. Really. It's just that…"

Painter sighed and lifted her chin in his hand. "I'm not like other men, Mikaela. You have suffered in the past, I can see that, but I'm different. You can trust me." He stared directly into her eyes and sensed that she was growing weak at the knees for him. It was a desire born of magnetism and lies and he was enjoying every moment of it. She wanted love, acceptance and desire. Someone to show her that she was wanted and protected. It was ludicrously the same every time. Human traits never changed and it made his pursuit of her easier than she could ever have suspected.

"Okay. I will. I'll tell Kev that I'm staying late to clear up. He'll probably be glad to get a break from driving me everywhere anyway."

"Good." He lifted her hand and kissed it. Her skin felt smooth as he gently rubbed the vein that was pulsing beneath it. The blue colour excited him, aroused his desires in a way that no victim had yet done. He was close, so close and she had no idea. If he could have taken her soul, there and then, in the horrid little kitchen, then he would have done so, but Painter wanted the moment to last and he knew it had to be done out of sight.

When Mikaela left him to go back into the main part of the Club, he went back to the Moriarty Suite and waited for her knock to come. When it did so, a few hours later, Painter was ready.

He lifted himself from his sleep as her voice called softly through the door. "Mr P? It's Mikaela."

"Are you alone?" Painter walked over to the door and carefully unlocked it. He eased it open and looked at her through the small gap. "Where is Kevin?"

"Gone. Everyone's gone. I'm not sure I should be hanging around really. Please don't tell me this is a way to get promoted, cos I'm not into this sort of thing."

"I wouldn't belittle you like that, Mikaela. You have no idea how important you are to me."

"But I hardly know you…" Mikaela leant against the door frame. "I like how mysterious you are but I'm not playing any games."

"Like your landlord?" Painter opened the door and stepped out. He had refreshed his appearance and looked immaculate.

Mikaela stared at him, open-mouthed. "Who told you about that? Was it Kev?"

"Oh, my dear, you and I are more similar than you think. I can sense that you are psychic and powerful. I, too, am…interested in…those attributes. I think we can be powerful together. You are attracted to me because I am like you. You and I know there is much more to this world than ordinary people can see."

Painter locked the door behind him and walked towards the

red curtain. "I have something I want to show you. You wanted to see my paintings?"

"Yes, but where are we going?"

"Somewhere fascinating. I want to show you how I actually create my paintings." He pulled the red curtain to one side, revealing the old wooden door. As he unlocked it, he made a point of taking hold of Mikaela's hand. "Come, there is nothing to be afraid of."

"What do you paint?"

Painter smiled as he opened the door and led her down the small flight of stone steps and into the tunnel. He breathed in the dank air with delight. It smelled of ancient foulness, of suffering and pox-ridden bodies and it heightened her rising uncertainty perfectly.

"I paint souls. Please don't be afraid. I know that you have courage. Do you remember how you felt when your landlord made his advances? Powerless and angry? Wouldn't you like to get your revenge?"

"Not…not in a bad way. Karma's a bitch." Mikaela looked around her in awe as he pointed to the dimly lit candles, placed sporadically along in the various niches.

"I made this tunnel. I forged it with my own power. And you can do that, too. You have more power than you imagine." Painter sighed and pulled her close to his chest so that she was held in his arms. He was careful not to be too forceful. "Karma is nothing. There are far more powerful forces in this universe that decide fate. Forces that determine where we are born, when we die…"

"I don't understand," began Mikaela in rising panic. "What are you saying? I'm not into any of the dark stuff. I don't worship

Satan or anything."

"You are adorable. Satan is a Christian invention, based on a much older Pagan god. Men just simply used it to further their control and put fear into the population. The amusing thing is, all the time they did not realise that very real demons walked among men. As they do to this day."

"I've changed my mind, Mr P. I want to go back. I don't want to know any more about this stuff."

Painter increased his hold on her and then put a finger to his lips. "Shush, my dear. It is too late now."

"What do you want from me?" Mikaela cried up at him as he suddenly dragged her along by her wrist. Her skin was on fire, the pain was so intense that she thought he would break her wrist, but Painter was not slowing down. "Please!" she screamed, begging him, "let me go! Please…" She gulped in air, nearly choking on her own tears, her boots scraping along the stone floor. It was rough and uneven and she kept slipping and Painter was losing patience.

"Just do as you're told, you little bitch. Shut that disrespectful mouth of yours and be thankful. I am going to save you."

"Save me? Save me from what? Stop...*please*." Grabbing hold of his fingers with her other free hand, she tried to prise them off, but he merely tightened his grip and Painter could see that she was nearly passing out from the pain. He needed to prolong her energy, to wait until the moment was perfect.

"Look!" he suddenly lifted Mikaela up off the floor in one violent sweep and pushed her hard against the wall so that her feet hung down, unable to touch the ground. "It will go much better for you if you just...shut...up. I want to enjoy this and if you stop your pathetic screaming then we can get this over with as soon as possible."

Mikaela nodded, mutely, stunned into terrified silence. Her eyes grew large in fear as she stared up at him. Painter closed his eyes for an instant, inhaling the delicious terror she was exuding, feeling its vapour penetrate every cell in his face. Her fear felt good, so good and for a moment he wanted it to last forever, to bathe in it and soak it up like plants soak up the rain. Her body was becoming more malleable in his fierce grip, her spirit growing weary from uselessly trying to fight him. Tears ran down her face and into the collar of her black and red checked shirt. Painter watched the rivulets in fascination and he suddenly bent his head to lick them with his long tongue from her neck. They tasted salty. He could hear her whimper in protest but he was beyond caring. Not that he had ever cared at all. He opened his mouth and began to take her essence, cell by delicious cell, and she crumpled in his arms in unconsciousness.

Painter stopped abruptly at the sound of noise. It was distant but definitely coming from somewhere further along the tunnel. It sounded like chanting and he knew instantly it was the annoying Pagan group who sometimes used the tunnels for their rituals. Furious, he bent his head back down towards Mikaela's unconscious body but he couldn't ignore the voices. The echoes were getting louder and the voices more urgent. The candles flickered, disturbed by the changes in the air around them. He pulled back his cloak and snarled. The urgency in his desire made him pant with uncontrollable thirst. He needed to finish. Dragging her body back with him along the floor, he heard them coming. Torch lights beamed around the walls and bathed them both in an ever-increasing glow.

With a howl of frustration, Painter dropped Mikaela's body and flitted up to the ceiling. He flattened himself there, hidden in the dark, waiting for them to turn down a different tunnel, listening to the chanting grow louder. He had to move quickly, faster than a human being could ever move, using every remaining surge of energy he had left. It agonised him to leave her lying there as fury raged into his muscles and he strained against his human shell; it slowed him, rendered him virtually useless and he had been so close to completing his task. Tears of rage flashed down his cheeks as he made his way back to the hidden wooden door of the Nightshade Club and locked it behind him with trembling hands.

When Painter got inside the Moriarty Suite, he bolted the door and fell onto his knees. *They* knew he had failed. The Ancient Ones. He could feel their anger around his head, filling his mind with torment. Sweat exuded from every pore in his body. He wanted to finish his meal, to go back and devour her fully but it was too late. Her body was going to be found and he now needed to lie low. It was more important than ever to hide himself out of sight. He needed to rethink his plans but, in that moment, he was utterly, extremely exhausted. He barely managed to pull himself on to the chaise longue. Collapsing, Painter closed his eyes and tried to mentally bargain with them for another chance. He begged them to give him more time, but their stony silence was more dangerous than their wrath, because Painter knew that his fate was being sealed.

Chapter 29

Tia sighed and turned over in her bed. She looked over at the clock. It was nearly three thirty in the morning and she knew that Mikaela had not come home yet. She stared up at the ceiling, used to not sleeping because of her nightmare, but now she felt worried. Maybe Kevin hadn't been able to drop her back and so she had decided to sleep in the Club all night.

Tia reached over to the bedside table and picked up her phone. The light hurt her eyes for a moment in the darkness. Scrolling down her text messages, there was nothing new from Mikaela at all. The last text had been sent to Tia a couple of nights previously with a link to a gig which Mikaela had invited Tia to go and see with her, but apart from that, nothing. Tia rolled over and put her hands comfortingly under her pillow and chin. Not so long ago, things had seemed relatively normal. Not always easy and definitely not perfect, but now everything had totally changed. She tried to close her eyes and tell herself that Mikaela was absolutely fine, but no amount of telling herself that worked and, in the end, sleep wouldn't come.

Tia finally gave in. Sitting up, she rang Mikaela's number. She felt bad about waking Mikaela up if she was actually asleep somewhere, but somehow it didn't fit Mikaela's character that she wouldn't have at least texted Tia to let her know what was happening. There was no reply. It just went to Mikaela's voicemail. Tia put the phone down and rang a hand through her hair in frustration. Something wasn't right. It felt different. She felt like a worried parent and on one hand that seemed crazy as Mikaela was an adult and able to look after herself, but Tia knew Mikaela was vulnerable and not as tough as she made herself out to be.

The clock moved slowly and painfully as Tia debated whether or not to ring Kevin. Almost pressing his number, she stopped and put the phone down, resting her head on her hands. It wasn't fair to wake up Kevin, especially when he probably hadn't even long gone to bed.

It was a long time spent in the early hours, mulling over what might have happened to Mikaela, and when Tia eventually got out of bed, she felt tired from lack of sleep. Even a hot mug of strong coffee and switching on the television to watch the morning news did nothing for her energy levels and in the end, Tia had to resort to an energy drink, just to finish getting showered and dressed for work.

She stood in front of the window looking out onto the gardens and tried to imagine what it would look like when the roses could bloom again and the borders were filled with beautiful cottage plants, box hedge and herbs. If she had any chance of ever seeing Redfield grow back to its full potential beauty, Tia knew that she needed a miracle. Nothing so far was filling her with any confidence that she was here at Redfield Grange to stay.

A short time later, after checking her phone several times again for any message from Mikaela, Tia locked up and began her drive to the Nightshade Club. All sorts of thoughts swirled around in her head and she felt sick with worry. Something was definitely wrong.

Kevin was already setting up the bar when she got in. He looked up and threw her over a tea towel.

Tia grabbed it. "What's this for?"

"Better look lively, mate. Mr P's on the warpath. 'He's in a right shitty mood. God knows what's wrong. He slammed his door on me when I went to 'elp. Apparently, he's got one of his 'eadaches again. 'E's such a diva."

"I'll go and talk to him in a bit. I need to ask him about the accounts anyway. The suppliers haven't been paid and I'm getting hassle. The accountant doesn't seem to know where the money goes, or where it comes from, for that matter. I don't want to get accused of being complicit in money laundering. Where do you think he gets his funds from?"

"How the hell should I know? Sorry…" Kevin scratched his head and looked frustrated. "I'm just fed of always getting a bollocking from 'im. I'd probably look for another job if it weren't for Mikky."

"Kev, have you seen her? Did she stay with you last night? She never came home and I thought I would have at least got a text from her. I've tried calling her."

"No." Kevin looked surprised and shook his head. "I thought she got a taxi back to yours? She said she wanted ter stay late an' clean up. I think she wanted the extra money."

Tia breathed in, deeply. "She never came home, Kev. And if

she didn't go home with you, and she obviously isn't here, then where on earth *is* she?"

"Beats me. Man, I feel so guilty...I should 'ave made her come back with me."

"I'll go and speak to Mr P. He might know when Mikaela left last night."

"Good idea. Rather you than me, though."

"Well, one of us has to do it. I'm getting really fed up with this guy never bothering. He has a team here and he should look after us."

"Rather you than me, mate," Kevin repeated, lifting up his hands, "that's all I'm saying."

Tia felt temper start to rise up within her. Anything could have happened to Mikaela and she getting annoyed with the inertia. "What are you so afraid of? He's not going to sack us just for asking."

"You don't know 'im. He's not like other people."

"Oh yeah, right, *he's a vampire...*"

Kevin took hold of Tia's arm. "Just don't say anythin' stupid. He's as tough as arseho...I mean, he's hard. Really 'ard. If you piss him off, he'll probably sack the lot of us."

Tia glared at him. "I get that, but he's a really crap boss if he doesn't care what happens to his staff."

"You've got your nice house, mate, you can live off more cash than me an' Mikky 'ave. We *need* our jobs..."

"Oh Kev, I know that, but I'm really worried about her. I'm going to take the chance. He's either seen her, or he hasn't. If he sacks me for asking, then at least we'll hopefully know, one way or the other."

"Okay…" Kevin sighed and acknowledged defeat. "You're gonna do it anyway. I can't stop yer." He dropped his arms and moved forward. "Come on, then," he said with resignation, "we'll do it together."

The two of them went out and down the passageway that led to the Moriarty Suite. They stood in front of the black door and stared at each other. Kevin's nerves were palpable and Tia felt his tension.

"You don't have to do this with me," she whispered. "I'm only going to ask him. That's all."

Kevin glanced back to the door. "I just don't trust 'im," he whispered back. His lips quivered.

Tia blew out her lips in defiance. Raising her fist, she thumped on the door. "Mr P, it's Tia. I know we haven't met yet but I really need to see you, please."

Kevin looked pale and he was already edging away from her. "Be careful," he mouthed, but Tia was determined. The longer they waited, the more annoyed she was getting.

"Mr P!" She thumped on the door, harder this time and Kevin very nearly freaked out completely. "Please open the door!"

"Leave it, Tia!" Kevin urged, through his gritted teeth. "He's not there. He would've opened it by now…"

There was a scratching sound coming from inside and Tia pressed her ear right to the door. "What *is* that?" She frowned and indicated to Kevin. "It sounds like something is dragging across the floor. *Listen...*"

"Nooooooo way...I'm not going near there..."

"You're such a wuss..." Frustrated, Tia put her ear to the surface again and winced. "It's so weird. It's like... like it's moving along the floor."

"Maybe he's ill. Collapsed, or something. Shall I call the police?"

"I take it there's no other key?"

"Nope. Not that I know of. Mr P has the only one."

"Mr P! Answer me! Are you ill? Do you need help?" Tia lifted up her hands in despair. "I can't help if you won't talk to me."

"*Go... away...*" Painter's voice was faint and rasping through the door. "*Get back to your work.*"

Tia pursed her lips. "I'm sorry to disturb you if you have a migraine or whatever, but have you seen Mikaela? She's staying with me at Redfield Grange and she didn't come home last night. Did she go home with anyone?"

"*Get back to work. I won't tell you again. Where is Kevin?*" Painter's voice was stronger now and more insistent.

"I'm here, Mr P. Right here."

"*How many times have I told you not to disturb me?*"

"*Now* do you see what you've done?" Kevin whispered in vehemence, and came closer to the door. He glared in nervous annoyance at Tia. "Sorry Mr P," he shouted, "this won't happen again, I promise."

"It's not Kevin's fault," continued Tia, determined not to leave until she had got an answer. "I just need to know if you've seen Mikaela, that's all."

"*No, I haven't. Now leave me alone. I need to sleep.*"

"Okay! Fine…" Lifting up her hands, Tia shook her head at Kevin. "At least we know. Best leave him to get on with it."

"You're lucky he didn't sack us on the spot." As they both walked back to the bar area, Kevin shook with relief. "He can be a right nasty bit of work… if you try ter cross him."

"Thanks for letting me know that, Kev, but you know what? He doesn't act like a decent, responsible employer. Maybe he's like a real-life Jekyll and Hyde. Either way, I don't like him very much. You could put in a grievance. Mind you, he's the only boss so that wouldn't work. That's how some employers get away with it. They could literally get away with murder and no-one would know."

"Yeah, alright…I need a stiff bloody drink… you want one?" Kevin walked behind the bar and rummaged for a glass. "Don't worry, *I'll* pay…"

"No thanks." Tia went over to her bag and took out her phone. "I'm calling the police. I don't feel right about Mikaela. Something's happened to her, I'm sure of it."

Kevin downed a shot of whiskey in one gulp. "How d'you know? Oh wait, yeah, you already told me. Yer psychic."

"Right now, I don't know what to think. What's the local police station?"

"Murray Road, I think. I don't know the number…sod it…I'm buying two bloody whiskeys."

As Kevin poured himself another measure and rested his elbows on the bar, looking exhausted, Tia found the number of

Murray Road Police Station and rang it. After a conversation, Tia ended the call and looked over at Kevin.

"They're coming out. Don't worry," she made a face at him, "*not to here.* Someone will call at Redfield as soon as they have an officer free. It's okay, Kev. I'll do it. After all, we don't want to piss off Mr P any more than we already have, do we?"

"You think I've got no balls, don't yer."

"I never said a word."

"You didn't 'ave ter. I can see from your face. It's better if you deal with it anyhow, you're the lawyer."

"I'm not a lawyer, Kev. I was a paralegal. I never got that far."

"But you know enough ter get things done, which is more than me. God, I feel sick. If yer need me, I've got me 'ead down the pan...."

"Lovely,"

"Whatcha gonna do now?" Kevin staggered away towards the toilet, scratching his head.

"Keep out of Mr P's way," Tia laughed, but, in reality, she wanted to go through the books again and make another study of the bank statements. Money came in and went out, but she still couldn't make proper sense of it. Even the accountant and the self-employed payroll woman didn't seem to know or care much about the way Mr P ran his Club. No doubt they were probably frightened of him as well.

Chapter 30

Later that evening, Tia heard the clang of the doorbell at home and pulled herself up from the sofa. She wrapped the large blanket shawl around her shoulders, more from defence than from a need for warmth, and walked along the corridor to the entrance hall. As the doorbell reverberated again around the walls, Tia sighed and slid back the chain on the front door.

"Yes?" She pulled the door ajar slightly and peered out. In the moonlight, she could make out a tall man with short, silvery hair. He bent his head and smiled at her.

"Mrs Olsen? Tia Olsen?"

"Yes, that's me." Tia felt a sudden flutter rise up in her chest. It was an unexpected sensation and it caught her by surprise.

"I'm Detective Inspector Chris West, from Murray Road Station. I understand that you have reported a missing person? Do you mind if I ask you some questions?"

Tia felt herself being quickly put at ease, despite not knowing anything about him, but she wasn't going to take any chances. "Can you show me your ID first, please?"

He smiled again, and she was aware of his hands as he lifted out his badge. "Of course." In the dim light, she could see that his photo looked enough like him to take a chance. She took the chain off the door and let him in.

"Thanks." Chris stepped into the entrance hall and was immediately impressed. It was lit with lamps and battery-operated candles, giving it a warm, cosy atmosphere. "It was getting a bit nippy out there."

Tia looked up at him and felt a surge of something…she didn't quite know what but it was enough to keep her quiet for a moment. She wrapped the blanket shawl more tightly around her without realising.

"I'm sorry, Mrs Olsen. Have I come at a bad time? If you would prefer to come down to the Station in the morning…" He took in all the details of her pretty face and auburn hair combed back into a pony tail. She looked like a fairy in her black jogging bottoms, sweat top and blanket. There was something ethereal about her and he felt strangely protective. "If I have disturbed you and your husband…"

Tia smiled and shook her head. "No, don't worry, it's good that you came. Would you like a coffee?"

"Yeah, thanks, that'd be great…" He followed after Tia at her indication, noticing afresh the large grandfather clock, the finely carved staircase and how quiet the house was, although he could faintly hear music somewhere in the background.

As if reading his mind, Tia turned and smiled at him. "I usually have the television on in the lounge, even if I'm not actually watching it. It's company for me."

"So, no Mr Olsen? Is he working?"

"Sort of." Tia felt the familiar urge to quell her anxiety again at the mention of Lars, and she desperately tried to push it back down and hold it under control. "It's just me here at the moment." She felt Chris's eyes follow her intently as they went into the kitchen. Turning on the light, Tia gestured for Chris to sit down on one of the kitchen stools, whilst she filled the kettle with water and switched it on. Taking two mugs from the cupboard, she spooned in some instant coffee. "Sorry, I don't have anything fancy. Do you take milk and sugar?"

"Just milk is fine, thanks." Chris looked around him with interest. "This is a big house to be in on your own. Do you have a good security system installed?"

"There is a burglar alarm system but I think it needs a service, to be honest. It doesn't really work." Tia eventually handed him his mug of coffee and Chris took it, gratefully. He was aware of how delicate and pale her skin was, and how the shadows beneath her eyes gave away the fact that she hadn't been sleeping well.

Tia felt his intense scrutiny and felt herself flush with embarrassment. "It should be fine, though. I'll get it sorted."

"I can ask one of our recommended firms to get in touch with you, if that would help?" He sipped his coffee whilst looking over his mug at Tia.

"Yes, thanks, that would be great." Tia could see just how blue his eyes were and how he never wavered his gaze from hers. Even though he was a complete stranger, something about him made her feel safe. "That would be really helpful. I, we, haven't been here long. I don't know many people enough yet to really ask."

"So, where are you from?"

"North London. Lars, that's my husband, and I, moved up

here a short time ago. He works in a local law firm. I used to work in the same firm but got made redundant." Tia sipped at her coffee, leaning back against the sink. Why was she even telling him that? He was here to ask about Mikaela, not her, but the way he spoke in his strong, capable voice both captivated and encouraged her, making it easy to confide in him. "Lars and I, well, he's about to move out. Things haven't worked out between us." She stopped short of telling him more and then immediately regretted being as open as she had been already.

Chris lowered his gaze, suddenly aware of his intense scrutiny, and frowned. "I'm sorry. Things must be hard for you at the moment."

"Yes, but you're here to ask about Mikaela, not me. I shouldn't waffle on, sorry."

"Don't worry. This coffee's good by the way. Better than I get at the Station," he laughed. He felt himself begin to wind down and relax more than he had in a long time, but he was conscious he had a job to do and just staring at the beautiful woman in front of him was not going to achieve that.

"It's Mikaela Stone. I work with her at The Nightshade Club and she's been staying with me. She needed a place to stay and I offered to help her out."

"And when did you first realise that she might be missing?" Chris watched as Tia pulled off her blanket shawl revealing her petite figure. "Do you have a photograph of her at all?"

"Er…yes…on my phone…we took a selfie a couple of nights ago. The thing is… although I haven't known Mikaela for very long, she is such a nice girl. Genuinely nice. And I don't think she would have gone off with anyone she had met at the Club. She wasn't like that. She's had some horrible experiences and that's why I took her under my wing."

Tia took her phone out of the pocket of her jogging bottoms and found the photo. She handed her phone to Chris. He studied it intently, taking in every aspect of Mikaela's identity, clothes and even the tattoo she had on her forearm.

"That's interesting..." Chris leant forward and opened up the photo so the tattoo was enlarged. "Was Mikaela into anything like Paganism, Wicca, Druidry? That sort of thing? What does this symbol mean on her arm?"

Tia went over to him and stood close over his shoulder to see the picture in more detail. She smelt his aftershave; it was a good smell. "Yes, Mikaela's a Wiccan. And that's a pentacle with a rose wrapped through it. A pentacle is a five-pointed star within a circle. Each point represents an element; Earth, Fire, Water and Air, encircled by Spirit. We are made up of all these elements. In Wicca, you can work with these elements to tap into the magic."

"Magic?" Chris turned and looked up at her. He saw how flecks of brown in her green eyes danced in the light. They were bewitching enough in their own right. "As in Merlin and Harry Potter?"

"Sort of but it is much bigger than that. It is the living essence. Magic is in everything. It is like electricity, neutral but powerful. It is the user of the magic that determines whether it is used for good or evil, white or black magic."

"You are very knowledgeable. Are you experienced in this sort of thing?" Chris was aware of Tia standing so close to him and of her own electricity. "Can you explain more of this to me? It may help me to find Mikaela and also assist with another on-going investigation we have."

"Of course. I'm not actually a Wiccan, more, um...eclectic, but I'll help in any way I can."

"Thank you. Are you able to come into the Station tomorrow?" Despite his reluctance, Chris knew he had to leave, even though he didn't want to. The pull to stay was very strong and he didn't really know why.

"I have a shift until 5pm. I can come along after that?"

"That's fine. Let me give you my card," Chris took out his wallet from the inside of his jacket and handed it to her. "Here are my details, mobile number and email. If Mikaela turns up for work in the meantime tomorrow, then let me know. And please forward that photo to me."

"I will. Thanks." Tia looked up at him and felt increasingly reassured. There was something steady, strong and calming about him. "I really appreciate it."

"That's what I'm here for. Don't worry. I'm sure there is a genuine explanation for her disappearance. It is still thankfully rare that people go missing and anything sinister is behind it."

"It's just...I have a bad feeling about it. It could be nothing, like you say but...I just have a feeling."

"Well, hunches are good things to take notice of. I do it all the time." Chris felt a weird sense of déjà vu suddenly. "Sometimes the gut feeling is the only feeling to rely on." He stared down at Tia. "We haven't met before, have we?"

Tia shook her head but she knew exactly what Chris meant. There was something familiar about him, something comforting. Like meeting a long-forgotten friend all over again. "No. Not in this lifetime, anyway," she replied, enigmatically.

Chris laughed. Her company was warm and entertaining, making him feel less serious. And he hadn't felt like that in a long time. It was enticing enough to make him want to stay longer, but he knew he had to leave. "That's intriguing. We can explore more of this subject another time, I'm sure."

Tia followed him out of the kitchen and back into the entrance hall. "Thank you so much for coming out. Especially on such a cold night. I never realised the weather could be so… changeable up here."

Chris laughed. "Didn't you get rain and wind and hail down in London, then?"

"It's not as spectacular, put it that way. I'd rather see the rain coming down from the glens than down the drainpipe of our old apartment. There is something very captivating about Scotland and I love it more every day."

"It's good to hear you say that," Chris was pleased and oddly reassured. "It is full of myth, superstition and history. And we have often been at war with the English. I'm glad those days are over."

"So am I," returned Tia, and she meant it.

After Chris had left, Tia locked the door again, made some hot chocolate and headed up to bed. She felt quite dreamy, and for a moment she was glad of the chance to close her eyes and think only of the rain-soaked mountains and misty purple glens of her new-found home. It was a welcome respite from any thoughts of the nightmare which lurked just around the corner of her mind. She felt so much better knowing that the police were now involved and actively taking care of the situation with Mikaela.

And she liked Detective Inspector Chris West a lot. She found herself thinking of his handsome face and lovely blue eyes again, replaying their conversation all over again in her mind. It was the last thing she did before finally switching off her bedside light and slipping into sleep.

Chapter 31

The following day, Tia sat in one of the interview rooms at Murray Road Station and raised her head as Chris entered. He was carrying a glass of water and a cup of coffee for her, which she accepted gratefully. "Thanks," she smiled, and sipped the water straight away. It had been a long day.

"You're welcome." Chris sat down on the opposite side of the table. "So still no sign of Mikaela? I assume she didn't turn up or call you?"

Tia shook her head. She felt exhausted from not having slept much and the strain of Lars moving out made her feel worse. "No, nothing. I've tried to call several times, left messages, social media, everything. It's like she's vanished completely."

Chris felt an uneasiness growing inside of him. He watched Tia sip her coffee and felt annoyed with himself that he had no instant answers. But he knew from many years' experience on the job that he couldn't provide one. He had to go through the process, step by step. "Can you let me have a list of anyone she has been in contact with over the last few days? We can start making enquiries."

"Yes, of course. I don't think there are many, to be honest. Not the ones I know of, anyway. Then again, you think you know a person…" She lowered her gaze and stared into her drink. All her thoughts for some reason seemed to be going to Lars and Sophie and she was fighting the urge not to cry. Everything was raw and jagged, like salt being rubbed into an open wound and she could think of nothing further to say for a moment.

Chris leant across the table towards her. He looked at his watch. "Have you eaten, Tia?"

"I'm sorry?" Tia looked up at him, miserably.

"I'm thinking of grabbing a bite to eat. There's a decent pizza place not far from here. You look tired and maybe that will help?"

Tia drew in her breath and sat back in her chair. She looked at him, afresh. His eyes, again that beautiful blue, were kind and there was something insistent in his manner that she couldn't, didn't want to, refuse. "Yes, that…sounds good. Thank you. Are you sure you can spare the time?"

Chris nodded and pushed back his chair. "Things always look better when I'm not hungry. Great. I'll grab my jacket and come back and get you in a minute."

Tia smiled and nodded. "Okay. Thanks." She wasn't sure if she felt like eating anything at all but he felt safe and easy to talk to.

A short time later, they sat at the window table of the pizza restaurant, watching as the cars drove past and talked about their respective careers and what had brought them to this point. Chris broached the subject of Lars and Tia finally opened about what had happened with Lars and Sophie. Tears threatened to flow but she restrained them. It was painful taking about everything but somehow cathartic at the same time.

Chris said nothing, instead watching her, intently. "That's pretty devastating, Tia. No wonder you feel so emotional. Worrying about Mikaela can't be helping, either."

"The worst thing is that, well…"

"What?"

"Lars always said I was nuts, but I can't help feeling that Mikaela is in danger. I read the Tarot cards for her and…we both saw something dark."

"And you think that is a warning? Do you believe in all that psychic stuff?"

Tia sipped her cola and nodded. She felt suddenly stupid. "Sorry. I shouldn't haven't said anything."

"I take it your husband didn't encourage you with this?"

"No. He said I was emotionally unstable."

"That's very harsh." Chris grinned as the waitress arrived with the pizza, divided into two different halves. "So, your side is the…er... weird side..."

"What's weird about tuna, pineapple and cheese?"

"Nothing if they're separate." Chris laughed. "I'll stick to the boring pepperoni, then."

Tia bit into a slice and struggled to swallow. She realised that she hadn't eaten much in the last couple of days and every bite felt like an effort. Whilst the taste was good and the food felt nourishing, she felt drained.

"So, how do you manage to do your job, Chris? Do you still get affected by what you have to deal with?"

"Every day. You never stop being affected. Just when you think you've nailed it, scraping the bottom of the criminal barrel I mean, something else comes along."

"It must be really hard. Seeing the worst of humanity. How do you cope with it?"

Chris shrugged and took a swallow of his alcohol-free beer. "I'm not sure I do. I just try and do my job and clear the streets of as many scumbags as possible." He looked down at his pizza and a wave of dread came over him. "Your friend, Mikaela. Why do you feel she is in danger?"

"I've always been…psychic. Sometimes I sense things…*know things*. Like I knew about the baby before Lars did. Sophie hadn't even told him."

"That's a real gift, Tia."

Tia made a self-deprecating expression. "Do you really think so? Lars never thought…"

"I think Lars has had his chance to understand you, and he didn't. You know, sometimes you have to draw a line under things, Tia. Under people. When they move on, it usually means you've outgrown *them*."

"Yes, you're probably right." Tia nodded and smiled at him. He had the ability to reassure her very easily. "You're so wise."

"I don't know if anyone has ever called me that," Chris laughed, and bit into his pizza. It was growing cold very quickly because they were talking so much. Strangely, his appetite no longer bothered him. He found he could listen to Tia and lose all track of time. "I think it comes from many years of seeing the best and worst of human nature. Good and evil, maybe?"

Tia leant forward suddenly. "Do you believe in good and evil?" Her eyes fixed on him, without blinking. "Do you believe there is evil? *Real* evil?"

Chris lowered his half-eaten slice to his plate, encapsulated by Tia's green-eyed gaze. "I've no doubt about it. Sure, there are mental conditions, and that isn't evil. But yes, I do believe that something is out there that can affect people and perhaps make them do evil things." He instantly thought back to the footage that Lucas Frain had shown him and he felt an involuntary shiver go down his spine. "I believe that I can deal with things I can see. What I can't see, well, I'm not so sure about that."

"I think…I think something is after *me*."

Chris studied her for a moment. "Why do you say that? Has someone threatened you? Has your husband threatened you?" He felt an unexpected flare of anger at the thought, which surprised him. He reeled himself back in.

"Oh no. *No*. Lars can brow-beat sometimes but he's definitely not a violent man. It's hard to describe. I probably sound like I'm going mad." Tia leant back and dabbed at her mouth with her napkin and gave Chris an apologetic look. "I'm sorry. I shouldn't have said anything. You have enough on your plate to deal with. I guess I just wanted another take on what I'm experiencing."

"Well, if I can help, I will. Look," he took another glance at his watch and signalled for the waitress to bring the bill, "I'll walk you back to the Station and you can tell me what's on your mind. I've got some calls to make and we need to find your friend."

Tia nodded and opened her purse.

"No, I'll get this. Perhaps next time, you can treat me?" he laughed, looking sideways again at her as he put his credit card into the card reader.

"Yes…okay, my treat," Tia responded. She liked the idea of a second time eating with him.

Chris grinned at the waitress. "We may be back here." He gave the grateful young girl a tip and put on his jacket. "Let's get you to your car. It's getting late."

"Yes," sighed Tia. She was beginning to feel the tiredness again threaten to overtake her body. If she could have slumped down, there and then in the street, she would probably have fallen asleep.

"So," continued Chris as they walked back, "tell me what's bothering you."

"It…doesn't sound like much," replied Tia, unsure of how much to say but his frequent glances at her were encouraging. "I…well…one of the reasons I haven't been sleeping is, I've been having a nightmare."

"Really?"

"Yes. Not every night but it's getting more and more frequent. It's the same thing. Something is trying to hurt me. I'm running away from it. I don't know who it is."

"That sounds pretty frightening. Do you think it could be because of your marital situation? Sometimes when we are going through difficult emotional circumstances, we experience nightmares. Perhaps you need to face something?"

"Maybe. That's what Mikaela said. But I don't know what else there is to face. My marriage is over and I've faced that."

"I don't know the answer, Tia, but one thing I do know.

When the time is right, your emotional state will settle down and the nightmare will stop."

"Yes, maybe." Tia stopped in the street and looked up at him. "I don't think it is Lars or Sophie, though, or even me. I think it is something else. I guess I'll just have to try and deal with it myself."

Chris sighed and felt a strange tug within him. Another hunch, perhaps. He wasn't sure but he felt compelled to go along with it. He smiled gently down at her. "Do you think it is something to do with Mikaela? Perhaps once we find her, you'll find it eases up?"

Tia nodded but, deep down inside, she knew that it wasn't that simple. "Perhaps. Thanks for looking out for me and the friendly ear. I really appreciate it. What will you do next, about Mikaela?"

Chris felt the coolness creep into their conversation, pulling it back around to pure professionalism, and he felt a deep pang of disappointment. "I'll use the contacts you gave me and get my team to start checking them all out."

"Will you let me know as soon as you hear something?"

"Yes, of course." Chris took out his mobile phone and was just about to call the Station to let them know he was on his way back, when he saw that Tia had stopped in one of the shop doorways.

Tia felt a sudden urge to be sick. She stopped abruptly and leant into the glass display window. The street began to sway around her and instantly she remembered her other vision, back in the cellar at Redfield Grange. She put her hands to her knees and bent over.

It was back.

The black presence infiltrated her mind, filling her inner vision with terror. It was massing, building in strength and intensity. Now its energy was growing as strong as her own. There was no way she was imagining it. The thing was filling up her senses and starting to overtake them. She gasped and struggled against it, squeezing her eyes tightly shut to try and make it go away.

"Tia? What is it?" Chris took a hold of her shoulders and lifted her up. "What's the matter?"

"I...don't know..." In her mind's eye, Tia felt the overwhelming dread and sense of darkness coming for her. "It's...nothing..." she managed to say, but Chris wasn't convinced.

"I should get you to the hospital. I think you are exhausted and ill."

"No!" Tia put a trembling hand on his forearm. "I'm not ill, I promise. I've had this before..."

"Then we should definitely go to the hospital..."

"I'll be okay." She reached out to the glass window and rested her head against it, desperately trying to bring any semblance of normality back, but all she could see through the window was a vast and terrible darkness. Everything around her suddenly tumbled, until she slumped against Chris and blacked out.

Chapter 32

Tia opened her eyes and was aware of the clatter of metal trolley wheels and lights around her. She was in a hospital ward and felt the thin blanket covering her body. She looked down at her arm and saw that she had a drip inserted into the soft, fleshy part of her inner arm. It was hooked up to a stand with a plastic bag of liquid and there was a monitor. She tried to sit up and then fell back down into the stiff pillows. It was like being in a vice and her own body was imprisoning her.

Gradually moving her other arm to the bedside cupboard, Tia picked up the sip cup of water. As the luke-warm liquid trickled through the spout and into her mouth, Tia felt some sense of relief and comfort. What she wanted more than anything was normality. She looked either side of her. One other lady was in the bed next to the window with her head facing away, the other bed was empty. Suddenly panicking, Tia reached for her bag which was in the bedside cupboard. She pulled out her phone, ready to call Kevin.

"Don't worry, I've told him already."

Tia dropped her phone on the blanket as Chris came around the corner and over to her bed. He pulled up a chair and sat down. He looked tired and worn out. "How are you feeling, Tia?"

"Did you…surely you haven't been here all night?"

"Not all night. Once I made sure you were being looked

after, I went back to the Station. We have a couple of sofas," he joked. "Besides, I was worried about you."

"Worried?"

"I'm used to people being sick over me, threatening me, verbally abusing me, but I have never come across...I want to help you, Tia. I just don't know how to do that yet."

Tia leant back in the pillows and closed her eyes for a moment. She felt weary and tired, but his words felt so good that she wanted to drink them in and keep them close to her. Tears of relief pricked her eyes.

"Would you like me to leave?" Chris went to stand up but Tia held out her hand and stopped him.

"No, I would be happy...much happier if you stayed. Even for a bit longer. It probably sounds silly but you make me feel safe."

"I can't talk to the doctors, Tia, but they *have* said to me that you can be discharged later today, if you feel ready. I've arranged for your car to be delivered to Redfield Grange. I'll take you home, myself."

"You've already been so kind, Chris. I know you have so much to do. I can get a taxi home."

"Too late. I've already arranged it. You need to tell me more of what is going on in your head, Tia. Maybe I help?"

"Help?" Tia felt her heart sink. "I'm not ill, Chris. Please don't make me out to be some kind of... lunatic."

"I'm not. That's not what I'm saying."

"Then what *are* you saying?" Tia dropped her hand and tucked it quickly back into the blanket. She remembered all of the unkind things Lars had said, how he had called her crazy, and ultimately found the gorgeous Sophie who was normal and everything she wasn't.

"Tia, sorry. I didn't mean it like that. I meant, well, I haven't been entirely honest with you and I can't tell you the details. I'm working on a case at the moment and elements of it are unusual, to say the least."

"Really?" Tia still felt hurt and bruised but he had piqued her interest. "What sort of thing?"

"I don't know enough myself, yet, but I'm beginning to think we may be able to help each other."

"Okay." Tia gave him a half-smile. "Chris, I'm really sorry to drag you away from your work. I feel so guilty. You don't need the likes of me getting in the way."

The likes of you keep me going, Chris wanted to say, but didn't. Instead, he just looked down at her with concern. "Just rest up and we'll take it slowly. You need to get some energy back."

As he left the ward, Tia realised that he was actually becoming a friend. There was no-one else who knew what she was going through and Lars wouldn't want to know. She didn't want him to know anything about her problems, any more than she wanted to know about his.

When Chris came back later, Tia didn't feel awkward about telling him her diagnosis.

"Exhaustion and anxiety? That's pretty understandable, considering what you've been going through."

"I'll be okay," Tia picked up her bag and followed him out to the car park. "It's strange, though. I mean, I've haven't been here long and already things are happening that are odd. Touch wood, I've never normally had to go to the hospital. I certainly haven't had episodes of passing out before. I feel like a right idiot."

Chris opened the car door for her and cocked his head. "I've seen worse idiots than you, believe me."

As they drove along, Tia looked at the medication the doctors had given her from the hospital pharmacy. "Beta blockers for anxiety. I'm not going to bother with those. I should have asked for some sleeping tablets, though."

"For your nightmare?" Chris looked across at her. "Are you sure it isn't the situation with your husband? You said he brow beats you? I call that bullying."

"Possibly." Then Tia shook her head, adamantly, in reply. "No, I just don't think it is about Lars but I can't get it to stop. I know it isn't normal. Anyway," Tia put the tablets back in her bag, "it is what it is. I'll carry on as usual. I've got no intention of stopping work or anything like that."

"Listening to me won't make any difference then?"

"Nope, sorry. I have a lot at stake. I can't afford to lose my job right now."

They spent the rest of the short journey back to Redfield Grange in congenial silence, apart from one or two minor observations on the weather and what news was on the radio. It was a comfortable silence, and Tia realised that she was more relaxed than she had been in a long time. There was an aura of positivity around Chris and it made her smile.

Chris noticed and grinned as he turned off the road into the lane that ran up to Redfield. "What's up?"

"It's just… well, you probably get told this all the time, but you have a really nice vibe."

"No, in all honesty, I don't think anyone has really said that to me. Most people are more upset that I've arrested them. I don't get that many compliments."

"Sorry. If it's any help, people didn't really like employment law advice, either. They needed it, but they didn't really want to ask for it and they hated having to pay the bill at the end."

"Are you glad to be out of the law?"

"I miss the structure of the day sometimes, and the training and chats in the office. But I don't miss the stress, no. Lars always said I was too soft for the legal world."

Chris carefully drove up to the front door, impressed again at how grand the house was. "I wouldn't take much notice of him, Tia. He's made his choice. Now you have to make the right decisions for you."

Tia unlocked the front door. "Yes, you're right. And I am. Would you like to come in for a coffee? It's the least I can do. You've been so great, bringing me home and everything."

"I'd love to, but I have to get back now. Promise me you will call me if you need anything?"

"Promise. Thanks, Chris. I really do appreciate everything you have done for me."

Chris smiled in response. He was fighting the strong urge to have the coffee, to stay much longer, but he knew he couldn't. He was needed at the Station.

"Stay safe, Tia," he said, nodding his head and watching as she disappeared inside.

When Chris's car eventually drove back down the lane out of sight, Tia closed the front door. She had a funny sort of sadness, as if he wasn't supposed to leave. Very odd, considering she had only just recently met the man. He was bringing up a lot of sensations that she hadn't experienced in a long time.

Chapter 33

Lucas Frain sat in the back of Chris's car looking pale. By the time they had reached Greyfriars, he looked distinctly queasy and even Chris felt a bit sympathetic.

"I'm sorry, Lucas, to drag you into this. But you may be the one person who can help us."

"You still haven't told me what's going on, though, have you?" His voice was accusatory and defensive. "If it's some paranormal thing you're doing, why not tell me?"

"We are investigating some…occurrences…and you being the expert, may be able to shed some light on them."

Chris got out of the car and waited for Ben to speak to the uniforms who had arrived as back up. Standing in the cold in front of Greyfriars Kirk, they huddled around, waiting for the next instructions from Chris.

"One or two aren't happy about it, Guv," said Ben as he walked back over to the two men. "Apparently rummaging around in consecrated ground is making them uncomfortable. Even though I told them we have permission."

"What's going on?" Lucas zipped up his black hoody and stared around. "What are we supposed to be looking for?"

"You can put everything you've learned into practice, Lucas. I want you to use all of your equipment to monitor these surroundings." Chris indicated at the perimeters of Greyfriars. "EVPs, orbs, anything."

"I've already told you I don't want to be a part of anything heavy. And this looks…heavy."

"Cheer up, mate," laughed Ben, slapping him on the shoulder. "At least they're not making you go down the tombs. That's apparently my job."

"Have you guys actually *heard* of the MacKenzie Poltergeist? Do you really wanna encourage that thing?"

"I don't believe it is a poltergeist we're looking for." Chris frowned and watched as the uniforms began their search. Torches flickered over various areas of the graveyard and he could hear their mumbling. "I want you to just keep your equipment rolling."

"So where will you be?" Lucas seemed resigned to his fate and began unloading his gear. Fumbling around, is was clear to Chris that he was dreading it.

"Ben and I are looking for anything that may lead to a tunnel."

"But that's not going to happen is it? Surely if there were any tunnels then I would already know about it. I've been doing this long enough."

"I think this is something recent. Something made for access and it won't be in any guidebooks, Lucas. I need you to watch and see whether we flush anything out."

"Flush anything out? What do you mean…*flush anything out*?" Lucas's hands shook as he got his camera ready. "I think you might just have the wrong guy to help you with this."

"But think about the evidence you might get," enthused Ben, "*and* you will be assisting the police."

"You guys are as cagey as hell. You drag me here, don't tell me even half the real story and then expect me to come up with the best evidence ever."

"You've got it." Chris indicated for Lucas to make a start over by the Covenanters Prison gates. Once Lucas had walked over, begrudgingly, Chris turned to Ben and took in a deep breath. "Are you ready for this?"

"Nope."

"Me neither. Let's go."

They both walked over to the entrance to the Kirk. "What about the crypt, Guv? A lot of old crypts had tunnels, didn't they?"

"They did, but this has to be something with easy access. Once the church is locked up at night, or whatever, then no-one can get in or out without an authorised key."

"So, what about the Black Mausoleum? The whole weird MacKenzie Poltergeist tomb? When that got broken into, didn't the whole activity start up?"

Chris shook his head and stopped for a moment. He felt the strange atmosphere as they both stood there, in the darkness. "That's also kept padlocked. No, this is different. I think whatever this thing is, it is using the whole Poltergeist story as a cover. This thing is masquerading as some kind of ghost but is something else, entirely."

Ben put his hands on his hips and then got a bleep from his radio. He put it to his ear, quickly. "Yep? What's up?" He listened intently and then blew out a deep breath. "We've found something, right round the back."

They reached one of the side walls of the graveyard where some of the uniforms were gathered. The row of ornately carved, box-like tombs, lined up side by side, looked like some kind of macabre street. Chris approached them and looked down with his torch to where he had been indicated. "Looks like something has disturbed the ground recently." He shone his torch onto the crumbling, grey stone and grass below. Quite a bit of stonework had fallen on the ground. He rubbed the edges of the tomb. "You would expect some corrosion over the years, but this looks fresh. Big chunks," he held them up to Ben, "they look like they've been cut away. Bag them."

Ben did as he was told and then watched as Chris ran his gloved fingers around, pushing as he did so. He eased the block of stone with the incumbent's name on and moved it slightly. Chris could feel the sweat start to drip off him. He felt as bad as a grave robber, exactly the sort of criminal that he disliked so much, but there was no other alternative. He was going to have to be the first man to go down there since the crypt, or tunnel, or whatever it was had been built, and he felt like he was violating something sacred.

"Don't worry, you won't get a curse put on you," Ben laughed, as if reading Chris's mind. "You're Saint Christopher, remember?"

"Hah bloody hah." Chris grimaced as another piece of stone came away in his hand. "For what it's worth, I do believe in good versus evil, you know. I'm just trying to remind myself that I'm on the good side at the moment."

Beneath his manoeuvring and manipulation of the stonework, the tomb began to give way and all of the police officers gasped almost unilaterally. Despite his bravado in front of his team, Chris was hating every minute of what he was having to do and his throat was dry from something akin to nerves and dread. He had thought about getting gowned up like Eric, but something made him feel that this wasn't going to be a normal tomb with a normal corpse. If something had made its home down there, then anything lying around would have been moved, or robbed out, some time ago.

The tomb front moved gradually, a centimetre at a time, until Chris was able to shine his torch into the space behind. "No cobwebs. This has been disturbed recently." He flashed the torchlight back around the grass area. "Strange, though. You'd think there would be footprints in the mud at least. The ground looks raked up, rather than trodden on."

"Well, we *are* dealing with a ghost," sniggered Ben and then caught Chris's expression. "Okay, well at least Lucas is here to confirm one way or another."

"Don't remind me..." Coming up amongst the waiting officers, Lucas held out his digital recorder. "All set. If I *have* to be. Hey," he pointed over to Chris, "you're not expecting me to go down there, are you?"

Chris found himself laughing. For a paranormal investigator, Lucas had as much courage as a rabbit in headlights, about to do a flit at the first chance of escape. "You need to stay here and record anything you see come out. Okay?"

"Fine, yeah. Good, just as long as you don't want me to go

down *there*. Whatever you're chasing, it's sick if it lives in someone's grave."

"Just think of what you can tell your grandkids, Lucas."

"Not that you're gonna let me tell anyone…" Lucas crouched down and began to check his equipment. "Don't want the batteries being drained. That's a classic." He rummaged around in the pockets of his hoodie and withdrew spare batteries.

"Drained? What drains them?" Ben looked at Lucas with rising nerves evident in his expression.

"Spirit manifestations," returned Lucas, clearly enjoying his brief moment of authority. "It's a common side-effect of investigations. It's believed that spirits use the power to help make themselves known. Good luck down there, if they do." He pointed towards the now fully open tombstone and shook his head. "You've still never told me what it is you're *really* looking for."

"That's why we need your help," answered Chris, preparing himself for the descent and looking into the darkness with distaste. "You're the expert. You can tell *us*."

His ego massaged, Lucas then shut up and watched Chris ease himself into the void. He edged further backwards to allow Ben to go in after Chris and gave them a mock Boy Scout salute. "Good luck then, cos I reckon you're gonna need it."

Chris smelt the damp, fetid air and brought up his face mask, which he had kept around his neck, hidden within the collar of his jacket. His feet felt the small, slippery stone steps going down below him. One by one, he pressed each foot sideways, not wanting to take any chance on the stonework's ability to hold him. He didn't even turn around to see if Ben was following him, he couldn't take any chances on safety. Each of them would have to fend for themselves. He breathed heavily through his mask. The material didn't make it easy but it was better than catching something unfathomable and disgusting. He felt cramped in the tight space, too tall for it but then again, he reasoned, he wasn't dead and the tomb had probably been tailor-made for someone much shorter. He blinked as a bug fell into his hair and he quickly brushed its horrible, tickly form out of his hair.

"Urgh, Guv, "came Ben's muffled, disgusted voice behind him, "do you remember when we had to crawl through that drain and pipework right out near the reservoir..."

"Yep..."

"This is so much worse."

"I know. Onwards and upwards, Ben."

"You always say that. But there's only downwards." Ben sneezed suddenly and coughed into his own facemask.

"Mind the forensics."

"Sod the forensics...it's all over *me*, thanks..."

As other officers climbed in carefully behind them, Chris suddenly felt his feet gingerly touch the surface of the floor. He couldn't quite stand up tall, he had to make do with an uncomfortable slightly crouched position and it made his neck hurt. He shone his torch around. The coffin had been partly ripped open and a putrid-looking shroud lay discarded over in one of the corners. Apart from some old bones, which Chris could see were a pelvis and leg bones, little remained of the once dignified casket with its wealthy occupant. He could see the blocks of stone which had been placed with precision in order to complete the tomb. It showed signs of having been made with care and decent workmanship, a masterpiece which had been constructed to last. It was a sad thing that someone, or something, had now desecrated it.

"I'm gonna see this in my sleep for a long time," moaned Ben, stepping down onto the floor beside Chris. "This is the stuff of my childhood nightmares."

"There's some sort of opening over here..." Chris wrinkled up his eyes. "Follow me."

"Well I can't go anywhere else can I…"

The opening in the iron grille was large enough for Chris to stoop through. He lowered his head and put out his hand to the stone wall to steady himself. Surprisingly, the passageway suddenly widened out and he found that he could fully stand up in it. Piles of rubble had been pushed to either side and a sloping recess made in the floor, which he had to climb into and through to the other side. Water dripped into it.

"Careful, everyone" he called out, "this is slippery." Relieved that he could stand up properly again, Chris took down his mask. The air was not so putrid, just damp and he aimed his torch up to the ceiling. In shock he saw the many stick-like bones sticking out, in all stages of colour and decay. "Welcome to the bones of the City's old dead," he warned, putting his mask back on quickly. Eric knew more than he did about how long plague could last and he didn't want to find out.

Easing themselves along the morbid passageway, Ben moved

himself nearer to Chris. "So where do you think this leads to?"

Feeling slightly safer, Chris eventually stuffed his face mask in his pocket. "Some sort of lair, I hope. If the killer is using this system of tunnels to get around, it would be really easy to hide down here."

"Yeah, if you're Nosferatu. "Most people, even nutcases, wouldn't even come down here."

They continued to walk along, each officer following through the deep recess and out into the long passageway. "Don't forget, we're not dealing with a normal human being, this is something else. We need to be on full alert."

The tunnels were narrow in places and leading off were smaller tunnels and chambers. As the officers shone their torches around each one meticulously, and found nothing, Chris could feel his frustration begin to rise. They were playing cat and mouse in a game of murder, and Chris didn't like being the mouse. Whatever it was that was toying with them, he wasn't going to let it gain the upper-hand, any more than it already had.

As they made their way along, Chris looked at his phone again. The map wasn't great; the detail was old and faded and made no mention of which tunnels led into smaller ones. He had to go on his hunch that the tunnel they were in would soon expand and lead towards the killer's base.

"Just thinking, Guv, you remember when we went to the Nightshade that time, for Deano's stag night?"

"Yeah, do you, though?"

"Very funny. I know I was pissed. But I do remember

thinking how cool the place was and how they had managed to put a nightclub down in the vaults."

"And?"

"Well, what if the club is connected in some way? I mean, all the victims we know liked to hang out and drink. Plus, they would probably have been attracted to the Nightshade, being into all the pagan stuff."

Chris stopped and shone his torch in Ben's face. "Well that does make sense." He thought suddenly of Tia and felt a pang of something, something new and unexpected. Growing unease began to fill his body. "I don't know why I didn't connect it before, Ben. Who's the owner, again? Painter, isn't it?"

"Yep. But I doubt it's him, Guv, I mean he's just a clever bloke hamming it up for the customers. And how old is he? Probably not more than forty, tops. That doesn't make him a killer spanning over a century."

"No, but we should question him. He may recognise our three victims, at least. Mikaela Stone has just started working at the Club. This fits, Ben."

Chris pinched his two fingers together an expanded the map. "If we carry on along this tunnel, we should reach another connecting tunnel. Let's hope it's not walled up. I don't fancy getting jack hammers down here."

They stepped over a pile of rags with some bones tangled up in them. "This is just pure desecration," moaned Ben, edging around them with his foot. "People should be allowed to rest in peace."

Their voices echoed around the tunnel as the beams of the

torches revealed blackened scorch marks where old candles and lamps had once lit the walls. Patches of green damp and odd pieces of stone, some hewn by hand, twisted and turned into openings with brick archways above them that went nowhere. Some smaller doorways veered off into small chambers, with rough dirty floors, rusting ironwork and old wooden shelves. It was a friendless underworld, soaked with impending threat, hopelessness and survival. Some tunnels led nowhere and had been blocked up, many years ago. Some had been broken into and people had carried out rituals inside them.

Amongst the storage spaces and dug out stone, Chris felt as if they were all being watched by unseen eyes and he geared himself up for some kind of potential ambush. It was easy for his imagination to get carried away and he reined himself back in, quickly. He bristled with anticipation and felt the prickling sensation of dread combined with adrenaline creep up his spine.

They all watched in silence as one of the officers pointed out a small chamber opening up to the left of them. As they entered the space, one of them recoiled as she pointed her torch down to the floor. A large pentagram had been painted on the surface of the stone, with candles placed at various points. They were burned down to almost nothing, giving rise to the assumption that the space had been well-used. There was a strange smell in the air, of heavy incense intermingled with something unidentifiable.

"No blood stains, at least. Seal this off and keep looking," Chris ordered, as he pushed down his distaste. "There's nothing else in there."

"Thankfully," Ben added. "I'll never understand the whole attraction of stuff like this."

"There's a lot we don't understand, Ben. We look at everyday life and forget there's a different level going on which we aren't usually aware of."

"Have you been watching too much Star Trek, Guv? You're the most common sense, down to earth bloke I've ever met. Don't turn all freaky on me."

"Once I would have agreed with you," Chris responded with a frown, "but whatever it is we're dealing with, I just don't feel it's something we have ever come across before."

"Or just been lucky, maybe."

Chris made a face and then wrinkled his nose. He turned around, trying to place where the sudden change in scent was coming from. "Can you smell it?"

"What, years of damp and slime and human waste?"

"No, not that..." Chris broke off from the group and moved further up the tunnel, cautiously. "No, it's like…perfume…" He couldn't quite grasp what is was, or where he had possibly smelt it before, but it was enough to go on and it energised him into action.

"Spread out," he shouted, indicating for the group to search alongside of him. Various small tunnels quickly showed themselves to be dead ends but one of them opened up into a longer tunnel.

"Down here…" Chris turned into it, closely followed by Ben. The tunnel should have been darker, more remote and impassable, but somehow there was a faint flicker of light coming from much further down. The scent wafted up to them and Chris sucked in air.

"It's definitely a woman's perfume."

Galvanised, they raced along the tunnel, with only the light and the essence of rose and musk to guide them. Chris mentally prepared himself for what they might find and he clenched his jaw in anticipation.

"Oh God, there she is!" Ben shouted, as he ran down the tunnel first. Mikaela's unconscious body sat against the wall as if she had simply slid down. Her head lolled to one side against her shoulder and her legs were crippled beneath her. "What the hell has he done to her?" Cupping her head in his hands, he sought the pulse in her neck. "She's alive, Guv! Just about…"

Mikaela moaned incoherently, her eyelids flickering. Chris crouched down next to them. "Yes, that's definitely her. Mikaela, Mikaela, can you hear me, sweetheart?"

She murmured something which neither of the two men could hear, but it was enough for Chris to feel some sort of relief. He signalled for one of the other officers to radio for an ambulance. In the meantime, he took off his jacket and wrapped it around Mikaela. As she lay down, Chris shook his head. "Not a mark on her that I can see, but she might have some internal injuries. Although, looking at her, she just looks like she is sleeping."

"Guv, look at this…" Ben beckoned for Chris to come over to the edge of the wall on the opposite side to them. "It's glass. Look like some kind of old bottle, I think." Ben knelt down to see more clearly but Chris pulled him back up immediately.

"No, don't touch it." Chris looked more closely at the shards of glass, which looked green in the torchlight. He could see from the biggest piece remaining somewhat intact, that it was probably Victorian. "Poison."

Ben stared down at it. "You don't think?"

"Yep, could well be. We need to get Eric down here as soon as. If there are any remains of acid, then he'll match the composition. With luck, we've got our killer."

Ben shook his head and put his mouth to his sleeve. "Thank God he never used it on her."

Chris thumped Ben on the chest with a grin. "Thank God even better that she's alive! She'll recognise him. But first we need to get her to the hospital."

Three hours later, Lucas Frain sat with Chris and Ben in one of the interview rooms at Murray Road Station. He had taken off his ESIP black hoody and hung it over the back of his chair. It was still caked in mud from where he had slipped on the damp grass and fallen over.

"It's way past my bedtime, you know," he moaned. "Can't we do this tomorrow?"

"Nope," replied Chris, sitting forward and clasping his hands together. "Show me what you've got."

"Bloody hell, you don't have to interrogate me…"

"Listen. You're starting to get on my nerves, Lucas. Put it this way, it could be a matter of life or death."

"What, for me?" Lucas looked startled.

Ben grinned. "You should be so lucky. You're not that important. Now show the Boss what you've got, or I'll do it for you."

"Bloody hell again, "Lucas rocked his head from side to side in sarcasm but then saw Ben's expression and closed his mouth.

Silently, he opened up his laptop and showed them both what he had downloaded. "My night cams have caught the usual orbs 'n' stuff, nothing mega. *But...*" He paused and fast forwarded the screen. "I caught a wicked heat signature."

"What do you mean?" Chris peered at the blank screen. "There's nothing there."

"Oh, but there is," grinned Lucas in triumph, "*just watch.*" Pressing a different key, he brought up a separate camera view of Greyfriars but in various shades of yellow, red and blue. "So, basically, blue means cold and red means hot. Most signatures fall somewhere in between. Like, you see this owl?" He pointed at the screen with his finger as an owl flew across. "The heat signature is pinkish. So, the little guy is alive."

"Yeah, that makes sense."

Lucas glared at Ben and then continued. "So, nothing much happens until you've started going down the tunnels or wherever the hell you *were* going. Anyway, I get this really creepy sensation. Can't describe it, except that it's worse than being in this police station. I keep the gear rolling and then, all of a sudden, something rushes past me."

"Like what?" Chris hardly blinked as he focused on the screen and the hairs on his forearms prickled.

"It felt like someone literally rushed at me, past me and out of the graveyard, but I swear to God and on my life, there was no-one in that graveyard but me. So, looking at this screen, you can see something..." he prodded at the computer with his finger, "... see how the heat signature changes into something about adult human size and coloured red, which is pretty much on fire. But I swear, I didn't see anyone. What the hell made that heat signature, I don't know. It was invisible to the naked eye but technically alive."

Chris stared at the footage. "Can spirits...ghosts...record a heat signature?"

Lucas gulped from his can of cola. "Not normally. Only something that is living and breathing. And unless we have developed some sort of cloaking technology, which is way too NASA for me, I've got no explanation for this anomaly."

"You mentioned before about demonic activity. Would this anomaly explain that?"

Lucas sighed and leant forward again. "Like I say, I've never come across anything like this. Usually with demonic activity, it's classed as paranormal, and you capture voices, some poltergeist issues, even shadow people. But a heat signature like this means that it's an entity that I've never come across before. Part paranormal, part human."

"A kind of alien, then?" questioned Ben, pacing up and down the room. "People reckon that aliens have walked amongst us for years. Would that be it? An alien of some sort?"

"Look, I'm not bloody Stephen Hawking. *I don't know*. But I can back this up with something else."

"Show me," ordered Chris, now getting frustrated but also unnerved. "A voice?"

"Hah, wait..." Lucas switched on the voice recorder and

linked it up to his laptop. "it's not just *any* voice…" He pressed on the graph which showed the two men the recording. The rhythms were steady as all of them could hear Lucas's voice asking questions. Then a big audio expansion on the graph suddenly leapt up the screen and Lucas pointed to it. "Listen to this…at 24:03… you can distinctly hear me asking *Who are you and what do you want here?* Then…"

As all three of them listened intently, Chris drew back into his chair, instinctively. His blood had just run cold. "It sounds like… like…a…"

"Howl," finished Lucas, with triumph. "Exactly what I thought. Listen again."

Ben looked worriedly at Chris as Lucas played the recording again. Without a doubt, the noise sounded like something between a human in dire pain and an animal.

"Bloody hell." Ben shook his head. "And you heard nothing at all at the time, with your physical ears? This was just what your recorder picked up?"

"Yep. This equipment can pick up audio that is out of the range of normal human hearing. Any audio that vibrates on a different frequency to ours. I think this confirms that our invisible friend is non-human enough to emit a howl that I couldn't hear and should have woken the dead."

"But can you be sure it is the same entity?" Chris pointed back at the screen. "Does the time of the howling noise and the heat signature tally?

"They do. And I've cleaned up the background. I can't detect any other anomalies either on the voice recorder or any of the cameras. I can pretty much guarantee that the two are linked."

"Thanks, Lucas. You've done a good job."

"Cheers. Praise indeed. Can I go home now? I'm knackered."

Chris glanced at Ben and then nodded. "You can. You've given me a lot of questions that need to be answered. Questions I didn't bargain for."

"That's the nature of the paranormal, mate," Lucas grinned, as he began to pack his equipment away. "I can't wait to let the guys in the team know."

"That won't be possible." Ben leaned over and started taking the equipment off Lucas. "I'm confiscating this until our lab has downloaded and wiped it from here."

"Hey! This is great evidence…" Lucas made a feeble attempt to hold onto it as Ben wrenched it from his hands. "You can't do this. That's not fair."

"One day, you might be able to have it back," grinned Ben, "but until then, this is classed as evidence of the police kind."

"Oh fine… take it then. All I can say is that I'd rather work with the paranormal than cops, any day."

Ben laughed and opened the door for Lucas. "You've done us a great service. You should be proud of yourself. Don't go expecting a medal, though. You're in for a long wait. I've been in the force for years and I doubt they even know my name."

Lucas made the whatever sign with his fingers as he exited the building, still clearly annoyed.

Once Ben returned to the Interview Room, he blew out his

lips and shook his head at his boss. "Blimey, what a night, eh? I need a decent shower. I look like one of the Addams Family, just crawled out of the crypt."

Chris held his head in his hands. All of a sudden, he felt about a hundred years old. "I'll question Mikaela later, if she's well enough," he sighed, looking up at the clock on the interview room wall. He wanted to call Tia and let her know about Mikaela but it was now the early hours of the morning and he knew she would be asleep. And he still hadn't worked out what to say to her. "The Nightshade Club..."

"Yes, Guv? What about it?"

"I want you to go down there first thing. Find out where this Painter is, and who else works there."

"No worries. By the way, Eric just texted me. He's found enough of the poison acid stuff and the lab are on it."

"Good. Let's get some sleep, Ben, for what it's worth. I've a feeling we're going to need it."

Chapter 34

Later that day, Mikaela lay in her hospital bed, looking washed out and pale. Her dark curly hair was spread out over the pillow and she barely managed to open her eyes, as Chris sat down in the chair next to the bed. He gave her a reassuring, apologetic smile, feeling bad that he had to question her so soon after her admission to hospital.
"Mikaela, I'm Detective Inspector Chris West of Murray Road Station. You won't remember but we found you in the tunnel…"

"I remember…" she replied, hoarsely, "…I remember you and…someone else…" She swallowed with difficulty and tears hung on the tips of her eyelids. "A man."

"Yes?" Chris leant forward, clasping his hands together and resting them on his knees. "Do you remember him clearly?"

Mikaela coughed and nodded. A nurse who was nearby came over straight away to her and held Mikaela's head as she drank some water from her cup. Once she had gone again back towards the nurse's desk, the young girl tried to sit up.

"Dark hair…with you."

"Oh yes, that was my colleague, DS Ben Miles, but Mikaela, do you remember anyone else? Do you remember what happened to you?"

Mikaela's face, already so pale, became ashen. "I…it was like I was…dying…I couldn't breathe…" She gripped the metal sidebar on the bed as if she would never let go. "Everything was spinning out of control. All I could think of was…that I'm going to die…" Tears trickled down Mikaela's cheeks and Chris reached up to the box of tissues on the bedside table. She took one, gratefully. "I can't remember how I got there."

Chris nodded in sympathy. He felt sorry for Mikaela and wanted her to take her time, but he knew that time wasn't on his side.

"It was like every breath was being sucked out of my body." She looked at him, miserably. "Does that sound stupid?"

"No, it doesn't. Not at all." Chris smiled, painfully aware that he wouldn't be able to push the questioning. "Mikaela, I need to find out who did this to you. I can't go into the details, but it's imperative that we find him. If you can remember anything about him, anything at all, it will really help our investigation."

Turning over slightly and resting on her arm, Mikaela winced and sucked in her breath. "It's…muzzy. It made me feel sick. I still feel sick."

"Would you like me to call the nurse?" Chris began to get up but she shook her head.

"No, I'm…okay. You know like when you've had a really bad nightmare and you can remember some bits and not others?"

"Yes. Yes, I do."

My mind…feels sort of hazy. Wiped."

Chris sat forward, flexing his fingers. He felt like he was on a hiding to nowhere. He couldn't force her to remember anything and even trying to might cause some irreparable psychological damage.

He felt a sudden flush of colour fill his cheeks.

"Do you remember Tia? She works with you. I understand you're staying with her at Redfield Grange. She reported you missing." He broke off, smiling, more to himself. "At least I can let her know you're safe now."

Mikaela closed her eyes in utter exhaustion. "Tia…Tia? Yeah…I do. Love her. She's brill…"

"Yes, she is," Chris replied, feeling a sudden surge of longing. He wanted to hold Tia in his arms and protect her. He needed to reassure her that all would be well. It was the only way he knew how. "She'll be so glad you're okay."

Fresh tears began to seep down Mikaela's cheeks. "She's my friend. She helped me and I've let her down."

"No, I'm sure Tia won't think that. She'll be relieved you've been found safe." Chris sighed and took out his phone from his jacket pocket. He had a thought. It was a long shot but it might work. "Mikaela, I'm going to show you some photos on my phone. It's of a night out I had with my colleagues at the Nightshade Club. It may just help you to remember."

As Chris passed over his phone to her, he gave her an apologetic smile. "You might get the wrong impression of the police force after seeing these, but all I can say in my defence was that I didn't personally get drunk."

Mikaela sniffed and laughed, weakly, struggling up the pillows to take the phone from Chris. "I'm sure they're not…that bad."

"Mmm, just keep an open mind", Chris teased. "They're

bordering on embarrassing." He hoped the photos would jolt Mikaela's memory of the place she worked. "Tia won't be in them, but some of the other staff are. You'll see Kevin hovering in the background."

"Kev…yes…" Mikaela frowned as if searching her brain for any signs of recognition. "Kev…"

Chris stood up and smiled gently down at her. "I'll leave you alone for a moment to scroll through. No pressure. Just take your time and see what comes. I'll be over by the nurse's desk."

"Sure." Mikaela smiled weakly up at him in return and there was a determined expression on her face.

When Chris got to the desk, Ben had just arrived from his visit to the Nightshade Club.

Ben nodded over at Mikaela. "Poor kid. She doesn't deserve what happened to her. Don't think she's had much of a life, going on what I've been able to find out about her."

"She's shocked and traumatised, Ben. I don't know if she'll ever remember… anyway, tell me how you got on?"

Ben retrieved his own phone from his pocket and scrolled through. "You know you think we've seen it all, Guv? Just look at this."

As Chris looked at the photo, he felt sick. "What the hell?"

"Hell's the right word. If Hell was a painting, this would be it," Ben stated, solemnly.

Chris leaned in further and felt almost violated. He could see where Ben and his team had broken down the door of the Moriarty Suite. The room was macabre, hung with red curtains and painted black, apart from the image that he was now looking at. It was the most grotesque picture he had ever seen and he almost vomited in revulsion. Across the wall were images, many faces, splayed in paint across the brick in such a terrible state of agony that he reeled.

Ben nodded, solemnly. "Don't ask me what he did to those poor victims before they died, but I think we can guess."

"Can we, Ben?" Chris looked up at his colleague, miserably. "Whatever was going through their minds, I don't think we'll ever really know how horrific it was."

"No," Ben sighed in agreement. "Well, we have a positive identification for Katie, Danny and Jessica, plus I've got background on the other acid victims being matched up. I'm willing to bet their identities will also be confirmed from this painting and their old photographs. It sounds sick to say it, but thank God this bastard is a good artist."

"I don't know what in heaven we're dealing with but it's beyond the realms of most psychopaths. What sort of artists paints people in the last stages of death? It's beyond any normal comprehension."

"You said it, Guv."

"Something I've never experienced in all my years in the force, that's for certain. Well, he's made sure he won't be ever walking free once the justice system gets his hands on him."

"Here's hoping, Guv."

"I know how you feel about the courts, Ben, but I don't think any judge or jury is going to let him off anything, do you? Not once they've seen this."

Ben took the phone back from Chris, with a visible shiver. He was uncharacteristically devoid of any humour or quips. "I've never felt so creeped out as when I went in that room."

"And don't tell me, our friend Painter has disappeared?"

"Yep. But it didn't look like anything was missing. Mind you, it didn't seem like he had the normal stuff anyway. No wallet, credit cards, paperwork.... nothing. Eric's going over it with a fine tooth comb, as ever. I've never known him be so quiet on a job. He took one look and has hardly said a word, since."

"It's him! That's him!"

Suddenly, there was a loud clatter and Chris spun around. His phone had dropped to the floor and Mikaela had gone into a full-blown anxiety attack. As the nurse went rushing over to calm Mikaela down, Chris also ran over and quickly picked up his phone from the floor. Although the screen had cracked, he could see the photo clearly. He showed it instantly to Ben.

"Guess who."

"Our buddy, the nightclub owner." Ben put a hand up to his hair. It was the photo of Painter standing over them, smiling his vacant smile, his sinister smile. "And all the while, I was too pissed up to notice..."

"Don't put any guilt on yourself, Ben," Chris replied, as his stomach turned over again at the image of Painter. The more he stared at the picture, the more everything was becoming clear. "Look at him. He's got the perfect cover. No-one would think he was real."

"Real? Real as in what?"

"I don't know exactly, but if I were a vampire, or demon, or something like that, I would place myself in the same environment. No-one would be any the wiser. All the time he hams it up and goes Hollywood, no-one would ever think he could be the real thing."

"Beyond gross, but yeah, I agree with you, it makes perfect sense."

After Mikaela had calmed down enough and the two men were allowed back over to her bedside, Chris spoke to her, gently. "Thank you, Mikaela. I'm very sorry that it has caused you so much distress."

"But I'm afraid." She buried her nose into a bed of tissue and tried to halt the sobs. "What if he comes after me again?" Her whole body trembled and the nurse hovered close by, suspiciously.

"It's normal to feel like that. You've been through a terrible, traumatising ordeal, Mikaela."

"But I can still see him," she pleaded, thrusting a finger into her head." In here."

"That's understandable, sweetheart. We have an excellent Liaison Officer, Pamela, who is very experienced with trauma victims. She will be assigned to you. You'll have nothing to worry about and you must focus on getting better."

"But YOU don't understand," Mikaela suddenly sat up and grabbed hold of the sleeve of Chris's jacket. Her knuckles were white. "He'll be in my nightmares. Like he's in Tia's nightmares. He knows where I live. He'll be coming for me."

Chris felt a sudden ice-cold chill run down his back, as if his blood had frozen. "What do you mean, nightmares?" His mind flashed back to what Tia had told him and he sat back in the chair as if he had been punched in the face. "He knows about Redfield Grange?"

"Yes. He knows everything. *I* told him. And now Tia's up there by herself."

Chris looked at Ben and it must have been apparent by his expression how urgent the situation had become, because Ben instantly got out his car keys.

"Please don't worry, Mikaela," Chris managed to reply, whilst trying to hold his wits together. "Pamela is on her way and will sit with you this afternoon. Nothing can possibly happen to you here. You are very safe."

"But what about Tia?" Mikaela urged up at him, still clinging on to his sleeve. Her face was racked with fear and terror. "What if he tries to do the same thing to her? She has no-one to help. And it's *my* fault…" She put a hand to her eyes in pain. "I should never have trusted him."

Chris carefully extracted her sleeve and signalled over for the nurse. "She has me. She has us. So please try not to worry. The Police team will be on hand for anything you need."

"Okay," Mikaela sniffed hard and leant back into the pillows. "I know you'll help. But what if he's there already? That crappy husband won't be there…"

"No, I already know enough about him," Chris responded. He had heard enough. All that kept him from going into a state of sheer panic was years of experience and training. But his heart was threatening to burst.

"How quick can you get us to Redfield Grange, Ben?" he

asked, as they ran from the ward and out of the hospital to the car park.

"Beam me up, Guv, that's how quick," replied Ben, as he whipped on the blue light and they screeched out onto the road towards the outskirts of Edinburgh and up to Redfield Grange.

"I just hope and pray that we're not already too late," Chris wiped around his mouth with the back of his hand, still feeling like he could vomit at any moment. The thought of Tia at the mercy of Painter made him almost lose his sense of rationality.

"You don't look well, mate," said Ben, glancing over at him. "It's normally you saying this to me. There's something different this time, isn't there? Is it Tia Olsen? You haven't said much. Which makes me wonder."

"Am I that transparent?" But Chris couldn't hide his true feelings any longer. He had fallen for Tia in a big way and now he was terrified that she had been thrown in the path of one of the most evil killers he had ever encountered.

"A bit." Ben gave him a half-smile. "I'm not going to say anything about anything. Just go for it. Life's too short."

"Cheers, Ben." It was on the verge of his tongue to say how the roles seemed to have reversed and now Ben was giving him the Dad pep talk. "You've done a good job on this investigation. You've really up your game. I'm proud of you."

"Blimey," Ben remarked, giving his boss a quick double-take. "Don't go soft on me, now," but Chris could tell by his smile that Ben was pleased with the compliment.

"Make the most of it, you don't get that many from me."

"That's true. I might just have it printed and framed. And whip it out every now and then to remind me that you don't always tell me off."

Chris allowed himself to chuckle through his fear, as he tried again to contact Tia on her mobile. As the automated service provider said once again that the call couldn't be connected, he sighed and pushed down his rising anxiety before it could get a hold and cloud his judgement. "Still no answer. There's no signal."

"Don't worry, Guv. If she's anything like you've already told me, she's not stupid. Have you got her landline number?"

"Yep. The line's been checked. It's dead."

"Just keep trying her mobile, it's all you can do. Don't worry, we'll be there soon."

Chris nodded and pressed his thumb on speed dial. The signal was intermittent, bordering on useless and he inwardly berated himself for not going fast enough. Not being there for her. Reaching down inside for every last ounce of courage and resilience he possessed, Chris knew that whatever it was would be waiting for them.

"At least back up is on its way. Whatever he's planning, this Painter demon, or whatever the hell he is, will wish he'd stuck to Hell Playschool by the time I'm finished with him."

Chapter 35

Painter situated himself, unseen, amongst the trees in the parkland, watching the lights go on in Redfield Grange. He had found it easy enough; he had followed Tia's car with ease and he laughed to himself. Humans had no concept of time and space; how it could be manipulated to his advantage. He could track any distance when there was a meal to be had.

Looking up at the dark sky, Painter watched the mist form over the countryside, and sniffed the air. It smelt ancient, of moss and heather and bracken. He drank in the rain on the wind, invigorated, aware that his own human body was fast failing him. He then sniffed the immediate air around him and sneered in response. He was turning rancid, like rotting meat. The cells that made up his human shell were dying, causing pustules of foul-smelling liquid to begin bubbling up on his white skin. It repulsed him and he felt rage torment him. This is what he had been reduced to and he was going to take out his fury on anyone now who got in his way. No amount of pleading or begging would stop him now from taking every soul in his path like a beast with prey in its mouth. He would tear the girl to shreds. There was no time for seduction and he had no taste for it. He was going to make her pay in the worst way possible. By prolonging her agony until she begged him to take her life.

Inside Redfield, Tia settled down in the living room to watch television. She didn't particularly like watching soap operas but for now it took her mind off everything as she curled up in the armchair. Just for a while, it felt like a kind of sanctuary; away from Lars and his demands, the worry about Mikaela and the whole stress of life in general. There was something calming about the house. It stretched its stone walls around her like protective arms and gave her enough comfort to feel sleepy. She felt her eyelids grow heavy and began to drift into light sleep.

The phone in the hallway rang loudly, its coarse bell shrill and unforgiving as it echoed down the passageway, rousing Tia from the first stages of sleep roughly. She knew, without even picking it up, who was at the other end. Half-minded to ignore it, but knowing that Lars would keep on ringing until he got an answer, Tia sighed and pulled herself up from the armchair, padding out into the entrance hall. She tried not to let herself feel on edge but it was hard; Lars still had the power to make her feel defensive and upset.

She picked up the receiver and tentatively held it up to her ear. "Yes, Lars?"

"How did you know it was me…oh forget it…*you know everything.*"

"What do you need to speak to me about?"

"I'm still your husband. *Unfortunately.* I've got a right to talk to you whenever I like."

"I'm not feeling great. Let's keep it short. I've actually been in hospital."

"What do you mean, you've been in hospital? You haven't done anything stupid, have you?" Lars' voice was angry on the other end of the phone.

Tia leant against the wall, eyeing up the banister with longing, wishing she could escape upstairs. "You don't have to shout, Lars. I'm on the landline. I'm not deaf."

"Well, it's pointless trying to contact you on your mobile with the shit signal up there. Anyway, you didn't answer my question."

"Because you haven't let me finish," Tia suppressed her mounting anger and looked up at the ceiling. He sounded like a petulant child. "I'm okay, just tired, what with the nightmares and everything going on." She stopped short of telling Lars about Mikaela because she knew he wouldn't be interested. "Everything here is just a…bit…odd."

"In what way? Don't say you've been holding a coven?"

"You are such a shit, Lars."

"It's all about you, Tia, as normal. You haven't asked about the baby or anything."

"It's not all about me. And the baby is nothing to do with me. Nor is Sophie, for that matter."

There was silence on the other end of the phone for a moment. "Well, we still need to work out what we're going to do, about the house and money."

Tia sucked in her breath. "So, what you mean is, you don't like living with Sophie and you want out of the whole thing?"

"Don't be ridiculous, I didn't say any such thing."

Tia felt the old dread creep up within her. She knew exactly, without Lars telling her, that he was finding his living arrangements hard and that he wanted her out.

"If you're finding it all too stressful, Sophie and I can sort something out with you. We could move in quickly. Make it as painless for you as possible."

Putting the phone down on the hallway table for a moment, Tia struggled to find the right words. Too aggressive and she would really piss him off, but she couldn't lie down and take what he was going to throw at her, either. "I'm not finding it too stressful, Lars. The hospital checked me out and I'm fine." Lying a little bit wouldn't hurt and she knew that Lars wouldn't need much to turn the whole situation to his own advantage.

"Maybe you should get a psychiatric appointment. That would be interesting." Lars's voice grew heavy and weary. "I've had enough of this. If you want a fight, Tia, then you can have one. I'm not letting Redfield go and Sophie *will* move in there with me, whether you like it or not."

"Look, Lars, I…" Tia broke off as she heard a loud bang coming from somewhere in the house. She looked up, abruptly. "Lars, I have to go."

"Fine!" he shouted down the receiver, "Hang up on me! I'll bloody be in touch…"

Tia put down the phone angrily and then unplugged it. She had had enough of Lars' abuse and rants at her for not doing what he wanted. Everything he now did was aimed at making sure Sophie and the baby were top of his list and she was nothing, merely the *ex* who was playing hard to control. Tia felt hot, angry tears stab at her eyelids. She had always been wary of his temper but she had never seen what a nasty side he had, until now.

Tia's heart skipped a beat as the noise suddenly came again, even louder than before. It sounded like a door being slammed at the back of the house but it couldn't be as she had locked it.

With her heart pounding, and still fired up with adrenalin from her conversation with Lars, Tia made her way cautiously into the dining room and sighed in relief. One of the French doors was open. The curtain lifted in the wind and rattled the glass. It had obviously worked its way open and Tia wasn't particularly surprised; the hinges and locks on several of the windows and doors were weak and needed replacing. It was another job to add to an endless list but Tia was buoyed up by her growing love for the house. It needed some tender loving care and she wanted to be the one to provide it. It felt like the house agreed; that it enjoyed her attention and that it wanted her to stay and look after it.

Tia drew back the curtain fully and stepped outside, briefly, onto the stone patio. No-one was there. The gardens were as quiet as they normally were. As she closed the door and turned around, she suddenly froze, rooted to the spot in fear.

A black shadow was out in the passageway.

Tia immediately crouched down by the side of the dining table, instinctively, her heart thudding. It moved out of sight and she felt her breath grow harsh. It looked like some sort of black mass, pulsating and rotating. The light from the hallway could be seen clearly behind the black shape, confirming to Tia that it was not a shadow. It was as real as she was. She felt her throat suddenly scratch with dryness and desperately suppressed the urge to cough.

Outside, the wind had whipped up again and threatened to once more blow open the French door. It rattled with increased urgency and Tia had to draw up all her courage not to move and steady the door before it drew unwanted attention. She felt a hard tightness in her chest as the black mass held itself within the doorway. Closing her eyes, Tia waited for the worst, imagining it coming into the dining room and attacking her. Her hands shook in fear as a sudden, ice pick headache entered her temples and made her wince in pain. The pain was intense, like the worst migraine she had ever experienced, coupled with a hangover, but then it went as quickly as it had assaulted her and, taking her chance, Tia edged herself forward, nearer to the doorway. Her eyes still smarting, she hurriedly brushed away the tears, focusing instead on the light shining in the passageway beyond. The black shape seemed to have dissipated; disappeared, moved on somehow. Tia wasn't sure where it had gone.

The noises then started loudly upstairs, crashing and banging, as though someone or something was throwing furniture around in the bedrooms. Tia gasped and swallowed air, almost choking in shock. The sound reverberated around the dining room, setting her nerves on fire like a dentist's drill, and she froze, deadly silent, unable to move or make a sound. All of a sudden, another crash came from her bedroom, as if the large oak wardrobe had been pushed over. Splinters of glass seemed to shriek over the wooden floorboards. Then footsteps, heavy thudding footsteps, shook the ceiling above her, and she forced her hand to her mouth in horror. Waves of sickness grasped her intestines and pushed bile up into her throat. Tia almost jumped out of her skin as another heavy crash caused the pendant light to swing in the passageway. Glass in the ornamental cabinet shook in response and she bit back a cry of panic. On all fours, Tia inched her way along the carpet, painfully aware of pulling on the tablecloth and the crockery off the table. Cursing herself for having unplugged the telephone, Tia managed to get to the doorway and edged her head shakily around the corner. The passageway was empty.

Struggling to get to her feet, Tia stumbled and ran along the corridor towards the entrance hall, intent on getting to the telephone. The noise upstairs had gone eerily quiet, too quiet, and this unnerved her even more. All the time the intruder was banging and crashing about, he was occupied, giving her time to get to the phone and alert the police. She virtually slid along the hall in her socked feet, grabbing on to the bottom of the banister as she did so. Her arm wrenched painfully in its socket and she cried out in pain. Tia fell onto the floor on her knees and grasped her arm. It throbbed intensely but there was no time to check it further.

Suddenly, and without any warning, the black mass appeared at the top of the stairs in the galleried landing, looming down from its prominent position over her. Tia stared in abject horror up at the heaving, swirling mass. It thickened and filled the gaps in the wooden banister rail, manifesting into the emergence of a human form. Tia's mouth fell open as Painter took on his terrible likeness, but as the pustules and rotting flesh overshadowed his appearance, Tia threw her arm to her nose. The stench was enough to make her vomit, without the knowledge that she was looking at the supernatural, demonic being who had been terrifying her in her dreams.

"You!" she cried out, pushing herself backwards. "You're the thing I've been seeing! All this time!"

"Hello, Tia. I'm delighted to finally make your acquaintance."

"Leave me alone. Get out of my house! I don't care who or what you are, get out!"

Painted laughed but his voice, racked with internal pain and fury, was not yet fully formed. He paused, aware that his breathing had not properly assimilated into his host body. He wheezed like he needed oxygen and every blood cell in his human form pounded to force life-giving air through his veins.

"You…don't…look…pleased…to…see…your…employer. What…a…pity."

Tia stared, aghast. "You? *You* are Mr Painter?"

"Of course I am, you stupid girl. I've been under your nose the whole time. And more's the pity, you have been under mine and I've not even realised. You are everything I have been seeking, Tia."

"Get out! I won't tell you again!"

"And what will you do if I don't?" Painter sniffed and took out his handkerchief. He saw the spots of blood and wiped them from his nose and mouth, fastidiously. As he did so, another pustule in his face burst, and a rivulet of green ooze trickled over his alabaster white skin.

Tia almost vomited at the sight in terror. "What do you want with me? Why have you been haunting me?"

Painter reached out to the banister rail to steady himself. He was now slowly moving down the stairs and growing in strength. "I am your worst nightmare. But I think we already know that, don't we?"

As he began to invade her mind, seeking to darken the recesses of her thought processes and weaken her resolve to fight back, Tia struggled to close down her senses and get back on her feet. "You leave me alone. Whatever you want from me, you can't have it."

"Oh, but I can. I want your soul, Tia. Since the very beginning of my existence on this putrid planet, I have longed for a soul like yours. You have astounding spiritual gifts and yet you don't even know it. You have been bullied, belittled, manipulated by your husband, thrown out of your place of work, treated like dirt. Why can't you see that you have power, more power than you could even begin to imagine? If I helped you, you would be able to make that husband of yours pay with his life. I could destroy him and everything he holds dear. I could make you mistress of this house forever. You would be invincible."

"How do you know all of this? I don't need your help! Lars has done enough damage on his own. I don't need revenge."

Painter was standing just two steps above her. He contorted his face into an expression of pity. "I've been watching you for hours. You want love, don't you, Tia? You want to be held, and caressed, and desired? All you humans yearn for such things. I could give you any man you wanted."

"Oh, like Satan? I don't think so, thanks." Tia edged herself along the passageway, carefully, holding her injured arm. "Whatever happens in my life, I'll sort it out. I'm not giving you anything. What *are* you?"

Painter dabbed again at his mouth and the fine silk material of the handkerchief was now a deep pink colour. "That's what your pathetic little friend asked me. If you truly knew who, *what*, I am, you would be looking on the face of Hell. All that is most evil, the most bestial, of humankind, lives in me. I *am* the dark."

Tia began to sob, hardly able to get her words out. "What have you done to Mikaela? Where is she?"

"Why should *you* care? You *abandoned* her."

"No! I didn't! I tried to help her."

Painter tutted and waved his finger as he reached the bottom step. "Try and tell yourself that, my dear, if it makes you feel better. You're selfish at heart. All human beings are selfish. Oh, they like to convince themselves that they are charitable but I know their souls, Tia. They don't care, really. They are conditioned to survive and will always put themselves first."

Tears now fell onto Tia's cheeks. "What have you done to her, you *monster*?" Her head swam as she tried to take in all that Painter was saying. The stench from him was making her retch and foaming spittle seeped out from the corners of her mouth. He was invading her, through her mind and her body, trying to exploit her weaknesses.

Painter expressed nonchalance with his long white hands. "She may be alive, she may not. I doubt there is much left of her. I was disturbed, you see, and that has never happened to me before. It was a novel experience, to say the least. Now I will finish the task properly. Once I have your soul, Tia, I will need no other. I shall be immortal. And *invincible*."

Tia swallowed a cry and spun around. Her slipper socks squeaked against the floor as she ran as fast as she could away from him. She could hear him curse and rake his long nails along the wooden banister. Almost breathless with fear, Tia ran to the kitchen and slammed the door behind her. Sobbing as she did so, Tia dragged the kitchen chair and forced the tall wooden back of it underneath the door handle. She knew it wouldn't hold him for long. All she could think of was getting down to the cellar.

Painter slammed his fists on the door, loudly. "Oh Tia, do stop with your silly games. I'm running out of patience and I'm very hungry, I've indulged you long enough…" he started pounding, heavily, "now open the fucking door, *my dear…*" The door handle moved up and down rapidly and she could see the whole door start to move within its frame. He would have the door down in seconds.

Scrabbling frantically in the kitchen drawer for the key, Tia grabbed it up between her shaking fingers and ran over to the cellar entrance. She fumbled with its jumping iron form, thrusting it roughly into the lock until the door eventually gave way. Diving inside, Tia locked the door back up after her with as much presence of mind as she could manage. As she switched on the light and it buzzed into life, half-heartedly, Tia could hear the kitchen door finally give way with a loud banging noise and she knew he was in the kitchen.

Hardly able to breathe, Tia crept down the steps as quietly as she could and leant against the dank wall, feeling dizzy with pain. It was as if he was infiltrating her mind and crushing all of her nerves, painfully. This was it. This was what her psychic senses had been warning her about for months and there had never been any ending to the nightmares. She had never been able to see the outcome. Leaning her head back, she squeezed her eyes shut as Painter crashed around the kitchen, opening the cupboards and throwing everything onto the floor. Turning her desperate gaze towards the back of the cellar, she saw the window which had once served as the coal chute and ran over. It was just about big enough to squeeze through and she prayed with all her strength that it hadn't been padlocked shut.

Pushing the large paint stripper barrel over the floor and grimacing in pain, Tia managed with difficulty to place it beneath the window and between the two racks of shelving. She clambered on top and it gave her just enough height to reach the glass. Tia managed to brush away the cobwebs with her sleeve. The glass was filthy and frosted with condensation but at least it came out somewhere down by the side of the house and would give her the chance to escape into the grounds. Almost crying with relief that it wasn't padlocked, Tia lifted up the old iron latch with her stronger arm and pushed it open with gritted teeth. A rush of dust, dirt and cold air swirled in and up her nose. Without thinking, she let out a loud sneeze and bit her lip in fear.

"Tia! You can't hide from me! I'm done with these extremely boring games and I'm getting very frustrated…"

There was a loud cracking sound and Tia let out a startled cry. He had splintered the wood of the cellar door. Pushing open the window as far as she could manage, Tia scrabbled up, her socked feet trying frantically to find a grip on the brick but they kept slipping. Her injured arm throbbed in pain as she pulled herself up as high as she could. Slipping back suddenly, Tia could hear Painter pulling the door apart. Sweat ran down her face as she tried again, pulling herself up with her elbow and grasping hold of the edges of the window frame. Finally, her toes found some hold in the missing cement in the brickwork and she heaved herself through the gap, gazing her chin and praying with all her might that the window wouldn't swing back shut on her face.

Painter was now at the top of the steps and he laughed. "Poor little pathetic Tia. You should give up any pretence of heroism. There's no-one here to listen to your screams. You're a nobody. A reject. Even your own husband doesn't want you…"

Tia grabbed on to the overgrown bush outside, wincing as the thorns pricked and cut her skin. As the thorns pressed in deeper, Tia closed her eyes and pulled herself free of the window with all of her might. As she lay on the grass, in the darkness, she could hear Painter thudding loudly down the stairs. He was banging the shovel on each step.

"I've lost patience now, Tia. I'm going to suck your soul dry and break every bone in your pretty little head so badly that not even your mother will be able to recognise you."

Tia rolled over onto her back and pushed her bloodied hands into the grass. She couldn't lie and wait for him. Eventually, she got to her feet and staggered down the side of the house, clutching at her badly wrenched arm. The trees and hedges were like some black ominous creatures on a supernatural stage, outlined with frost, their bony and misshapen forms leering over her. Tia kept her eyes straight ahead, knowing that she had to run down the track towards the main road and hope to God someone would stop and help her. She had no time to get her phone or car keys. He could be anywhere in the house. The gravel bit through her slipper socks and she limped down the side of the drive towards the iron entrance gates. She thought she saw random lights coming through the parkland, but it wasn't long before her hopes were dashed.

He stood there, taller and now fully formed, in front of the gates. Painter grinned, lasciviously and licked the bloodied spittle from his lips. "Did you really think you could escape from me? You're my destiny, Tia. You might as well accept it."

"No, no...I don't..." Tia fell onto her knees and shook her head as he came closer. "I don't accept it. I'll never accept it!" She flung her head furiously up at him, picking up a handful of the stone gravel and threw it hard in the direction of his face.

Painter laughed at such a weary attempt of defence, but it had given Tia a split second of time to run across back into the gardens. She fell between the hedges and out onto the lawn, stumbling against the broken stonework of the rose garden wall. Her slipper socks squelched in the damp grass and cold water seeped between her toes. The contrast in temperature, compared to her hot and sweating body, snapped Tia out of her terrified daze and forced her through the dry fountain and out into the trees beyond. It was at that point, as she neared one of the bare oak trees with its sturdy trunk offering her some protection, that her hair was suddenly violently pulled back and she fell against something hard and unforgiving.

His white hand caressed underneath her chin, tenderly. "Pretty, silly Tia. You are so amusing. I'm going to love doing this to you." He spun her around with such force that her eyes rolled back in her head. "Look at me and see who I really am."

"No!" Tia tasted blood coming through her lips as his grip on her twisted and fragmented every cell of her mind and drove nails of burning fire into all the nerves in her body. She felt Painter lift her up as if she were made of paper and knew that she was being carried back towards the house.

"I want this house to be the last thing you see before you die. I know how much you love it. I want to make you see its snivelling wreck whilst I burn it to the ground. I haven't done that since your World War, London, I believe, oh that *was* fun. Everyone thought it was the bombing that caused it. I just happened to…enlarge the spectacle a little after feasting. What was one fire amongst so many?"

"Evil bastard…God will know…what you did."

Painter twisted Tia's hair tightly in his hand and put his stinking, oozing face to her neck. "What has God got to do with it? No-one can stop me, least of all some creation of frightened little humans in desperate need of a saviour. Listen to me, don't you think I would have been stopped by now if your so-called God did exist?"

"*Let…me go…*" Tia wrenched her face away from his and felt his hands grip her jaw like a vice. Her teeth ground together as he slowly brought her around to face him.

"Now Tia, we can either do it nicely, or I can torture you

first. Which would you prefer?" He coughed, suddenly and it seemed to wrack his body.

Tia found herself laughing, hysterically. "You're sick. You're going to die before I do…"

"An amusing observation, my dear. Somehow I don't think so…"

As Painter coughed again and his whole body shuddered in response, Tia took her chance and got to her feet. Picking up the shovel, she brought it down as hard as she could across his head, cutting into his white skin with a shot of crimson. He murmured and feel sideways to the ground, stunned but not unconscious.

Without a second look, Tia limped back across the garden and out onto the gravel drive. It was then that she was blinded by a sea of car headlights and she stopped dead in her tracks. After that, it was a hurried blur of activity and shouting, and Tia felt a familiar voice close to her and strong arms enclose her tightly.

"Tia, speak to me. Look at me," Chris lifted Tia's head in his hands and brushed back her damp hair. "Sweetheart, tell me what happened. Where is he?"

Tia sank down to the ground and buried her face in his chest, her strength gone. She could hardly bring herself to speak.

Chris said nothing for a moment, but she could hear people in the distance as her ears rang with cold and shock. She smelt his skin close to her and felt comforted.

"He's gone from here." Tia felt the familiar psychic tug and squeezed her eyelids shut for a moment. "I can see him. I can see him now. There are tunnels and a churchyard." Tia fully closed her eyes and let her mind completely absorb her in the mental picture that was forming. "He's desperate. He's growing weak." She clung on to Chris's forearms, using his strength to help her focus hard. "He's running out of time. If we get to him now, we may have a chance."

"I'm not putting you anywhere near him!" Chris pressed his mouth against Tia's head. "Don't even think about it."

Tia struggled to fully stand up. She turned to face him, desperately. "Chris, you have to understand. I've connected with him. I've *bonded* with him in some way."

"Like hell you have. No! I've said no!" He gestured for Ben. "Code Red. You know what to do."

"Where are we going, Guv?"

"Back to Greyfriars. That's the only place he has left. Where I can face this son of a bitch once and for all."

"I'm on it." Ben raced off, speaking on his phone as he did so.

"Please, you have to let me come with you. He needs me."

"Oh, and you think that I don't?" It was the closest Chris had come to tears in a long time. "Don't ask this of me, Tia. It's my job to keep you safe."

Tia buried her face in his shoulder as he held her tightly. She could feel his tense muscles, and sense his humanity. "If you don't let me do this, then no-one will be safe. He will come after me, again and again, until he gets what he wants."

Chris kissed Tia's head and found himself shaking, with fear and anger. "I thought I was too late. I would never have forgiven myself. I'm not taking any more chances with your safety."

"I'm what he needs to fully regenerate. He wants *me*. *My* soul. *I'm* the bait you need."

"You're no-one's bait!" Chris pulled Tia gently up, taking in every horrible detail of her injuries. "I'll kill him myself."

Tia took Chris's face in her bloodied hands and steadied him. Her eyes held his and she spoke, calmly, softly. "I know that you want to save me, but no-one can. Trust me, please."

Chris buried his face in her hair and locked his jaw. Every bone in his body was screaming in denial but he knew that Tia was right. On a level, some kind of spiritual level, he knew that she was the only person to bait the trap. He held her away from him slightly, looking deep into her green eyes. "I don't know what it is about you, but even since I met you, I felt that we were meant to be together. That I needed to protect you. And now I know why."

Tia stared into his face. "You won't let me down, Chris. I know that. We *will* defeat him. Love can conquer anything, even demons and death."

"Love..." Chris held her close again, as if it was their last moment on earth together. "I think you got that right."

"We'll go together. And I will lure him out. Chris, I don't know how this is going to end, but if you're with me, I know I can face it."

Chris brought down his mouth gently on Tia's lips. As gentle as he could be without hurting her. "I guarantee that the only end is going to be for him. Now, let's get you in the car with a blanket and if you disobey my orders on that much, Tia Olsen, we'll be having words."

Tia nodded and allowed herself to be put into the police car and wrapped up warmly. As Chris started up the engine and radioed that he was on his way, she gave him a small smile, trying to reassure him. But inside, deep inside, even with Chris's protection and the rest of his team behind them, Tia seriously doubted that they would be strong enough for Painter. His connection in her mind was growing stronger again and she could see him in her third eye, scratching his way through the tunnels to get back to Greyfriars. He was growing steadily weaker and was now far more dangerous than he had ever been. He was desperate, goading her, luring her back to him and as terrified as she was of the outcome, Tia knew that she was the only person who could potentially destroy him, once and for all. It had always been her destiny, she realised that now, and she was going to face it, regardless of the consequences.

Chapter 36

As Painter slipped into Greyfriars Kirkyard, he saw instantly that the whole area was deserted and he was consumed with rage so vitriolic that bile spilled out of his mouth and ran down his chin. He fell against the wall of the church and grimaced as fresh pain flooded through his body. As he looked down at his forearms, he saw the flesh peeling off, the bloody layers of skin tissue catching in the ruffled cuffs of his silk shirt. He was drenched in sweat and bodily liquid, drawn up from his oozing sores and every move was agony. He did not know what he looked like now; what form his human body was taking. As fastidious as he had been over his human shell since it had been created, he now saw it as a plague-ridden, sodden mess of useless tissue and bone and he had no wish to see how revolting his reflection was. The Ancient Ones had turned their disgust and vehemence fully on him, on his continued failure, and he felt crushed and broken by their contempt. It had been terrible enough living with their silence; how they had turned their backs on him whenever he pleaded for help, for more time to accomplish his dreadful mission. Now they drilled into his mind, into every cell of his being and condemned him to a fate worse than anything he could endure. He would be dissolved, consigned to nothingness, until not even one tiny speck of his existence remained. He had outlived his use for them and would be destroyed.

He felt the bloody tears seep from his sore eyes. If the bitch had not escaped then he would laughing now, knowing that his victory would have been complete. The Ancient Ones would have revered him, even tasking him with further destruction and suffering to inflict on humankind. They would have accorded him his rightful place in the Dark World, recognising his contribution to the greater cause, the total annihilation of all who resided on the planet they called Earth.

Painter slid down in the hidden recess of the wall, and crouched in agony as another wave of pain tore through him, like an injection of fire being forced through his veins. He cursed the human weakness of his body, baring his teeth in torment. He was so close and he knew that she was coming. He sensed her fear and wanted to laugh but it caused him too much pain to do so. He had to content himself as much as possible with the knowledge that she was being lured to her fate and she wasn't strong enough to resist him this time. Her body had been battered, bruised and wrenched in pain; now he would see to it that every last ounce of protestation would be crushed out of her like a dried leaf in hot summer. Her will to survive had been strong; all humans were possessed of the trait as it ensured the continuation of their dismal species; but she was special. Her psychic ability and spiritual gifts of love, courage and compassion, were now his for the taking. Tia Olsen would be the one consigned to the dust, trodden into the mud and dirt of Greyfriars Kirkyard, not he.

As he waited, Painter was suddenly, hauntingly, aware of all the hundreds of souls calling out for retribution from centuries before. Their blood and tears had been washed away but their suffering remained. It swirled like a torrent of agonised crying, caught on the wind of history but he could feel it acutely. He saw the destruction that man had inflicted upon man and it encouraged him. It made him almost dizzy with pleasure at the vision of their torture, their barbarity to one another. And on top of such a place of suffering, stood a monument to a God they would turn to, time and time again, for deliverance from their evil, which was such an amusing joke. There was evil in the Universe far stronger than anything that humankind could conjure up, but when they did, they unknowingly tapped into such dark forces and made the work of the Ancient Ones so much easier. No amount of stupid brick with a cross painted on the door could ever save them.

Painter rested his head in his hands for a moment. It was excruciating enough to fail, let alone at the hands of a race of beings whom the Dark World had long held in utter contempt. He should have acted more quickly, consumed more souls to feed his strength. There was no mercy now from the Ancient Ones, nor did he expect any. He knew, as they had enforced it in every atom of his human body, his string of borrowed DNA, that failure was abhorrent and would never be tolerated. He ached in vain for their consuming darkness to surround him in comfort, like it had done for so many years, until it had started to wane and been withdrawn. It had been the only sense of belonging that he had ever known.

The noise of footsteps alerted him to danger, and Painter leant back further into his cover of darkness. He could hear low murmurings, voices talking together but he was unable to make out what they were saying. His human senses were dying, slipping away into the vast ether where such things were no longer needed. He followed them instead with his mind, sensing their teenage giggling, feeling their idiotic drunkenness. He saw them kiss, young inexperienced lovers, and felt revulsion. He could have taken them instantly, biting into their bodies and sucking out their souls. It would have granted him a small reprieve, but he had little energy left. He needed to conserve every portion of it until he had finally extracted all of Tia Olsen's screaming, frantic soul until nothing remained of her but a shrivelled, discarded, miserable carcass. She would be his reprieve, his salvation at the midnight hour, his stay of execution. And she was now so close that he could almost taste her.

Eventually, the teenagers made their way out of the Kirkyard, laughing, and he saw them throw a discarded empty lager can at one of the gravestones. He bit back a groan of amusement. There was no respect for the living or the dead in such a place.

Painter struggled to his feet, cursing inwardly as needle-sharp pain shot through his entire system. More piles of skin lay at his feet, discarded like unwanted rags and he looked with renewed horror at the mass of throbbing rawness which his wounds had now revealed. Layers of human flesh now lying around him in a sodden reddened mass, suppurating into the stone of the ground. As the tissue began to evaporate, Painter shivered. He knew the end was close at hand. It waited for him like the black dog at the gate; eyes following his every move. Waiting patiently. Straining his fading vision, Painter could see the lights flickering around the Kirkyard, he wasn't sure where they were coming from. Voices again, but this time they were louder and he recognised the woman, instantly.

Painter lurched along the wall and felt a thrill of expectation shudder through his failing body. Longing for her reactivated his appetite and saturated his being. He knew the man was there; the one who had been trailing him for some time, and he snarled in hate. As the two of them made their way up the path towards the Kirk, he came quickly out of the shadows and hurled himself at Chris, who tumbled down onto the grass and over towards a grave.

"That's where you belong! Stay away from me. I will not let you interfere!"

Tia stepped back with a cry as Chris got back onto his feet. Chris wiped away the mud from his jeans with a brash smile.

"It's going to take more than that to floor me, you bastard. Is that the best you've got? You look disgusting, by the way." Chris strode over and stared Painter in the face. "I've got something for you. It's what us Scots call a tiodhlac. A gift." With a grin, Chris pulled up his clenched fist and punched hard into Painter's face, splitting his lip. With the force, it hung off and Chris found himself laughing with adrenalin. "You look even better now."

Painter touched his mouth with shaking fingers and lowered his gaze. With a snarl, he rushed at Chris and they both fell to the ground.

"Stop!" Tia limped forward, her face stained with tears. Holding her injured arm, she moved into Painter's way. "Take me. *I'm* what you want, not him." She felt herself tremble uncontrollably, terrified that Painter would not go along with her. And even more terrified that he would. "Leave him alone. You and me. We can be powerful together."

Painter snarled and licked the blood away from his streaming nose. "You think you are clever. All of you think you are so much better than you are. You have nothing. You *are* nothing."

"You're wrong!" Tia edged closer to him, even though every part of her screamed not to. "We have love and compassion and all the things in this world that you will never experience."

Painter tried to shield his vision from the stabbing pain in his eyes. "Oh, spare me the sermon! You think you know what's really going in this pathetic world of yours? You have no concept of the forces fighting for all of this..." he spread out his hand and saw that it was shaking. "Pathetic, useless little species! You haven't got the power to stop this battle. It has been going on for centuries! There are thousands of others like me, walking amongst you every day, and you think you are in control with your stupid little religions and gods?"

Tia staggered in front of Chris, blocking him from Painter's advance. "Now's your chance! Take me to the Covenanters Prison. If I'm to die, let me die there, where hundreds of other souls have died. Use my energy. Use the energy of those unfortunate souls."

Chris looked down at the grass as Painter began to laugh. "So easy. You are even weaker than I imagined. You love this man and you are trying to save him. How sweet," he mocked, sarcastically.

He strode over to Tia and grabbed her by her injured arm, making her cry out. "Let's get on with it, then! I've had enough waiting. I'm done with you and your whole entire fucking human race."

Pulling her along the grass and gravestones, Painter screeched horribly as more pain gripped his body. "We are so close now. Can't you feel it?" he cried, as bloody tears ran down his face. "You should be pleased. You will make me more powerful than you can ever imagine... mmm, the smell. Can't you smell it?"

Tia felt his terrifying grip harden on her arm, digging his bloody nails into her skin. She sobbed with pain as he flung open the gates of the Covenanters Prison and pulled her inside. The smell of dead meat, rotting with maggots, ran up her nose and she heaved. Groaning, she felt Painter push her over to the mound of earth at the end of the Prison. She smelt the mud and moaned as the loose stones grazed her cheek. He was tugging at her, forcing her to turn over.

Painter grinned as he knelt down over her. As Tia fought and kicked him with all her remaining strength, he grabbed her jaw and forced her to look straight into his eyes. The ice blue contact lenses had been dislodged during the struggle with Chris and now she looked into the depths of blackness. Pure evil.

"Tia, why make it so difficult for yourself? Just let me feast. You will feel release. I am stronger than you. You are nothing."

Tia grit her teeth and turned away her head, straining with all her strength not to look him in the face. "If I'm nothing..." she cried, her limbs in agony, "...why do you need me so much?"

Painter smiled and wrapped his long fingers around her skull and then down her cheek. "You and I connected. You *know* me. You are the one I have needed for so long. You understand me."

"Because I can see who you truly are and the Hell you exist in?" She screamed as Painter knelt his body on her forearm so that her head would twist up at him. "Why don't you go back there…"

"Oh, I will, my dear. But first I have to become who I was created to be. I will become immortal. An Ancient One. One of many who have tormented humankind since the beginning of existence. It is a battle. Begun since the dawn of time and it will continue until we have crushed the light completely. *You* will help me achieve this."

Painter leant harder on Tia's body as she writhed beneath him. He breathed in her terror and agony, relishing her torment and failing strength. In some ways, he wanted to make the moment last, to absorb every last groan and make her reach the pinnacle of pain before he devoured her soul entirely. But he was ravenous and close to the end, himself. It was now that he had to use all of his own strength to pull her face up to his and fix her with his hypnotic gaze.

Tia felt her body begin to give up on her. Her strength was failing and she could no longer hold him back. As she screamed out towards the unfeeling, unmoving tombs of Greyfriars, she found the strength to bring up her knee sharply into Painter's groin. Her foot squelched into his weakening mass of muscle and rotting bone. Clenching her teeth, Tia tried to push him off but he gasped in pain and fell sideways on top of her, motionless for a moment before he began to stir again. Seizing her chance, Tia cried out with every last drop of resolve and determination she had and pushed him off of her. As she rolled over and began to crawl away, Painter grabbed hold of one of her ankles and began to draw her closer.

"No!" she screamed, grabbing at handfuls of grass and leaves, feeling him pull her back. She slid further backwards, clutching hold of a black iron grate of a mortsafe, built over tombs to deter body snatchers, the Resurrection Men. One of her fingernails caught on the edge of the metal and ripped it down to the below her finger line. It started to bleed profusely. Pain coursed around her arm and for a moment it dulled her wits.

Clinging on with all her might, Tia buried her face in the grass. Perhaps it was better to suffocate, before he had the chance to kill her. It was the only option left, and tears of exhaustion and pain flowed down her cheeks.

As Painter finally seized his last chance, he snarled in surprise at a row of bright lights suddenly switching on and glaring straight into the black pits of his eyes. He was aware of black-clothed men surrounding him and the tall, silver-haired one in the middle. Painter raised his head in exclamation and confusion as the terrible harshness of the combined white light stabbed through his brain. His horrific, dissolving features, now almost completely devoid of any last vestiges of human form somehow managed to fix a disbelieving gaze on Chris.

"Armed response unit," said Chris, sarcastically, raising his eyebrows. "Whilst you are still in a human body, whilst you are *mortal*, you won't leave this place alive."

Chris gave the order and immediately the shots rang out in the air, echoing around the graveyard with intensity. Each bullet hit Painter and lifted him up into the air on impact, throwing him backwards. Blood poured instantly from his wounds.

In his agony and rage, Painter thrust out his hand, railing against the moonlit, scudding sky and moaned. The last words he could see in his mind, before the terrible blackness finally took him, were those he remembered seeing etched once on a tombstone in Greyfriars; when the words of humans had seemed so amusing and trivial.

NON OMNIS MORIAR

He screamed the words out as loud as he could, grasping at nothing but the sky, as chunks of his body flew off and locks of his pure white wig ripped themselves from his scabbed, encrusted skull and were grabbed upwards into the night air.

"What is he saying? Chris shouted against Painter's howling, picking up Tia and holding her as close as he could. Her long strands of auburn hair whipped up into his face as they watched Painter finally give himself up to the powers that had come for him.

"It means *Not All of Me Will Die*," she whispered, staring in horror as the demon known as Painter began to twist into terrible contortions. Chris looked down at her, taking in every detail of her face and summoned up all the last remaining courage and strength he had.

"Like hell it does," he shouted back, suddenly pushing Tia to one side and taking out his gun. "Go back to where you came from, you bastard." He fired the last shot and it rang out, reverberating around the graveyard. And then silence.

Painter arched his back, twisting grotesquely in the moonlight as the bullet entered his heart. He saw the tombs hurl past him, felt the Judgement coming and knew he was dying. For a second, he relished it; an end to his torment and suffering. He was not wanted and he knew, in that final moment of breath, that he had stood in front of his Accusers, the Ancient Ones and had failed. As he fell onto the grass and stared up at the dark sky, his one last sight was the moon going behind the clouds. He almost laughed as the wind brushed past him, taking his essence away into the dark.

Chris and Tia watched in silence as Painter's mortal body finally disintegrated and became a pile of dust, which was finally whipped up in the wind and blown away.

No-one, not one single officer said a word. They had all been stunned into silence and incomprehension. Where Painter's body had once been, now only a few strands of black cloth remained. The wisps of velvet quickly unravelled themselves in the wind and flew off also, leaving no trace of Painter behind. A strange echo emanated from somewhere out in the Firth of Forth, lost quickly on the escalating storm that was coming.

Tia clutched hold of Chris tightly as he pulled her carefully to her feet. He enfolded her protectively in his arms and kissed the top of her head, tenderly. "It's okay, Tia. It's over. He's finally gone."

Tia lifted her face up towards him, tearfully. "I thought…I thought we weren't going to make it…"

Chris wiped the tears away from her face with his fingers and smiled down at her. "I knew we would. I had every faith in you. In us."

Ben was shaking his head in disbelief as he came over to them. "Well, *that* was bloody mental," he said, pale as a ghost himself in the bright lights. "How the hell will we ever explain *that?"*

Chris smiled gratefully at him. "Good job, Ben. All of you have done brilliantly tonight."

"I'd like to say it's worth a beer, Guv, but right now, I've kind of gone off drinking."

Chris looked down at Tia and grinned. "Never thought I'd hear you say that, Ben. If it's any consolation, I've gone off watching horror films for the foreseeable future as well."

Tia closed her eyes and allowed her body to finally relax, despite the pain searing from her various wounds. She felt herself drooping with tiredness but allowed herself to scan her mind for one final moment, terrified that he would still be there. The blackness.

"No more nightmares, sweetheart?" Chris caressed Tia's hair and pressed his mouth again to her head. "You'll never see him again. He can't hurt you anymore."

"No more nightmares," she managed to say. And it finally seemed as though the darkness had gone. Nothing of him remained in her mind, in her vision, and she felt fresh tears of relief form in her sore eyes. "Wherever he's gone, he's far from our world. He can never come back."

After that, there was another whirlwind, of police activity and more cordoning off. The last memory Tia had of Greyfriars Kirkyard was the tape being wound around the site. As she got into the car with Chris by her side, she closed her eyes and let her head roll onto his shoulder. She had utterly depleted of energy and sheer exhaustion overwhelmed her. As peaceful rest came at last, finally devoid of nightmares, Tia gave in to the welcome darkness and allowed herself to let go of everything. All of the trauma, worry and terror now receded as she felt Chris's arms envelope her, encouraging her to sleep. She distantly remembered the hum of the car engine and conversation between Chris and Ben, and then nothing more.

Chapter 37

Later the following day, Chris, Tia and Ben stood in the Moriarty Suite. The Nightshade Club had been closed down and a sign pinned on the door 'Management Gone Away'.

"If only they knew the truth," mused Tia, standing in the room with a shiver running down her spine. It gave her goosebumps, even through the bandage of her arm sling. "Now you've told me everything, I still feel like part of me dreamt the whole thing. It almost feels like it didn't happen, it was so surreal."

Chris smiled down tenderly at her. "Eric matched Painter's blood samples from you and the gravestones. It was the same blood in the acid, which confirmed that Painter had been the killer all along. Eric wants to retire, I think. He says he's getting too old for all this lark."

"All this will be classified for a very long time," stated Ben, staring around again at the room. "No press, no danger of any of this getting out to the public. Our very own Roswell," he laughed, but it didn't quite reach his eyes. "All this time, he put on an act. Made us all think that he was this enigmatic nightclub owner who threw free drinks around the place and looked cool. I don't think I'll ever look at anyone in quite the same way again."

"We all fell for it, Ben. All of us." Chris stared around at the black room, the chaise longue and the mirror. "It looks like a theatre dressing room, doesn't it?" White pan stick makeup, contact lenses, luxurious robes. Even white wigs. We'll never know what he really looked like, under all this."

"Don't think I want to know, thanks." Ben shook his head. "What a monster."

"He was more than that," said Tia, feeling emotion welling up inside of her. "He was the true incarnation of evil."

"Look at this. I need to show you." Chris went over to the far wall and pulled back the curtain. When he did so, Tia gasped in shock and horror. "These are the portraits of all the victims," he continued, solemnly. "Katie McGlynn, Danny Logan, Jessica Barker, and many more who'll soon be confirmed by the old records and photos."

"But no Mikaela Stone," interrupted Ben, with a thankful smile. "She's coming out of hospital next week and going to stay with Kevin and his parents in London. They want to be as far away from here as possible and I can't say I blame them. Mikaela is going to call you when she is well enough, Tia."

Tia felt a surge of relief, only for it to be replaced by a sudden wave of intense sadness. "I can't explain how grateful I am that you both found her before…" She closed her mouth for a moment and let the swathe of feelings flood through her. "But what about the souls of the dead? Of all these victims?" Tia felt Chris's arms enfold her as she stared miserably at the painted wall. "I wish we could help them."

Chris kissed the top of Tia's head, gently. "Maybe we already have in some way. I don't know, there's too much about all of this that we'll never really understand."

"I'll pray for them," said Tia, looking at their agonised faces in pity and sorrow. "I still believe in good. That there is a God somewhere who loves us. I don't believe that they have been abandoned."

"Of course, sweetheart." Chris held Tia tightly again. "If I didn't believe in something good either, I couldn't have done this job for as long as I have. We'll have this place blessed and put to rest. Maybe it will help the souls in some way."

"Thank you." Tia smiled up at him and leant her head on his arm. "Maybe that's all we can do now."

"Come on, let's get you out of here." Chris took hold of Tia's hand and they walked towards the door. They hadn't got far when Ben gave a shout in surprise.

"Hey, look, Guv…" Ben exclaimed, urging them back into the Moriarty Suite, "Look at the paint on these faces! It looks like…like….it's…*dissolving*…".

All three of them moved back, closing in on the wall and staring incredulously as the paint began to bubble up softly and, one by one, the images of the poor victims began to disappear.

"Looks like they are finally free," said Chris, pulling Tia tighter to him. He could hardly believe that he had been so close to losing her and adding her soul to Painter's other victims. "I'm no expert, but it looks that way to me. What do you think, Tia? Maybe your prayers have already been answered?"

Tia nodded. Tears were running down her cheeks as she felt their souls release, one by one, and find their way into the light. She felt gratitude and love from each of them, and in that moment, she knew all of them were finally safe. Every one of them could now go home. Into the true Light.

"They're gone," she whispered, "I can see it. And they are at peace now."

"What's gonna happen to this place now, Guv? If it were down to me, I'd gut the whole thing and brick it up."

"Best thing for it," agreed Chris, "but it probably won't be. Some businessman will no doubt buy it, turn it into a tourist ghost attraction. We can never release the true details. It would panic people. Not to mention bring the wrong sort of tourists here."

"Then how do we know that it won't ever happen again?"

"We don't, but I'm not going to dwell on it any longer. We focus on the everyday criminals again, Ben. That's what we're here for."

"I'm not sure life can ever really go back to normal after something like this," murmured Tia. "It changes people. I don't know if my mind will ever be safe again. For all I know, something else might attach itself to me."

"Perhaps that's your gift, Tia. You can help us with your psychic gifts. The police don't always admit it but they always need extra help. And you've proved your worth, I think." He smiled down at her.

"Have I? That's praise, then. I'll have to go with that." She reached up and kissed him. "I don't come cheap, though."

"Hey, lovebirds, once you have finally finished, let's go for a curry. And I'm paying." Ben took out his wallet. "I'm starving. I think we've earnt it, don't you?"

"Lead on, *Guv,*" gestured Chris, laughing as Ben rubbed his stomach. "And you, sweetheart, are you ready to put this all behind you now?" His blue eyes were full of concern as he took Tia's hand and led her out of the Moriarty Suite. "Now that you've had a taste of what life is like for a copper, I would very much like to get to know *you* better. Perhaps you can teach me some psychic skills. I might be quite good at it. You never know."

Chapter 38

A few weeks later, Chris drove Tia back to Redfield Grange. The house now seemed at peace and Tia knew her nightmares had finally ended.

"It's a mess, I'm afraid. I need to do a lot of work to repair the damage. I told Lars it was storm damage. He told me to get my act together and get a real job."

Chris gripped the steering wheel. "I've taken on a demon. I can take him on, too, Tia. No problem."

"Oh, don't worry. Apparently, Lars had a change of heart anyway. I've no idea why but he got a call at the office and the Board have decided to transfer him back to the firm's office in Cambridge. He's always hated the Cambridge office. He said it was for the rejects of the firm as it was in the back end of nowhere. Weird, don't you think?"

"Very weird," replied Chris, turning the car up into the lane that led to Redfield. "Can't think what must have happened." Chris rendered a small smile to himself.

The dark looming form of Redfield Grange came into view as they drove through the open iron gates. Tia felt herself visibly relax. The house, which had seemed so threatening to her at first, had proved to be her saviour. And now she didn't have to leave. Happiness, true happiness, bubbled up within her and Tia realised that she had not truly felt that way for many years.

"So, are you sure you can put up with me, living here with you, Tia? I mean, I'm not a regular office worker – I don't work normal shifts" he laughed. He looked lovingly down at her as he finally brought the car to a stop on the driveway.

"I think I can handle that," she laughed, looking up at his handsome face with a fresh surge of love and desire. "Of all the things I have managed to deal with, I'm sure I can kick you out of bed when your alarm goes off."

Chris bent his head and kissed Tia deeply, caressing the back of her hair with his hand. "I'm not sure I want to be kicked out of bed," he laughed, softly, urgently. "In fact, why don't we try it out now? I don't have another shift for…" He glanced at his watch, "…oh, another twelve hours."

Tia sighed and pretended to scowl. "I'm not sure about that, DI West. Surely there is a law about fraternising with members of the public. A terrible crime."

"Well, in that case, I consider myself arrested. And as long as I serve my full life sentence with you, then that's all I care about."

Tia found herself laughing as they both got out of the car and she stepped up to the front door. She handed Chris the keys.

"You're so cheesy, but I'm willing to go along with that."

Chris grew quiet and paused for a moment, before accepting the bunch of keys. "This won't do, you know. This really won't."

Tia felt her heart lurch. "Have I said something wrong?" The thought of hurting Chris in any way made her panic. "Have you changed your mind?"

Chris bent down and kissed her lips, laughing as he did so. "Nope. No chance. What I meant was, how am I going to carry you over the threshold when I'm wrestling with a bunch of keys? Have you seen the size of these things? You open the door and I'll carry you in."

Tia felt an overwhelming sense of relief and began laughing, too. "You don't have to do that..."

"Actually, it's too late..." With a sudden flurry, Tia was pulled up into his arms and she fell against him, giggling. "I've had training in opening doors of creepy houses, whilst carrying a beautiful woman in my arms."

"No, you have not," Tia chuckled, as Chris manfully got the main key in the lock and opened the door whilst holding her close. "You're fibbing."

"Okay, maybe, but at least you don't weigh a ton."

"Thanks."

"You're welcome." He eased her to her feet, gently and watched as she switched on the entrance hall light. In an instant, the house was bathed in serene, comforting light, and Tia smiled up at him.

"Welcome home," she whispered. "This is your home now, Chris. I hope you will always want to stay with me."

"Try getting rid of me, Tia." Chris bent down and kissed her, longingly. "You and I, and the dog, well, we can get a dog, and the house, and maybe kids in the future. Who knows where it will take us?"

Tia closed her eyes as waves of love and contentment washed

over her. "If that's an offer, DI West, then it is the best offer I have ever had and I accept it, one hundred per cent."

Chris smiled down at her, taking in every detail of her lovely face. "You dazzle me, Tia. Right from the first day I met you, I thought you were beautiful. And now I know you are, inside and out. Just promise me one thing, though?"

"What's that?"

"No putting any creepy gargoyles on the roof, okay? Any décor is great with me, but that would seriously make me want to work late at the office." He curled her auburn strands around his fingers, lovingly. "Anything that keeps me away from you will just have to go, I'm afraid."

"Don't worry," laughed Tia, playfully punching him in the chest. "No gargoyles. But I can't promise anything about the Tarot cards, or the seances in the cellar."

"You are kidding?"

"Nope."

"Okay, well, maybe the Tarot cards but no seances, please. I'm far too young and innocent for all that."

Tia took his hand and pulled him forward. "Agreed. Now, *come on*, no more talking. Now you've only got *eleven* hours until your next shift…"

The End

Printed in Great Britain
by Amazon